SKY CLAD JAIMA

KAREN L. MILSTEIN

Sky Clad Jaima

Cover Design by Kenny Calderon, Wild Inx

Cover Art by Magdalena Almero Nocea

Sky Clad Jaima

Sky Clad Jaima

For anyone who's ever looked to the stars and
wondered…..

To my family, for putting up with me and my constantly
running ideas past

them and demanding feedback.

Sky Clad Jaima

PROLOGUE

Lord Jaima of Taburon, head of the King's Guard, second-in-command of the King's Armies, groaned softly again. Squeezed into a vehicle made for people much smaller than his six foot, seven inch frame, his knees were pulled up to nearly touch his chin and his sword was shoved uncomfortably by his side between his seat and the driver's. Give him a decent *crufa* any day, he mused, and he could move as fast as this mechanical beast was currently.

He glanced back through the window as the car was driven through the streets. This city was old, the buildings worn and aged, their paint chipped and fading, the corners cracked. Nothing like the buildings on Taburon. At home they were meticulously maintained and repaired, kept clean by their owners who had pride in their buildings, homes, and city. Jaima would not have enjoyed living here – the people were too crowded together, too busy, and too noisy. The air smelled of noxious fumes that burned his throat.

It was also quite dirty. Debris and trash littered the curbs and sidewalks. He watched a person with an animal of some sort on a lead, waiting as the animal dropped its feces into the small planted area from where a measly twig of a tree grew. The man continued on his way as soon as the animal had finished, not bothering to clean up after his animal or at the least bury the droppings. On Taburon, he would have been severely fined for his actions.

He saw people, raggedly clothed and apparently drunk, sleeping against the buildings. They were unshaven and miserable looking. The car passed a woman, who, dressed as though she was wearing everything she owned, was pushing a grate-type cart that was piled to overflowing with items, some clothing, some trash, some unidentifiable. Jaima shook his head in disbelief, that these people would permit such disrespect to each other without helping.

Sky Clad Jaima

But King Radine had come to Earth to bring McKenna, his queen, back to show the people of her former home how she'd fared over the last two years. Humans were wary of outworlders and suspicious of what had become of those humans who'd elected to migrate to another planet over the last five or so years. Becoming queen of the planet and the mother of the heir couldn't be all that bad.

Jaima didn't fully trust these humans. They had only been nine years since their last war. The conflict had devastated the male population. Those who were left were possessive of their women because they now had the option to pick and choose, or discard, from the abundant number of females. And they didn't want anything to upset the balance that gave them those options. With the arrival of non-human races from off world, women were given the opportunity to make their own choice.

Such had been the case for the Queen. Having been working for a man who wanted her to become his mistress, McKenna had decided to go with Radine to Taburon, marry him and become his queen. The king had come to Earth to find a woman, essentially to get his mother off his back about finding a bride. He had lucked out when he'd found McKenna's car stalled on the roadside and stopped to help her. Thoroughly smitten almost from the beginning by the dark haired beauty, Radine had brought her home.

And gotten her pregnant within the first three days. Luckily for him, it was before she had kneed him in the royal balls for not telling her the whole truth about his trip to Earth. Rather than coming right out and admitting to who he was, he'd beat around the bush, causing her to think that he, Radine, had been some sort of marriage broker for the king, who'd not been named up to that point, though he'd been sleeping with her and sharing nadryl – sex – from the time they'd boarded the ship. She had, enraged, kneed him firmly.

But that was after they'd shared nadryl and he'd gotten her pregnant, yet they hadn't found out about the pregnancy until after a particularly vile Taburon woman had kidnapped the Earth woman and tortured her, intending to kill her for usurping what she thought was her place beside the king. Then one of the lords of the king's council – an outspoken xenophobe - had created false letters for each of them telling the other that they'd wanted to end the relationship. McKenna had been taken back to Earth almost immediately. Radine, upon finding out about the deceit, followed, finding her, explaining what had happened, and bringing his love home, marrying her even before they'd landed on the planet.

But it was all in the past. The royal couple was deliriously, and sometimes sickeningly, happy. Which, during some of his more profound emotional times, made Jaima jealous.

For he had no woman of his own, just the occasional *skala* with whom he might relieve his needs and then leave her, after leaving the appropriate amount of coin. He was almost certain he was ready to find himself a wife and settle down, and he would begin looking through the available and suitable Taburon women as soon as they returned home.

The driver glanced at him as he sighed again. "Sorry about you being squished up there. We weren't told you folks were so big. Could have gotten the Hummer instead."

Jaima wondered what a hummer was. He knew what humming was, it felt good around his cock if when deep in a woman's throat she hummed. The vibrations on his flesh were exquisite. But to ride in one? Had this Earther offered him a chance to share nadryl with a woman? He merely nodded. "I will survive."

9

"Another block or two and we'll be there. We'll pull up right in front of the White House so you can go right inside."

This White House must have been very important, perhaps like the palace. McKenna had said that this was where the head of this United States of America lived. He was pleased that at least the King and Queen were being treated properly. He was certain the king of an entire planet outranked the president of a land the size of one of Taburon's small continents.

He hoped the men behaved themselves. With a full squadron of the king's palace guards, who had been given leave to visit the city, this Washington D. C., he had instructed them, indeed emphasized, that were they to cause any problems, the punishment would be severe once they returned home. No one, not a single soldier, was to upset these meetings and sully the name of the planet, the people or the royals of Taburon. The king's wrath would be fierce. His – Jaima's - would make the king's looked like a slap on the wrist.

There were people lining the streets of the path they were taking, gawking at the vehicles, necks straining to see if they could get a look at the 'aliens.' Jaima snorted softly. 'Aliens, indeed,' he thought. People were all the same the galaxy over. If this 'parade' were taking place on Taburon, the people there would be just as curious to see how different the 'aliens' were from themselves. They had, in fact done that very thing once McKenna had been crowned and introduced to the people. Radine had only taken her into the city once prior to her crowning, so she was an oddity to Taburons, but welcomed with enthusiasm and love. The people loved their king, and if he was happy with his choice for wife and queen, then they would be, too. Unless she hurt him. Their protection for the royal family was fierce.

The vehicle made a turn through a tall gate into a grassy area, the lawn surrounded by a fence, a pair of guards saluting as they passed through the gate. Up a long drive the vehicle glided, towards a three story building the size of the Taburon winter palace, then under a rounded canopy of pillars where the vehicle pulled to a stop. Double doors to the building faced the vehicle, armed soldiers standing guard on either side of the doorway came to attention as the vehicle stopped. The driver cut the engines and opened his door. Around them, the guards who had escorted them along the route stopped their two wheeled vehicles and dismounted, surrounding the cars.

Jaima unfolded himself from the front seat, stretching his back as he stood, righting his sword at his side. He reached down to make sure his laser weapon still hung attached to his belt. He glanced around, taking in the surroundings before his attention returned to his king. There was but one man on the grass to their right, standing near a bush with white flowers, looking intently into the bush as though he was searching for something inside the foliage. Someone reached for the passenger door on the side of the car where Radine sat.

Giving the young prince to his mother, Radine hunched over and stepped out of the car. He extended his hands to take the boy so McKenna could exit, followed by the President and his wife. McKenna took the child back, holding him against her shoulder. Prince Rakenn couldn't see enough, his head swiveling from side to side, babbling excitedly. At the invitation from the President, everyone turned to begin entering the building.

From behind them, a shout was heard. On the grass, his arm waving madly, a man approached, the one who had been staring into the bush, screaming about the pestilence of aliens and the whoring human women who betrayed their race by sleeping with them. Explosive noises came from something the man held in his hand and everyone around the vehicles began to duck for cover. Some of the armed men who had escorted the entourage raised a weapon, looking for the shooter, not sure where to point at first, then hesitating for the shortest of seconds.

Jaima pushed the king to the ground, who bowled his wife and son over at the same time, huddling over the two of them, covering them with his body. Standing, calling on the hours and hours of training he had and his quick reflexes, honed to perfection, Jaima pulled his laser weapon and pointed to the man, who'd gotten dangerously close. The king's life was in danger, and Jaima would protect him and his family to his last breath. The tall Taburon felt something like a punch to his left side, a second following quickly after the first and the onset of a excruciatingly burning pain, but he pushed it aside as he rebraced himself and pulled the trigger of his weapon and fired. A thin stream of blue light was emitted, hitting the man dead center in the chest. The man fell instantly, his voice cut off abruptly.

Sky Clad Jaima

Everything was deathly silent for just a heartbeat. Rakenn began to wail as Jaima faced his king. The burning wasn't easing, but he had a job to do. "Your Majesty, are you hurt?" He leaned against the hood of the presidential car, the flag bending under his elbow.

The king looked confused, but offered a smile. "We are fine, Jaima, thank you."

The queen, however, was looking at him closely and her eyes widened in horror. His face had paled and he was beginning to slump over, finally reacting to the fact that he had been injured somehow. Feeling a warm wetness soaking his shirt, he tried to hide it, but she was too smart and observant. He started to take a step towards the queen and swayed. "Jaima?"

Radine followed the glance of his wife. His face paled in stunned surprise at the spreading stain of blood on the left side of Jaima's shirt. "Jaima!" he cried, grabbing his friend and brother as the lord collapsed, his legs folding under him. The laser weapon he'd been holding clattered to the ground. "Jaima."

Together they sank to the ground, Radine cradling the injured man. "As long as you're safe, Radine."

The queen screamed. "We need help!" she yelled. "Please, somebody help us!"

Jaima's side throbbed, he could feel the blood pumping from the wound, his body not answering to his commands. He didn't know what had happened, but it was better that he took whatever the injury was than the king. Taburon needed Radine, he was beloved by the people, and he was good for them, a fair and just king. He had known that someday he might have been called to make the ultimate sacrifice, he had just hoped it wouldn't have been so soon. He would have liked to have seen the young prince grow up to become a man, or at least close to becoming a man. He would have liked to have had a son of his own to befriend the prince, as he had young Radine when they were young. A best friend was worth all of the armies in the galaxy.

Men were gathering around, peering over the shoulder of the king. One man was speaking into a device, giving orders, asking for emergency help. Radine looked so lost, glancing up at McKenna, then back to his friend.

"You will survive," he ordered softly, his voice tremulous. "I command it." Radine placed his hand over the spot where Jaima was bleeding his life away and pressed –

hard. Jaima grunted as the king's attempt to help only increased the pain.

"You have always been so tyrannical," Jaima replied, his voice a whisper.

"How else would I have gotten you into so much trouble if not?" Jaima thought he saw the king's eyes fill with tears. Radine never cried, except for the time when he'd thought McKenna lost to him and when Rakenn had been born. He'd not cried when his own father had passed away, standing proud and stoic, the heir apparent, the soon to be king, leading the funeral procession. But he teared up now. "I need you with me to teach my son."

Jaima tried to laugh, but a cough came out instead. Blood bubbled through the king's fingers. "He's in trouble then."

"He needs you. I need you."

Pain ripped through Jaima and he groaned. "Gods' rods, Radine, this is quite painful, like the Fire Pits of Koloda," he ground out, grabbing onto Radine's sleeve and holding on tightly. He was sorry he was bleeding over the king's uniform. Blood was so hard to remove. "More than getting stuck with a sword, I should say."

"You are not thinking straight."

No, his head was clear. "No, I know what I'm saying. I do not recommend you trying this, Radine. You let yourself get stabbed just to see how it felt. Do you remember?" The prince, fifteen and untried in battle, had believed that he should know what the men experienced when a sword went through them. He convinced the sword master to stab him, shallowly and not to kill or maim. Jaima, having gotten word of Radine's plans, had not arrived in time to stop it, seeing the prince run through the side with a blade. A flesh wound, but enough to bring the prince to his knees in agony. The king and queen had been furious, with both their son and his friend. The sword master spent a month in the dungeon.

"I do. Not one of my better ideas." Radine's hand, the one not covering the wound, clenched and unclenched at the material at Jaima's shoulder. Jaima could feel the king's body quake.

"Your mother nearly took my head off when she found out I was involved and didn't stop it."

"She was rather put out with you."

"She sent me to the dungeon." His voice was getting softer with every sentence.

"She was being lenient because she knew I had told you to leave be. You could have stepped in."

"I would have taken the blade and disobeyed my prince had I."

"Gods' rods," Radine prayed, his eyes slanting skyward for a second, "save me from stubborn friends. Please be still. You need your strength to fight, to live."

Jaima would try, but darkness was taking over his sight, squeezing in from the sides of his vision. "I shall do my best, Radine, my king." He really did not want to leave the king. Dying, here and now, would tear Radine apart. He would have rather been hurt someplace where if he was going to die, it would not be in the arms of his best friend while his wife and their child looked on. But he couldn't help himself, shock setting in, his blood still pumping from the wound around the pressure of Radine's hand. Unable to fight it anymore, he gave into the blackness and let it overwhelm him. His body went slack, draping over the arms of the king.

"No," Radine whispered. His head tilted skyward. "Gods be damned," he cursed. "Don't take him," he pleaded.

Sky Clad Jaima

Sky Clad Jaima

Chapter One

"Your Majesty, I'm very sorry, but we can't keep your man here any longer. Those protesters and curious onlookers have blocked the doorways and our staff and regular patients are having trouble getting in. We can't keep the hospital on lock-down any longer." Dr. Martin Tripp, Chief Surgeon of the Washington Medical Center in Washington, D. C., shoved his hands into the pockets of his white coat, sighing with exasperation. Standing beside him, a nurse watched with anxiety as the physician and the queen spoke. The Taburon, Jaima, had been in his hospital now for three days and had yet to recover consciousness. Shot by a mad man in front of the White House, he had been rushed to the hospital where they had removed the bullets, put the man on life support and sat back to wait for him to regain consciousness. Which had yet to happen. Why, at this point, was anyone's guess.

That he was an alien had made his care somewhat a challenge, and may have been near impossible were it not for the Taburon physician brought down to the planet to help in treating the injured man. Sistan, the Chief Medical Officer on the king's ship the *Veleda*, quickly learned the equivalent Earth medicines and directed which ones might help the best in treating the warrior. The Taburon anatomy was basically the same, lending more credence to the theory that a super race had, eons upon eons ago, seeded the planets with peoples who adapted to their own worlds as needed, but were basically the same. For some reason, the Taburons grew big, at least six and a half feet tall, and evenly proportioned. This man, Jaima, a soldier and close friend of the king, considered a brother, was in tip top condition, a factor in his favor in the present circumstances. Muscular and broad, he filled the hospital bed to overflowing, his shoulders nearly touching from side to side and his feet almost hanging over the end.

Sky Clad Jaima

An emergency back on Taburon had called the king back home. He'd left two days ago with his son, Prince Rakenn and all of the troops that had accompanied the king to Earth, leaving his wife, Queen McKenna, a human formerly of Earth, and Sistan, to oversee the care of their friend. She'd argued with her husband that it was logical that she remain, being human and easily fitting in, and that the rest of the troops return to Taburon, since the huge warriors stood out like sore thumbs. She also wanted her son, the crowned prince and heir, someplace where he would be safe from the xenophobes who were against any alien from another world coming to Earth. She had argued that their child was more important than any danger she might face, frightened at what could happen to him should he fall into the wrong hands. Earth may have gotten rid of the Middle Eastern terrorists, but there were still abominable people on the planet.

But those gawkers and protesters were making life at the hospital difficult, especially the protesters. Once they had found out where the huge alien had been taken, they began to show up every day in droves with signs and bull horns, picketing the building, demanding that the alien be turned over to scientists for examination and ultimately, dissection.

They demanded the physician be imprisoned and the queen locked in a mental health facility. McKenna had warned Radine that this could happen, justifying her decision in sending her husband and son back to the safety of their own world while she stayed to be close to and oversee the care of their mutual friend to his benefit and insure nothing untoward happened to him that could be considered a mistake. If he were destined to die, it would not be because he did not receive the best medical care possible.

For two days she'd had to fight her way through the crowds to get into the hospital to be with Jaima, surrounded by Secret Service men provided by the President. She'd finally been given a room in the hospital to avoid having to fight the crowds. Soon the guards that had kept the crowds under a rough semblance of control would not be enough as the number of people grew. And she was in real danger - she, Sistan, Jaima and the unborn child she carried. If these people ever breached the doors of the hospital, the staff would quickly be overrun and the Taburons captured for certainly an unsavory outcome.

"If you feel that strongly, then we'll have to make other arrangements. But we can't just walk out the door. They'll follow, and Jaima still needs care. My husband

24

won't be back for at least another nine days. Then we will go home, no matter what Jaima's condition. But until then...."

"You have the ear of the President. Call him. I'm sure together you can find somewhere safe to go, to keep your friend until the king returns. I'm willing to send supplies with you, even the monitors, if it will help."

"It will, and thank you. But I know nothing about running these things, and Sistan only has a basic working understanding. We wouldn't know what to do if something goes wrong."

"I'll go with them," the nurse volunteered, speaking up for the first time. McKenna gave the woman her attention.

The nurse was a blonde, her hair the color of ripened wheat. She stood a few inches taller than McKenna, about five foot six and had a lush figure. When Jaima had come in, she'd been the nurse on duty, asking questions about Jaima for the record, then changed her schedule to become his floor nurse once he'd been moved out of the recovery room.

She'd watched the woman over the last two and a half days, caring for Jaima, administering medicine, bathing his body, just sitting with the Taburon and watching. She seemed fascinated by the man, her bottom lip sometimes caught in her teeth as she contemplated his sleeping form. The queen had wondered if it was genuine care the nurse felt, was she caught up in the fascination of an alien, or perhaps it was the simple knowledge that like many Taburons, Jaima was a beautiful man.

Taller than Radine, Jaima had the toned and muscular body of a soldier who practiced his profession every day. When not training new troops, he could be found on the practice field keeping his skills fresh with the rest of his men from the guard. He would tie his long golden hair back with a ribbon and shed his shirt, drawing sighs from the ladies that gathered to watch the handsome men as they swung their heavy swords at each other. Jaima, a ladies man from the day he came of age, had not been above sending scorching grins to the ladies as he scored hit after hit on his men, their sighs drifting down over the field and causing him to grin with cheek. He was well aware of the picture he painted, naked save for his short legged training togs, which left little to the imagination, and boots. The sweat highlighted the muscles of his chest and back as he swung his sword, and plastered his thick hair to his scalp. The queen had, on occasion, joined the woman when her husband took up his sword to join his friends, giggling at their audacity when both men showed off.

It wasn't just his body and looks that made Jaima attractive. Being a lord in his own right, he laid claim to lands and estates inherited from his parents after they'd died when Jaima had been but six years of age. Taken under the wings of the then King Tylene and Queen Inoa – Radine's parents – Jaima was quite a catch for some deserving woman. So far he'd avoided any trap set for him by a diligent and aspiring mother, having vowed to take a wife when he decided.

The rumors of his sexual prowess only added to his mystique. Jaima did not deny himself the pleasures of a woman, but had learned to be discreet in his dealing with them, following the example of the king who also had to remain fatherless until he married to insure the validity of his heir's claim to the throne. But of course women talked, as all people did and after a particularly adventurous rendezvous the giggles he would hear that would follow him through the palace at times made him uncomfortable.

So for this woman to pay particular attention to her friend and husband's adopted brother did not surprise the queen. McKenna had caught her yesterday gently combing Jaima's hair, running her fingers through his tresses as she worked. She always spoke to the unconscious man, telling him what she was doing and why. When McKenna had asked, she had explained that she believed that even unconscious, the patient heard what was being said, perhaps not the actual words, but the tone of voice penetrated. She professed to give the same treatment to all of her patients and was convinced it helped in their healing.

McKenna's brow furrowed. "I'm sorry, but I don't remember your name."

"It's Jo, Joanna Simon, Your Majesty. I've been Jaima's nurse since he came in, and I think I can help him." She flushed. "I know I can."

"Are you sure, Jo?" Dr. Tripp asked, concern in his voice. "If it's found out you're with them, you become a target as much as they."

"What most of those people are doing outside is wrong, Doctor. These Taburons have done nothing wrong. And Queen McKenna is obviously happy with her husband.

She's not mentally unstable like they say she is. She and the other two should have a chance to go home." Her chin lifted as she drew a deep breath. "I'm not afraid."

McKenna's touch on the other woman's arm was gentle. "Thank you," she said. Having someone who knew the medicines and machinery would improve Jaima's chances. Having another woman would give her someone to lean on and talk to, especially since she was carrying the next princess of Taburon.

"All right," Dr. Tripp agreed after a moment. "You make the arrangements, I'll make sure you have enough to last you several days, including antibiotics, fluids, pain meds and bandaging. You'll take the bed he's on now, it's on wheels, and it'll be easier to transport him if you don't have to move him out of the bed. It's the biggest one we have. So you'll also need something big enough to transport it. I suggest you don't go far, just in case he needs to be returned to the hospital. There should be places nearby you can get to. It's just a question of how."

"I'll speak to the President and see what arrangements he can make. It'll probably best if we create a diversion."

"Several, if you can. There are several entrances to the hospital as well as a helipad. We can also move him at night. That should cut down on the crowds."

"Let me make that call. I'll let you know." She faced Jo. "Will you stay with Jaima?"

"Of course, Your Majesty."

"If we're going to be stuck hiding out, I think McKenna will do. Please also tell Sistan the plans. He's been reading your medical texts while watching over Jaima."

Jo smiled. "I will, McKenna." She left the two people to rejoin her patient.

Sky Clad Jaima

Sky Clad Jaima

Chapter Two

The room was silent when she entered, the only sounds the soft beep of the heart monitor and the gurgling noise of the drug pump monitor that controlled the fluids and meds going into Jaima's arm. Jaima lay still on the bed, his eyes closed, his breathing steady, his chest rising and falling rhythmically. In the corner, under a lamp, reading, sat the Taburon physician, Sistan. He glanced up briefly as she entered then went back to his reading seeing she was no threat to his patient. Jo glanced at the monitors quickly, there had been no change. Picking up the chart, she quickly scribbled the readings down before replacing it on the foot end of the bed. Why he wasn't waking no one knew. Perhaps the shock of the injury and surgery had taken him. Perhaps the shock of simply being shot had proved too stressful for someone who'd never known about such things as bullets. McKenna had said that they had no such thing as guns on Taburon. Instead they used swords and laser weapons, like the one he'd used on the shooter.

She had hoped every time she entered the room to see that he'd awakened, making an effort to check on him every half hour or more as her schedule permitted. She did have other patients on the floor. But in her mind, his case took priority considering the seriousness of his injuries and that he had yet to awaken. She was profoundly disappointed when he had not.

Partly disappointed, truth be told. The longer he remained unconscious, the longer Joanna could spend time with him to leisurely observe him. He had caught her attention from the first time she'd seen him. He was probably the most beautiful man she'd ever seen. He was certainly the biggest. His chest was the envy of every man and the wet dream of every woman, his pectorals hard and sculpted. His stomach and abdomen were washboard perfect. He had a trim waist, lean hips and long legs full of hard corded muscle that tapered down to long feet. She'd discovered calluses on his hands, the mark of a working man. And he had no body hair, anywhere, save that on his head and groin.

His face was softened planes, strong jaw, high cheeks, and full lips. If he knew how to kiss, he would devastate a girl with those lips. His hair was the most unusual color – a golden honey wheat shade, and it was the softest, silkiest hair she had ever felt. She couldn't wait to see his eyes. If they were anything like the ones she'd observed on the Taburon physician Sistan, she was a goner. The gold was the most alluring color, and they seemed to sparkle at times. Alien, yes, but still so beautiful.

This was a man whose body showed that it was honed by everyday hard work and not by a twenty dollar a month membership to a gym. Had she ever had a picture in her head of ancient Viking warriors, he would have eclipsed them exponentially.

And her washing him had given her an intimate look at his genitals. His cock, laying dormant on his thigh, a urinary catheter inserted, was long and thick. Engorged, it would be a most formidable weapon, and once a girl got used to it, if he knew how to use it, an absolute mind-blowing experience. He had two large testicles, the size of extra-large hen's eggs. A woman would certainly feel those seed keepers pounding against her while his cock shafted her pussy.

But it had been her experience that size didn't necessarily mean the man knew how to use his equipment. Her husband – now ex - certainly hadn't. Wham, bam, off to sleep – that had been her husband, straight missionary for the most part and only enough foreplay to insure she wouldn't be dry when he penetrated. Almost always at least.

Jo felt the same rush that ran through her every time she entered this room and stood, a heartbeat or two, at the foot of the bed. Was he married? Was there a woman back at his home waiting for him to return, or mourn him if he did not survive? Jo decided his wife, if he had one, was one very lucky woman. She hoped his wife felt that she was a lucky woman. Sometimes men took to soldiering because they received no affection or attention at home and better to be part of a fighting unit than an ignored partner in a relationship.

She wondered if he was as affectionate to his woman as it appeared the king had been to his wife, since McKenna seemed delirious happy with her big Taburon. Most men hung out with men of like mind. Radine had said that Jaima was not only his best friend, but a brother to him. That meant they held the same values. Her heart wanted to find out, whether he had a wife or not. Her head said he wasn't staying long and she would be a fool to get involved. Her body – damned traitor - had already made up its mind, heat and moisture flooding her pussy until it was nearly uncomfortable. Discreetly, she pressed her thighs together.

She acknowledged the man sitting quietly to the side, watching her. Her silence had caught his attention and when she merely waited at the foot end of the bed after writing in the chart instead of attending to her duties, he'd closed his book and looked to her. "Dr. Sistan," she greeted.

"Not a doctor, Nurse, just Sistan."

She nodded once. "All right. Dr. Tripp and Queen McKenna wanted me to tell you that Jaima has to be moved out of the hospital. The gawkers and the protesters…They're making it impossible for the hospital to function, for patients and visitors."

Sistan's brow furrowed with concern, his glance landing on the unconscious man he'd known now for over five years. "I don't think it's wise to move him just yet but I understand. Your hospital has been more than gracious in taking care of Lord Jaima."

"Your queen is asking the President for help in getting him moved. Dr. Tripp will provide everything he needs for a stay of several days, even the monitors and bed. They just have to figure a way to get him out without letting the crowds know. They're going to try to create a diversion as well. Hopefully soon." Jo caught the glance that Sistan slid to the monitors. "I'll be going with you to help out. I'm well-trained," she added in case he had any doubts.

Sistan eyed the young Earth woman. He'd watched her over the last few days, seen the looks that had crossed her face while tending to Lord Jaima, and he recognized the signs. After all, he'd gone through it with the king when the human woman, McKenna had been brought on board the ship as Radine's intended. The king had been besotted by the human, so enamored that he'd forgiven her for the cruel kick she'd delivered to the king's genitals after being misled as to his intentions. Joanna had the same 'I'll defend him no matter' what expression in her eyes the more time she spent in the room. Though this nurse had been very professional, her interest was growing to be more than professional. Yet he wouldn't say anything unless it interfered with Jaima's care or endangered his life. If, and when, Jaima awoke, the two of them could work it out between them, if she was brave enough to admit to it to the warrior. And if they left before then, well... What Jaima didn't know could never hurt him. Far be it for him to jeopardize the health – physical or mental - of any of his patients. Jaima would never hear of her interest from him.

"Very well," he agreed.

Sky Clad Jaima

Chapter Three

The arrangements had been made. Throughout the afternoon after her talk with the President, three women, McKenna lookalikes, covered in long coats, floppy hats and sunglasses, entered the hospital and were secreted into a room. Three teams of four agents, to be dressed as physicians and orderlies, would escort a bedded man through the hospital and out to waiting vehicles, the 'queen' and an unknown Taburon at his side. Two ambulances had been parked near the doors at the front of both the hospital and emergency entrances, and a helicopter waited on the roof. Each would take a decoy out, at midnight, when most of the protesters went home for the night.

Sky Clad Jaima

The real Jaima would exit via the loading dock at the back of the hospital. Already a white paneled van was parked as tight against the rolling door as possible, dummy boxes being emptied from the back to be replaced by cartons filled with the medical supplies they would need. When the word was given, the monitors would be unplugged, the equipment placed on his bed, and Jaima would be rolled into the van, the back pulled down and he would be on his way.

A single story house had been rented in the name of the nurse's maternal grandmother, located just outside the city proper in a small town called Springfield. The street was a quiet residential one where mostly working families resided and who were normally at work during the day and sleeping during the time when the van would arrive. It had three bedrooms and two baths, enough for the small group to be comfortable and not crowded. Its best feature was the huge garage into which the van could completely disappear so Jaima could be unloaded directly into the house and settled.

And for once, McKenna mused, as Jo and Sistan set the equipment up in the larger bedroom, things were finally going their way. The plan had gone off without a hitch, the van driving away apparently unobserved into the night,

Jaima totally unaware of the effort to keep him safe. There was no change in the big man's condition, the transfer had not hurt him. McKenna smoothed over the slight bulge of her stomach. Her baby was restless tonight, momma not having eaten since lunch. "Is he all right?" she asked Sistan. Joanna was checking the monitors and entering information onto a chart.

"All seems well, Your Majesty. You should rest, have a care for yourself for your child's sake."

She sighed, rubbing her belly. "I'm going to, after I've had something to eat. Can I make anything for you two while I'm at it? It appears some food was stocked in the kitchen."

"No, thank you, Your Majesty," Sistan replied.

"Thanks, but I'm okay," Jo answered.

"Then I'll say goodnight," McKenna finished and left the room. Jo would take the first watch over Jaima until morning.

As the queen left the room, Sistan burrowed into a leather bag he had brought from the ship, retrieving a long pencil like device. It was thicker than a pencil, silver colored and metallic. Standing by the side of the bed, he watched as Joanna plugged in the last machine and checked the readings, making a slight adjustment, then wrote onto the chart that had accompanied the group.

Joanna hung the chart from the end of the bed and straightened, pulling at her uniform shirt, glancing to the instrument Sistan held. "What is that?"

Sistan enclosed the device deeper in his grip, making Jo wonder just what it was he held and how much danger it posed to the sleeping man. "There is something I must do, if you would leave for a few moments."

"Why? What is that thing you're holding?"

"It will aid in his healing. But you should leave. It is not for humans to know."

"No, sir, I won't. Not until you tell me what you plan to do."

"Lord Jaima is Taburon. It is no concern of yours, nurse," Sistan said firmly.

Jo stood taller, ready to defend her position, to cover Jaima bodily if needed. Her expression firmed and her eyes narrowed just the slightest. "He is my patient, sir, he is my only concern."

The determination in her eyes was enough to sway the Taburon physician and he nodded once sharply. "Very well," he conceded, "but you must never tell anyone what you are about to see." He reached for the blankets covering the ill man and started to draw them back. "Would you remove the bandaging please?"

Joanna frowned, hesitating for only a few heartbeats in indecision, but after donning a pair of sterile gloves, she began to gently peel the tape and bandaging from the wound in Jaima's side, revealing the angry, puckered skin beneath. A light seepage moistened the wound, the stitches starkly dark against his skin. From the medical box kept near the bed, she withdrew several sterile gauze pads and with sterile water cleaned the wound of the seepage and blood that had dried around it.

Sistan made her move out of the way, taking her place beside Jaima. After examining the wound carefully, he moved away again. "Can you remove the stitching for me, please?" he asked.

"He'll bleed if that wound opens, infection will set in," she protested.

"While I fear he may not escape the infection, it having set in already or during the surgery, I can guarantee he will not bleed and the wound will not open unless someone does it for him. Proceed, please."

Joanna ripped the gloves off from her hands and dug out a pair of forceps and scissors before donning a new pair of gloves. Pulling the light closer so she could see better, she carefully lifted each stitch and nipped it with the scissors, dragging it through the skin slowly so as not to cause any pain or tearing. When the last stitch was remove, she again stepped aside for the Taburon physician to take her place.

Sistan held the device over the injury. "While our medicines are not completely the same, we preferring to rely on herbal remedies instead of the chemicals you humans use, we do have some very advanced knowledge when it comes to wounds." He flipped a small switch on the side of the device. A blue light shot forth, aimed at the incision. "Watch," he ordered.

Little by little, he scanned the light over the incision, slowly and precisely, from one end to the other. Joanna's eyes widened as the line where the skin had been incised and cut fused and healed, leaving behind a reddened line of what appeared to be a healed incision at least a few weeks old. As he continued to shine the light on the wounded area, even that began to fade until the slightest pink line remained, the only indication that an injury had occurred.

Joanna softly ran her fingers over the wound. There was no thickening of scar tissue, no swelling of abused skin layers. The area felt warm to the touch. "That was amazing. How does it work?"

"Lasers," Sistan replied. "It is quite useful in shallow cuts, healing the wound quicker to keep infection out and prevent bleeding. However, it only works on shallow incisions, anything deeper than a few centimeters or larger than your palm with ragged edges cannot benefit from it."

"Could you have used it during the surgery, closing the internal incisions, cauterizing the bleeding arteries?"

"Had I been summoned soon enough, most probably. Since he had already been operated on by the time I came planet side, there was nothing else I could do."

Joanna plucked the instrument from the Taburon's hand. "This would have been so useful during the war. The lives it might have helped save…"

"It is technology your world is not prepared to handle. In the wrong hands, it can be a weapon as much as a device of peace." He pulled it back and replaced it in the bag from where he'd gotten it. "I have your word you will never mention this to anyone from your planet?" he asked again.

"Of course. My concern is for my patient, as I said a moment ago. Whatever helps him recover the best he can."

"Very well. I am going to rest. Rebandage that just in case. It will be a reminder to Lord Jaima when he awakens that he has been injured and may keep him in bed for a few days. There is no reason to tell him otherwise. Keep an eye on him. I believe we are not through with our Jaima quite yet."

Sky Clad Jaima

Chapter Four

From across the street, hidden in the shadows, a lone man watched the house as lights blinked out, leaving one room to the side dimly lit. Ever since her face had appeared on the television, he'd been watching from the safety of the crowds to gain a glimpse of her, only to find she was surrounded by Secret Service agents and city police whenever she entered or left the hospital. Then he'd not seen her for an entire day and his suspicions grew even stronger that something was in the works. Only with his highly suspicious mind combined with careful observation and a burning need for revenge had he been able to determine that the paneled truck parked at the hospital loading dock was being used for a secretive purpose, so he'd followed it at a discreet distance until it had disappeared into the garage of the house across the street from where he hid. A barking dog startled him for a moment, afraid that he'd been discovered and his plans thrown all to hell, but he relaxed as soon as he realized the bark was coming from a house two doors down from where he watched. Even if it had been meant for him and the dog's owner come out to investigate, he would not have been seen from his hiding place.

He smiled in satisfaction as he melted into the night. He would bide his time to finish formulating his plans.

Sky Clad Jaima

Chapter Five

Jaima's hand clenched reflexively, his breath catching in his chest. He didn't understand the smells that filled his nostrils, they were certainly ones that he did not recognize, acrid and unpleasant, and the noises he heard were not ones to which he was used. The constant 'beep, beep, beep' he was finding annoying the longer it persisted. A soft gurgling noise with an underlying hiss wasn't any better. He wanted to rise to see to the sources of the sounds, but his body wasn't cooperating.

To his left he heard a soft click. An even softer hiss followed and a band around his upper left arm began to tighten. The pressure increased until it became painful. His hand and fingers started to tingle as the pressure continued passed the point of painful then held for the space of slightly less than a few seconds. With another soft hiss, the pressure eased, backing off in increments until it retreated completely. He flexed his hand, his fingers throbbing with tiny sparks of exploding energy.

Forcing himself to take a deep breath, he shifted on the bed and stilled immediately. Pain ripped through him, radiating from his left side, spreading up his chest and down through his hip. He could feel a pull on his side and thickness that he recognized as heavy bandaging. He groaned softly, his head lolling to the side. He could feel as someone took up his right arm and was holding it, running their fingers over the skin around something that was attached to the inside of his elbow.

He grabbed blindly, his hand clamping around a slim wrist. He heard a woman cry out softly, a surprised whimper as his hold tightened. Forcing his eyes to open, blinking against the light, he searched out the source of the whimper, finding a young woman staring at him, her brows furrowed in concern and fascination. She wasn't Taburon, but a beautiful human who might have been Taburon had she been taller and her eyes golden. Her hair was the same gold color of the women on his planet, draping down her shoulders and back in soft curls. Her lips were kissable, full and berry red. Her nose was turned up somewhat, cute and delicate. A nondescript terrible green shirt hid whatever curves she may have had. He couldn't see below the edge of the mattress on which he lay. But her eyes were the bluest eyes ever, the color of the deepest part of the Sea of Taburon.

With the grip he held on her wrist, she should have been frightened. Any tighter and he would bruise her skin. But instead he saw only curiosity. And was that happiness? How could this complete stranger, a human as well, be happy at seeing a Taburon warrior? Most humans were, if nothing else, respectful of the large men from his planet – he'd seen their reaction when the ship had landed in the city and his troops, members of the King's Guard, had smartly marched down the gangplank. Even with their weapons holstered, the humans had flinched just the slightest amount at the Taburon troops. The humans had visibly backed off a step when the guard had drawn their swords. Jaima trained his troops well.

"Who are you?" he whispered hoarsely. "Where am I?"

She flinched now at the harshness in his voice. "I'm Jo, Joanna, your nurse. You're safe." She twisted her wrist a little. "Could you please let go? I won't hurt you."

Jaima glanced to where they had connected and after a heartbeat, released her wrist, dropping it abruptly, his eyes scanning the room. "Where am I?"

"You were in the hospital, but we had to move you. You're in a house in a city called Springfield. It's early morning, not yet sunrise."

Jaima felt panic set in as memory returned. "The king? Queen? Are they safe?"

"Yes, they're fine. The queen – McKenna - is sleeping right now. So is Sistan. They should be up soon." Jaima winced again, the pain having backed off, but still unrelenting with every breath. "Are you in pain?"

"My side, it burns and throbs."

Jo turned away from Jaima for a moment, searching through a container placed on a small table near the bed. Pulling a bottle and hypodermic needle free, she opened the sterile hypo package. Wiping the end of the bottle with an alcohol pad, she pulled the cover from the needle, inserted it into the bottle and pulled out some of the liquid. Placing the bottle back in the container, she located an access point in the iv tubing, inserted the needle and pushed the plunger.

He watched with fascination at her actions, not understanding any of it. Within a few heartbeats, Jaima's head began to swim, his vision wavered. "What have you given me?" he demanded.

"It's a pain killer. It may make you sleepy." She discarded the used syringe. "Let me know if the pain doesn't ease."

"I feel dizzy." He struggled to sit up, fighting against the vertigo.

"It can make you feel that way." She laid a hand on his shoulder, pressing down. "Lay still, don't try to move or you may reinjure yourself."

"How long have I been ill?"

"You were shot four days ago. You've been unconscious since then. I'm so glad you finally woke. Everyone was so worried." Jo was pleased to see that she had been right, his eyes were more gorgeous than the physician's, a dark gold color, though the spark she'd been looking for and expected was dulled, most likely because of his injury and pain. "Pain better?" she asked.

He nodded, his eyes closing to stop the spinning. A deep breath did not ease the twirling feeling and he hated that he was flat out on his back, unable to rise or move without possibly causing himself some discomfort. He was a soldier, a warrior, and the word 'invalid' was not in his vocabulary. His chest expanded in another breath and he forced himself to look around and ignore the swaying.

The room was sparsely decorated. A dresser was opposite the bed he was on, it was piled with towels and blankets and assorted medical items. There was a chair to his right with a lamp above it, the light on, but muted. Beside the bed was a waist high table on which sat the container of meds. A window was behind the container, the curtains drawn, darkness beyond. Above the bed, there was a pole with several bags of liquid hanging, tubes running from them to a spot taped over on his arm. The tubes ran through a machine, the source of the gurgling noise he'd heard.

To his left another machine emitted the beep sound that had disturbed him, lines wavering across a small screen. To the side of the screen, luminous numbers flashed, changing every now and again, but steady for the most part. Below it was a tank with a tube attached, the line leading to his face where a part of the tube curved around his head, two prongs pinching in his nose. His left arm rested next to his body outside the covers.

Lifting his left leg slightly, he felt a pull on both his thigh and his cock, his brow rising in puzzlement. He moved his leg again. There was definitely a tug, and he could feel something hard and cool draped across his leg that ended in his cock. "Gods' rods, woman, what is wrong with my cock?" he demanded. He felt a rise of panic that he tried to subdue until he knew more and could decide what he would do. His wound hadn't been that low or centered on his body; that much he remembered.

"What?"

"Something is pulling on my cock. What have you done to me?" He started to lift his left hand to pull the blankets up to see how he had been damaged.

Jo stopped him by grabbing his hand. "It's a urinary catheter. You can't take it out."

Horror crossed his face. "Have I been unmanned?"

She swallowed her laugh. How like a man. His first concern being for his precious genitals instead of the injury that had nearly killed him. "No," she assured with a smile. "It's there so you can pass urine without wetting the bed." She bent slightly and lifted a bag to show him. "See, it goes in here and we can empty it as needed." She replaced the bag to the side of the bed. "Don't you have such things on your planet?"

Jaima shook his head, regretting the movement instantly and fighting the dizzying feeling. Once his head settled, he slowly turned his head to look at the pole. "And these?" he asked, indicating the clear bags hanging.

She pointed to each one as she explained. "This is to keep your fluid levels up so you don't dehydrate. That's why you have the catheter, you may have been unconscious, but your body still functioned. Fluids in means fluids out. This one is your antibiotic, to prevent infection. These lead directly into one of your veins, so when the medicine is administered, it goes right into your bloodstream. The medicines can work faster that way." She pointed to the machine with the blinking lights and wavering lines. "That one keeps track of your heart beat, breathing and blood pressure. There are electrode pads on your chest, and a cuff around your arm to check your blood pressure every sixty minutes, at least while you were unconscious. I'll change it now that you've awakened." She took a place near the monitor and began to make adjustments to its programming.

"Thank you for explaining."

"You're doing quite well. I think the fact that you were in such great physical shape has helped, though why you were so unconscious for so long, we may never know. The doctors took out the bullets…"

"Bullets?"

Reprogramming done, she turned to face him. "You were shot twice, nearly in the same place. You lost a lot of blood, so we typed it and found out your type so some of your soldiers donated blood to replenish quite a bit of it."

"What is a bullet?"

"McKenna said you don't have guns either."

He started to shake his head then remembered. "No."

57

She thought for a moment to construct an explanation. "A bullet is a metal projectile that is fired from a gun due to a controlled explosion in the gun. The guns look a lot like the weapon you were carrying. Bullets are meant to kill by ripping into a body, tearing it apart, and causing massive bleeding and internal damage to the organs. You were fortunate you weren't killed."

"Was anyone else hurt?"

"No, and you killed the man who shot you before you collapsed."

"Am I to be arrested, for killing one of your citizens?"

Her head shook vigorously. "Not a bit. He would have been shot by one of the Secret Service guards if you hadn't gotten to him first. He was aiming at the President as well as your people." She leaned on the railing along that side of the bed. "Of course, they may have tried to simply injure the man, take him prisoner in order to question him, especially to find out how he managed to get onto the grounds of the White House and hide a gun on the property." She patted his arm reassuringly. "But you're safe from prosecution. The President made sure of that days ago."

Tiredness washed over him suddenly. "I am tired," he murmured. His long, blonde lashes fell onto his cheeks.

"Sleep. It's the best medicine." Her words fell onto deaf ears. Jaima was already sound asleep.

Chapter Six

When he next woke, early morning was slipping into early afternoon, the birds outside the window were singing happily and loudly in the trees around the house. He blinked twice before his vision cleared and he turned his head. McKenna, rising from the chair in which she had been seated, smiled broadly. She leaned over the bed rail, a hand on his shoulder.

Jaima swallowed, his mouth and throat dry. "It's good to see a familiar face," he croaked.

"It's good to see your face," she corrected. "You had us worried there for a few days."

"Is there something for me to drink? I am thirsty."

"Of course." McKenna poured water into a glass from a pitcher on the night table beside the bed and helping Jaima to lift his head, allowed him to sip from the cup until he had had his fill.

"Where is Radine?" Jaima asked, laying his head back against the pillows. His side hurt, and his head throbbed, he felt as though he'd been thrown from his crufa – twice.

"He had to go home," she answered as she set the cup back on the table.

Shock crossed his face, his eyes widening. "He left you here?"

"We got a message the day after you were shot that Inoa had taken a fall from a *crufa* and was seriously hurt. He had to go home."

"And Rakenn?"

"Went with him. They're safer there. And it was my idea, before you think otherwise."

"But are you safe here? You carry a child."

"And I'm human too, or did you forget?"

"You have become such a part of Taburon that you are Taburon."

She pulled the chair closer and sat back down with surprise. "Why, Jaima, that's probably the nicest thing you've ever said to me." She wrapped her fingers through his, a connection of friendship and sisterly love. "I'm glad you've come back to us. Radine will be beside himself with happiness."

"He cried. He never cries."

"I know he did. Even with me and Rakenn, he'd be lost if anything happened to you. He loves you, you know."

"I know." He tried to lift his head, letting it drop back when the muscles in his side and the swirling in his head protested. "When can I get out of bed?"

"When you can stand up without falling on your arse or face. Give it a few days, Jaima, there's no rush to be the big, bad warrior again. Heal first."

"What about all of these things attached to me?"

"Sorry, big guy, you'll have to put up with them a few more days as well. So deal with it," she ordered in her best queenly voice. She loved him, too.

"You have become a cruel woman, McKenna." The queen laughed, delighted that Jaima was awake and seemingly on the mend. "Who is this woman, Joanna?"

"She's been your primary nurse since you were brought into the hospital. When the decision was made to move you, she volunteered to come along, even though she may have put her life in danger."

"How?"

"Unfortunately, humans, a number of them, are a 'shoot now, ask later' species. Some of them fear change more than life itself, and the unknown doesn't fit into their ideal of life. Those people don't like Taburons simply because you're different, unknown, and they fear you with everything they believe. They're calling for you to be turned over to scientists for study. That means taking you apart piece by piece until they understand every nuance of what makes you, you. What makes you tick, cutting your chest open to watch your heart beat and your lungs breathe, make you do things they would never do to a human if for no other reason than to be perverse. They also don't care for anyone who supports Taburons or gives them aid. We got you out of the hospital without incident, but sooner or later we'll be found out. As long as she stays, she's a target."

"When will Radine return?"

"I'm hoping in eight days or less. It all depends on how bad Inoa is and what she needs from him." She sat back in her chair, rubbing her tummy. "Anyway, I think your nurse has a crush on you."

"Crush? Is that good?"

"She finds you fascinating. She's smitten." McKenna smirked. "I don't know, there's something about you big, handsome guys that just gets a girl's panties wet."

Disbelief showed in his widened eyes. "She has told you this?"

She snorted in a very unqueenly and unlady-like way. "I'm not stupid you know. I have eyes *and* I remember how I felt the first time I saw Radine."

"I do not think I wish to know that Radine got your panties wet, my queen. Besides, Taburon women do not wear these panties." It was an interesting possibility though, a way to know if he had such an effect on a woman. Just check her panties to see if they were wet. Panties were something women wore over their pussy, Radine had told him during one of those times when men shared some of their secrets. And while the king had told his wife he had destroyed the pair she'd been wearing when she joined him on his ship, he'd secretly kept them for those days when he wanted a remembrance of her scent.

But wouldn't panties become a barrier to that treasured place that men valued nearly as much as their own cocks? He didn't think he liked that idea. He frowned in thought.

McKenna's laugh was full throated. "I can see where your mind is going, my friend, and I don't think you're quite up to that yet. Nor would any woman wearing panties appreciate you sticking your hand down there to check."

Sistan came into the room, smiling. "The last thing you should be thinking about is putting your hand anywhere it does not belong," he scolded. "I heard laughter. It is good to see you awake, Lord Jaima."

"He's feeling a little confined," McKenna explained.

"He was seriously injured. He needs to heal," Sistan added firmly, speaking to McKenna as though Jaima was not there. He knew the injured man listened.

"*He* has gotten the message," Jaima replied sarcastically, "though *he* is not content."

"Give it time, my Lord. You'll be back at your swordplay soon enough."

A single eyebrow lifted in distain. "Did he just call it sword *play*?" he asked McKenna.

"Indeed he did, my Lord," McKenna confirmed, hiding her smirk behind a hand. Jaima was an accomplished swordsman, the best on Taburon, and quite proud of it.

Jaima growled softly. "When I am better I shall introduce him to how I *play* with my sword," he promised.

Sistan grinned at the innuendo. "Sorry, my Lord. I much prefer women." Stepping to the side of the bed, Sistan folded back the covers on the left side. "Let me take a look at your wound. Your Majesty, if you would give us a few minutes, please?"

McKenna now raised an eyebrow, folding her arms across her waist. "Really?" she asked. "I think I've seen a few wounds in my day."

"How is your stomach this morning?" Sistan asked pointedly.

McKenna swiveled on her heel. She was still suffering morning sickness and nasty things, like blood and injuries, tended to make her toss her cookies. She preferred not. "I'll be back in a few," she called over her shoulder as she headed for the door.

"*Fendet*," Jaima called after her, bringing her up short in the doorway. He'd just called her a wimp. Well…worse than a wimp really. When she turned, her eyes flashed in challenge.

"I tell you what, *my Lord*," she said with the same amount of distain he had shown moments ago. "You carry a baby in your body, throwing up every day for three months straight, putting on enough weight to cause your ankles to swell, have your sense of balance shot all to hell, and have a living being the size of a *veramid* thrust out of your hole, then, and only then can you call me a *fendet*." She shot him a significant look, huffed and left.

Jaima continued to stare after her retreating back for several seconds before he turned his glance to the physician with a look of puzzlement. The other was grinning in glee. "Sounds painful," he commented.

"And be glad you'll never know," Sistan agreed reaching for the bandaging. "How are you feeling?"

"Like my first day of training when I first joined the army. How badly injured was I?"

"You might have died." Sistan peeled back the bandaging from the bottom where Jaima could not see how healed the incision was. "Were it not for the fact that the physician here was very skilled and it appears our anatomy is mostly similar to humans, you would not have survived." Sistan recovered the site, tapping down the tape to make sure it stayed stuck. "These bullets did a lot of damage internally, but he repaired it quite cleanly and several of the guard provided blood to replenish much of what you had lost. You should remain in bed for at least a week in order to insure you ate completely healed, but…" he added, seeing that Jaima was about to argue, "give it three more days before you get up. I will not permit you to rise any sooner." Straightening the covers, he shoved his hands into his pockets with a deep sigh. "I know it will be hard for you to stay confined, but please try to bear with me. Neither Radine or the queen would ever forgive me if we lost you."

Unhappy, but placated for now, Jaima conceded to the physician with a scowl, resting against the pillows, covering his eyes with his free arm and a sigh.

Chapter Seven

Things couldn't have gone more predicted than if Sistan had injected infection into the prone warrior himself. Despite being given antibiotics and with consideration to the repair made by the laser device, infection reared its ugly head by that evening.

His fever rose quickly, topping out at a dangerous high. After consulting with Dr. Tripp, Joanna increased his antibiotic's strength, instructed to wait twelve hours to see if that had any effect. She added an antifebrile to his meds and began wiping him down with alcohol.

Jaima tossed and turned with fever, searching for comfort. He never lost consciousness, yet his eyes showed his distress every time he glanced at his caretakers. A warrior, unused to confinement and now more ill, he silently pleaded for help to end his misery. Jo's heart broke every time his glance fell on her then slid away upon realizing she could do no more for him than what she was doing already.

While he didn't thrash about at the fever's peak, he did require restraint as it reached its highest point, for he sought to leave the bed, threatening to dislodge the monitors and pull out the catheters. As Jo and Sistan held him down, McKenna, with consideration for her pregnancy, attached the straps to the bed then belted them over the feverish man explaining in a soft voice all the while her actions and reasons even as she tied him down. Unable now to move more than the smallest amount, Jaima settled, though he threw an accusatory glance at the three people trying to help him.

When it became apparent the current medicine was ineffective against the infection, Jo was instructed to switch to a more potent antibiotic and begin the wait again. Diligently she bathed him while keeping watch, refusing to leave his side until his fever broke despite the pleas of both McKenna and Sistan and their offer to relieve her.

Though her head knew better, in Jo's heart she felt she'd let her patient down - that she'd somehow, somewhere overlooked something. She was wrong to consider involving herself more than professionally, to create a conflict that was proving more harmful than pleasant, no matter her heart's and body's desire. So she would dedicate herself to getting him well, to let him return to his planet, his home, and his life.

Up then down his fever played out for another twelve hours, finally breaking twenty-four hours after its onset, the medicine finally kicking in to defeat the infection. Jo breathed a sigh of relief as she wiped his neck, sweat pouring off him as he slept peacefully for the first time in that time period, releasing the restraints from his arms, legs, and across his chest.

She herself dozed fitfully in a chair nearby for several hours, stirring at mid-morning to refill the bowl she'd been using, making a soothing concoction of water and lavender to wipe him down once more. Turning her back to him after rinsing the towel that had warmed, she was surprised to see him staring at her when she faced him again, and she smiled in reassurance. "Hi."

His voice was soft from disuse, his throat dry from fever. "I have been ill."

"You developed a fever. But it's broken now, so you should get better." She dabbed at his throat, stopping when he took her hand into his.

He studied her fingers closely, rubbing against each one individually. "You have such small hands."

"Compared to yours, I guess so."

"Soft. Your skin is perfect for one with hands that work." He brought her hand to his face and rubbed her fingers against his lips. "I like your scent."

"It's lavender, a flower. It's supposed to help soothe and calm. I think Sistan approves since it's herbal so I've been using it in the water."

"Men on Taburon would never allow a flower scent on their body. But I like this."

73

She flushed. "There are some men who don't mind a sweeter scent, especially if it has restorative properties. I remember you smelled kind of wonderful when you first came in. Of course, it disappeared after a day or so, especially after a sponge bath. But I liked it."

"McKenna said Radine reminded her of a Turkish market, whatever that is."

For a moment, Jo contemplated his description. From what she had read about Turkey, it had been and most probably still was even after the war, a land of exotic spices and scents, cloths and foods. She'd never been to a Turkish market, she'd not even been far from where they were presently hiding out, but if her imagination was anywhere close, then McKenna had described Jaima's scent perfectly. He reminded her of harems and sheiks, desert sands and tents, veiled dancing girls and genies in magic bottles. She couldn't help the flush that darkened her cheeks at the image of him standing over her, the naughty harem girl, he wearing only a pair of blousy trousers, cuffed wrists, and a large gold amulet on his chest hanging from a heavy gold chain. Shaking off the image, she brought her wayward thoughts under control, smiling sheepishly.

"She had it right. That's exactly how I would describe it." When he frowned, Jo thought it was because of her words. In truth, her flush had not escaped his notice and he wondered what thought had crossed her mind to cause such a reaction. He promised to himself that he would try very hard to root it out of her. "We don't have a computer here. Maybe when you're feeling more up to it, if you stay around for a little longer, I can check and see if I can find pictures to show you. You might like it."

"I would like that. I have read about your world, but have only seen what little passed by as we rode to your White House."

"I would love to show you around. There're a lot of wonderful sights to see here in the Capitol area."

"We won't be staying," McKenna said from the doorway. "Once Radine returns and we go home, we won't be returning until the people here prove they are more ready to accept people from another world." She entered to stand on the other side of the bed. She didn't miss the flash of disappointment that shot across Jo's face at her announcement. She knew the young woman had developed an attachment for Jaima. She just hadn't been aware of how

75

deep it may have actually gone to until now. And with Jaima being ill, and Radine expected to return, there was little chance of the two of them having much opportunity of exploring any relationship. Of course, it wasn't fair to judge, since she'd joined Radine to return to Taburon after only one day together.

"That decision has been made?" Jaima asked.

McKenna nodded. "The night you were shot. And I agreed. Neither Radine or I will allow any of our people to go through what you're going through now." She scowled. "Earth doesn't deserve us."

"As you will, my Queen," Jaima conceded.

She slid her glance to Jo, an eyebrow raised at the way Jaima still held her hand. Her head tilted to the side slightly. "Do you think he can handle some soup? I've got a pot going for dinner but can bring in a bowl of broth so he has something to eat."

Jo pulled her hand free. "I think if he doesn't eat too much, he should be able to handle it."

"Good, I'll bring in a bowl. And some watered down juice."

Once they were alone again, Jo dropped the towel back into the bowl of water she'd been using to wipe Jaima of sweat and bent by the head end of the bed. Releasing a bolt, she pushed a button on the side rail of the bed, the head end lifting. Jaima watched with surprise, dying to try the buttons out for himself, a new toy for his masculine curiosity. Smiling, Jo pushed his hand away. "You can play with it later. Here, this one lifts the head end, this one the foot. Push the ones next to them to lower each end. You can adjust the bed until you are comfortable." She adjusted the covers that had slipped when raising the bed, tucking them back into place. "You should change position anyway soon to prevent bed sores. I've been massaging your body and limbs, but it's best if you change positions. If it's not too painful, maybe you can sleep on your side tonight."

"It would be better if I could get out of this bed."

She shook her head, rolling her eyes, stifling her giggle.

Jaima frowned. "What do you find amusing?" he asked suspiciously.

"There must be truth to the theory that the galaxy was populated with the same kind of species and the same mindset. Men could have holes the size of a fist in their sides, but think of their genitals first and must be stubborn the galaxy over," she mumbled. "Here," she continued, folding back the covers to the tops of his hips. He was nude beneath, wearing only a short hospital gown that stretched across his shoulders and barely reached his thighs. Taking one leg in hand she pulled it over the edge of the bed, then reached for his other leg, pulling it to follow the other. With a hand to his back, she helped him to sit up. "Easy," she instructed. "Nice and slow." His hands grabbed for the edge of the bed and gripped tightly, his head spinning as the room tilted. Hunched over, he took several deep breaths before straightening. His face had paled. "Now do you understand?" she asked pointedly.

Defeated, he nodded. "You have made your point, Jo. I am sorry to be such trouble for you."

Guiding him, she helped him to relax back, lifting his legs to return them to the bed. The blankets were resettled over his legs to his chest. "You're not any trouble, Jaima. I love my work, and I know what I'm talking about. Give your body time to heal. It's been violently violated."

He snorted. "I have never been violated."

Jo gasped softly, her breath caught in her chest before she seemed to shrug in the slightest way. "Yes, well, it's not very pleasant, is it?" she asked, busying herself with straightening the blankets. The way she asked raised his suspicions. She sounded like someone with first-hand experience. Her face had paled and her lips thinned as they tightened, pressing together, her eyes hooded and the laughter that had been there a moment ago fled. She seemed to draw into herself.

Jaima took her hand again. "Have you?" he asked mildly, curiously.

Pain flashed across her face which she quickly disguised as McKenna returned with a tray. Jaima dropped her hand like it had become burning hot. "Ah, you're sitting up," the queen exclaimed. "Good." She set the tray across his lap, putting the bowl directly in front of him. "If you want to grab something to eat, I'll stay with Jaima," she offered to Jo.

"I would like Jo to stay, if she wants," Jaima implored. He could see the hesitation in her face, but she finally nodded. In truth, Jo wanted to hide in her room for a while, curl up and chase away the memories that his question had brought back. She'd spent a lot of time driving the demons from her mind, but they had come back full force just moments ago. She needed to purge them again, but her concern for her patient, and her fascination for him, came first. She would take care of herself later when he didn't need her.

"I'll stay until he's finished. Then he should rest again." McKenna nodded her approval.

"So, tell me more about yourself," he asked as he spooned the soup.

"What do you want to know?"

"How old you are, where did you grow up? Do you have any family? Everything."

"Turnabout is fair play," she reminded him.

"I understand."

Jo pulled the chair closer and sat. "I'm twenty nine. I grew up here in the Capitol, not far from where we are now. My life as a child was fairly normal, school, college, nursing school. I have a brother who disappeared four years ago, no one knows where he is. My parents have passed. I like nursing, it gives me a chance to help others who really need it at a time in their lives when they're the most helpless."

"Have you never been in love?"

She hesitated. "I thought I was, once. It didn't work out the way I expected."

"What happened?"

"He wasn't what he presented himself to be when we first got together. What about you? Have you ever been in love?"

"I have loved three women," he replied and waited. The frown on her face pleased him. She was thinking about him in terms other than a patient. Otherwise why would she have frowned at his confession? "My mother, the Queen mother Inoa, and McKenna. Radine is as a brother to me, his wife as a sister. Does that please you?" he asked when she visibly relaxed.

"It's none of my business except for making conversation. I shouldn't have asked."

"My parents died when I was but six years of age. The king and queen, Radine's parents, took me under their wing and raised me as an adopted son. I started in the army at sixteen and worked my way up the ranks until I became Commander of the King's Guard and second in command of the King's army. I have several titles that I inherited from my parents, and several estates I visit four times a year when my other duties allow. I have never had a wife. McKenna says you have crushed me."

"What?" she squeaked, her voice rising. Talk about an about face. "She said what?"

"Is that not the right term? She was quite sure."

Jo shook her head in disbelief, her brow furrowed as she tried to figure out just what the queen may have told this man. When the answer dawned on her, she turned as bright red as if she'd taken a serious sunburn. Her hands lifted to cover her tell-tale cheeks. "Oh no," she groaned softly. "She said I had a crush on you?"

"That is the way she said it. I am sorry if I have misspoken."

"Oh my god," Jo whispered, hiding her face and bending over.

"What is wrong? Am I not attractive to you?" he asked, oblivious. "I find you very attractive, beautiful even.

Would you not want to know this?" To give him credit, at least he was honest.

Jo straightened, taking a deep breath. She couldn't believe she'd been that obvious in her interest for the tall Taburon and that even if true, that the other woman had discussed it with him. "You're my patient. Whatever I might feel about you doesn't matter. My job is to care for you, send you on your way when you are well and move on to the next patient."

"But are you being truthful to yourself now, Jo?" He pushed the tray down his legs reaching out to take her hand. It was so small, his hand encompassing it completely. So soft, yet strong, one of his fingers scraped gently along the back of it. "Will you be able to just walk away this time?"

"You'll be going back to your planet soon. It's wrong to start something when it can only last a few days. Plus, you're not well yet."

With her hand in his, he pulled her close enough to slide his other hand behind her neck, under her hair, gently massaging her neck, holding her close, her lips less than an inch from his. "Let me show you just how ill I am," he offered, pressing her mouth to his.

Sky Clad Jaima

Oh, god, she was in heaven. His kiss was everything she had believed it would be and more. He was an expert in the art of kissing as his mouth traced over hers, sliding sensuously around her lips, sharing with her the taste of the broth he'd just eaten. Pressing his lips tightly to hers, he slid his mouth back and forth across hers, making her open. Once given access, he speared her mouth with his tongue, exploring inside, coaxing her to battle with him.

Her ex had never taken time to make love to her mouth the way this man did. He poked and probed, coaxed and demanded, sharing an intimacy two strangers should have never had so soon in a relationship. If his kiss was any indication, his love making would be superior, thoughtful and complete, and she would walk away a very satisfied woman.

She felt her breasts swell, her nipples tighten. Her blood rushed through her and a pulsing started in her groin that spread to her pussy, expanding her intimate flesh and filling her with moisture, preparing her for sex. Her body softened and relaxed, her breaths were caught by him and returned to her, hot and humid. Anymore and she would soon be climbing into the bed with him.

If she gave in. If she could accept in her heart that this would last but a few days, enjoy it, and forget it as easily as a man could. Her ex had walked away and forgotten her easily enough, marrying within months, a father within the following year. Could she take a lesson from his book and do the same?

Jaima was an artist with a paintbrush, a sculptor with a fine block of marble, a musician with a Stradivarius and she was soaking up every second of his massacre of her mouth. When she finally came up for air, she knew no man would ever be able to surpass or even compare with his kiss.

"Can you walk away from me now?" he asked, his mouth still close to hers, his breath warm on her wetted lips.

She hung her head, her forehead braced against his chest. She could feel his chest rise and fall with his breathing. Turning her head just so her ear rested against his muscular breast as his heart beat strong against her ear. "This is so wrong, and I shouldn't," she murmured into his warmth. She smiled for him. "I can't let you pass through my life without seeing what we can have, even for a short time."

He growled deep in his chest. "Take this Gods' forsaken thing out of my cock so when I am feeling better I can share nadryl with you."

She straightened, though he kept her hand in one of his. "Nadryl?"

"Sex." His grin was wide as she flushed again. "You are so appealing when you turn red. For a woman who deals with men and their wayward cocks in a sick bed, you are very shy."

If it were possible, she darkened even more, pulling her hand free. Her tone was haughty and flippant. "It's been my experience that after a while, once you've seen one, you've seen them all. Though none of them are built quite like you, Jaima." She moved the tray to the bureau.

"I should hope not," he replied, indignant. "It would appear that Earth men are sadly lacking in the size of their better parts." Jo let that pass. If porn stars were any indication, there were some men on Earth that could rival these Taburon men in a pissing contest, but he was more than likely correct when it came to Earth men in general. There was no comparison there. The Taburons held all the first-place, best in show prizes.

Of course, it was a given that no matter the size, if a man didn't know how to use his equipment, couldn't please a woman with his nature given endowments, then size made no difference between a bad and good lover. And like it as not, Jo knew that making love was more than a cock shuttling in and out of a woman's pussy. She'd had enough of that from her ex.

"Are all non-Earth species like you?" She flushed, not realizing her faux pas until after the words had left her mouth. She coughed once to cover her mistake. "I mean, humanoid in body shape, two legs, two arms, and so on?"

"And with a larger cock?" he guessed, watching her turn even a darker red. "I do not know. It is not my habit to check in order to compare."

She laughed, going to the container next to the bed and opening it. "You know this means you'll have to get out of bed to use the toilet." She took out a needleless syringe and pack of sterile gloves.

"I know. If you or Sistan will help me keep my feet, I will manage."

Sky Clad Jaima

With the blankets at his knees, she lifted the gown to his hips, revealing his cock, tube inserted. Gloving her hands and with the syringe, she fitted the needleless side into a small tube that dangled beside the larger one and pulled the plunger back until it was fully extended. Releasing the air inside, she again pulled air from the bulb that held the catheter in place in his bladder until the plunger wouldn't move further, an indication that all of the air was out of the bulb. Holding his cock firmly, she began to pull the catheter. "This may sting a little," she warned, tugging gently and slowly. "Don't move now." He hissed, ready to fold up and protect his precious manhood, but she pulled more and with a feeling of relief, it exited from his body. Jo held the end up, there was urine in the tube. He didn't hesitate to wrap his hand around his cock and rub gently, easing the sting that remained as she took the bag and tube and went into the bathroom attached to his room. By the time she'd returned, he had soothed his mistreated favorite body part enough to lay back, covering himself with the hem of the gown.

"When will the sting stop?"

"Oh, it should be better in a few hours." She put the used syringe away and tossed the glove. "You may feel the urge to urinate, but that's residual. If you want or need to go, just call for me or Sistan." She hooked a urinal on the edge of the bed. "Or you can use this."

He eyed the container with distaste but ignored it after a minute. "I warn you Jo, when the time is right, you will not escape me."

She laughed, leaning into the side of the bed, her lips close. "I might just let you catch me," she challenged. Bussing his mouth, she turned, grabbed the tray. "Get some rest," she tossed over her shoulder and left the room. Not until she was in the kitchen did she realize she'd come really too close to giving in to his allure, promises and sex appeal and she would have to be more on her guard than ever.

After she'd cleaned Jaima's bowl and washed the glass, she joined McKenna and Sistan at the table in the dining room where they were enjoying their breakfasts. She set her own meal down.

"Did he eat everything?" Sistan asked.

Jo nodded, taking a seat. McKenna giggled softly, causing Jo to look up at the other woman. "I know it when I see it. You've been thoroughly kissed."

Jo touched her lips with her fingertips. "It shows?"

"My dear, I've seen the same thing on me in the mirror any number of times. These Taburon men know how to knock a woman's socks off with their kisses." Her smile was loving, reminiscent. "I know Radine did it for me the first time."

"Are you really happy with your husband? I mean, it's not just because you got a chance to marry a king and became a queen?"

"I fell in love with Radine before I knew he was a king." Sistan snorted and McKenna shot him a dirty look. Rather than come right out and tell McKenna that he was the king, he'd led her to believe he had been searching for a bride for the king and had chosen her for the part. Of course, before his confession, they had been sleeping together for three days, and she had assumed he was meaning to turn her over to the king when they reached Taburon, having tested her 'qualifications' and approving. She'd been so angry that she'd kneed him in the crotch, felling him instantly. It had been Sistan who'd treated the injured, and deeply embarrassed king. "Never mind," she ordered the physician. She faced back to Joanna. "Anyway, those two are like peas in a pod, so alike that sometimes it's hard to tell them apart. So I assume he has the same skills as my husband."

Jo smiled. "Oh, he's skilled all right. It's just I shouldn't be getting involved with him. You said you'll be leaving in about a week or so, and I'll be here. He's my patient. It's unprofessional and so totally out of line." Her sigh was heartfelt and full of longing. "And I so want to do it."

"He is recovering from his injuries," Sistan reminded her.

"Which is why it's so wrong. By the time he's able to do anything without causing himself harm, you'll be gone." She dropped her fork onto her dish, her appetite gone. "By the way, I removed the urinary catheter. He wanted it out, and he seemed so determined. He promised to ask for help to use the bathroom."

McKenna snorted indelicately. "He'll ask when he falls flat on his face, that's when he'll ask," McKenna revealed. "They're not only the picture of stubborn in the dictionary, but the whole damned book."

"The queen is right. Lord Jaima is as stubborn as the king, as any Taburon warrior. Lying about just because you've had your insides scrambled is still an abomination to them."

"I could always keep him sedated," Jo suggested.

Sistan smiled to McKenna. "I like this woman," he declared.

She practically gleamed. "So do I," she admitted.

Jo flushed prettily at the compliment, taking a deep breath. "What is Taburon like?"

"Not anything like Earth. They don't have the pollution we have here, they live fairly simple lives comparatively. Travel primarily by an animal called a *crufa*, which is kind of a cross between a horse and a very large sheep, though they have space travel. If needed, they can utilize the shuttles for emergencies, and they communicate via modern methods, better than Earth's internet. Picture Earth around the eighteen hundreds, and you've got it pretty close. They have a monarchy, Radine's family has ruled for ten generations. Jaima was raised with Radine, his parents killed when he was very young. Radine's father took him in and the two of them got into as much trouble as two young boys with the power of the throne behind them can. I've heard some pretty far out tales, but knowing Radine as I do now, I tend to believe them. And in fact," she remembered, "I owe him a sound verbal thrashing when he comes back for something incredibly stupid he did as a young man." Jo waited for a moment, but the queen was obviously not telling.

Coming out of her wayward thought, she continued. "I met Radine when my car stalled in the middle of the road on my way home. I'd just quit my job because my boss got way too handy. He, Radine, was kind enough to give me a ride home. He stayed the night, we did not have sex," she emphasized, "but when my ex-boss showed up the next day and started to attack me, he saved me, beating my ex-boss with his bare hands. That's when I knew for sure I loved him. He's been my hero ever since."

Jo's voice was wistful. Didn't every girl these days want to be swept off her feet by a handsome prince? A king would do if there weren't any princes available. Or just a handsome warrior. "It sounds like every girl's dream."

"It turned out that way, but I certainly wasn't looking for it."

"And you have a son?"

"Rakenn. He's his father's pride and joy. He spoils him ruthlessly. Now we're going to have a girl, and I just know Radine is going to be wrapped around her little finger the minute she's born." She giggled. "Picture that man in there flat out mushy over a child and you've got the idea."

Jo laughed as well. "'The bigger they are the harder they fall,'" she quoted. She looked to Sistan. "What about you?"

"I live on a starship. It is no life for a wife and family. I live vicariously through others. I am content." He concentrated on his food.

McKenna scowled in disapproval. Sistan was hiding behind his position as the ship's chief physician and not fooling anyone. Any wife who loved her husband wouldn't mind living with him wherever, as long as they were together. There was someone out there for him, if he'd only get off the ship on occasion and look. "Have you been married, Jo?"

"I was, but he divorced me. You know, get unhappy with the one you have, get rid of her and start anew."

"I'm sorry, Jo. It sucks, doesn't it? We finally get a little bit of the upper hand in life, but the men still rule. They don't need women on Taburon, but if any were to emigrate, they'd certainly find things different there. Of course, the men can be a bit overbearing and chauvinistic, but they do it because they really love their women and really want to protect them."

"Females are precious," Sistan remarked as if it explained everything. McKenna's eyes rolled at the blatant statement, men were alike the universe over. Jo smiled in return.

"We'll have to be careful with our idioms," Jo said. "He thought I crushed him."

McKenna laughed. "Did he tell it to you like that? Oh, that is so deliciously ridiculous. I will never let him live it down."

"Why did you say anything?"

"Because it's too easy to get swept off your feet, and he is a bit of a lady's man. He is very sought after by the ladies at court, and all of the others just look and sigh dreamily. Mind you, he's been very discreet, but he hasn't denied himself either. As much as I don't want him hurt, I don't want you hurt either."

"Are they always so blunt?"

"Yep. Well, except for that one time, which my husband is not likely to forget for a long time."

"Someday you'll have to explain that to me," Jo hinted.

"I will tell you one thing. They will never hurt you, physically or mentally, not if it can be helped. Radine would give his life for me. As I would for him. And if you get involved with Jaima, he'll be the same way as long as you are together."

Jo kept her thoughts to herself, but nodded. "That's good to know."

Sistan, finished with breakfast, gathered his plates and rose. "I'll go see to Lord Jaima before I settle to reading. If you will excuse me, madam, Your Majesty."

McKenna watched Jo's face for a moment. "Was there something else?"

Jo squirmed in her chair. For a nurse, she was rather shy. Her face reddened. "He's all but come right out and said we'll be having sex. But, lord, even relaxed, he's big. I've never known a man his size let alone had one. I don't know your history, and smack me upside the head if I'm being too presumptuous, but was it difficult for you, that first time?"

McKenna thought back to her first time with Radine. He'd been thoughtful, aware of their size difference, and took penetration slow and gradual until she'd adjusted to him. "He was gentle and considerate. If, and mind you that's a big if, you do share nadryl, have him come at you from behind, doggy style. It's easier on you. Or you can ride his cock and control the penetration at your pace. It'll drive him crazy – they can be so impatient - but that's not your worry, at least not the first time. Might be easier on him, considering his injury. Just make sure he's prepared you beforehand, lots of foreplay."

Jo stared off at a distant point, her body responding to the memory of just a half hour ago. "His kiss is foreplay," she announced softly.

McKenna giggled. "Aren't they though," she agreed. "I'm not trying to pry, but it might help. When was the last time you had sex?"

Jo flushed dark red. "It's been a while," she confessed.

"Longer than a few months?"

"More like a few years."

"Then you should definitely make sure he gives you a lot of foreplay before he penetrates. They're large relaxed and much larger engorged. I'll be honest, it took me a while to be able to take my husband comfortably. But I'm used to him now, and sometimes things get a little hurried..." She waved her hand, sure Jo would understand, woman to woman that sometimes you just can't wait to enjoy the pleasures.

After a moment of thought, Jo nodded. "When you had your baby, wasn't he large for you?"

"A little. Rakenn was only slightly bigger than a normal human baby at birth. The labor was long, and the actual birth well watched by our physician. He came out fine, and so will this one." She absently rubbed her stomach. The baby was awake and kicking, a wonder that filled her with joy. "Don't get pregnant, Jo. If you do, you'll never get rid of him if you're only interested in a fling. If you're not on birth control, it may not be a good idea to follow through with this thing."

"I'm safe. No chance of pregnancy." In the final year of her marriage, she'd not gotten pregnant once, despite her husband screwing her at every chance. When she'd suggested seeing a specialist, he'd refused, threatened her if she made an appointment for herself, and tried harder to get her pregnant to no avail. It was when he threatened to bring in the extra men that she'd drawn the line. She wouldn't whore for him, for any reason, believing their marriage had been for love, not because he wanted a brood mare.

The truth, once he'd screamed it at her during their fight, had cut to the bone. He'd kicked her out, left her homeless, divorced her and promptly remarried. He now had four children, and who knew exactly which ones were his, if any, but that was not her concern any more. Her ex-husband's words still resounded in her dreams, accusatory and cutting. And though she used barrier birth control religiously since, for the few times she'd engaged in sex, she blamed herself then and now for the failure of not being able to conceive.

Jo stood, gathering her plate and utensils. "I'm tired. I'm going to sleep for a while. Thank you, McKenna, for being so candid with me. I have a lot to think about."

Sky Clad Jaima

"Sleep well, Jo."

Chapter Eight

In the shadows, the man watching the house snapped his phone closed with an audible click and pocketed the device. The plans were set, the safe house secured, a nice quiet place where no one would hear her screams and wonder. He only had to get through the two hulking aliens in the house, but one of them was still recovering from a gunshot wound and most likely out of commission. No matter, his Glock would quickly discourage the bastard if he dared to interfere or stop him in his tracks if he did. The car would be left for him in the back alley behind the house, there would be rope and other such devices tucked into the trunk he would use to make her beg for mercy. But he would have his day to sink balls deep into her, fuck her like he'd always wanted, then kill her for betraying him.

Soon, he promised himself. Soon he would have his day.

Chapter Nine

Lord Jaima, Commander of the King's Guards and second in command of the King's Army never realized that being shot, operated on, spending four days unconscious and fighting a fever could take so much out of him. Soon after kissing Jo senseless, he dropped into a deep sleep filled with pleasant dreams – dreams of a golden haired woman stretched out on his bed, naked, offering herself to his perusal before he sank to the root of his cock deep into her pussy. Of how she would look without her clothes, her breasts heaving in anticipation, her pussy dripping with her dew. Dreams of sharing nadryl with this woman until both dropped from exhaustion. Of lying next to her, her body flush from sex, only allowing her a short period of time to recover before he started all over again.

Normally an active and robust man, when he wasn't in his office taking care of military business, he could be found on the practice grounds training with his men. Jovial and enthusiastic, he gave as good as he got, never excusing a man from using the best he could when sparring with his commanding officer. Wielding his sword with the ease of many years usage, he was considered the best swordsmen on Taburon, and expected little else from his troops. Nothing stopped him from demanding and giving his best.

So when he woke with a full feeling in his bladder, his cock hard with a semblance of a morning erection, not the way he might have preferred, the fact that he couldn't rise to care for himself frustrated him beyond frustration. Stuck in the borrowed hospital bed, tubes attached to his arms, things taped to his chest, he refused to even consider the urinal hanging from the side of the rails. He was a full grown man and full grown men stood to piss. "Jo," he yelled. "Joanna," he hollered when the first call didn't work.

Instead of the woman he wanted, Sistan answered the summons, pulling a shirt over his head as he entered the room. "You don't have to bellow," he complained.

Irritated, his voice was gruff. "Where is Jo?"

"She is sleeping. She spent the entire night with you while you were feverish and only took a short sleep after. Then spent the night watching you last night while you slept. What can I do for you?"

"I need to use the bathroom."

Sistan unhooked the urinal and placed it near Jaima's side. "You may use this."

"*That*," he replied with distaste, "is for invalids. I am not an invalid."

The physician shook his head knowingly. He'd treated so many soldiers through his entire career, he could read most like a book and knew their habits. "No, you're a stubborn, irritating male who is going to end up in bed longer than necessary because you're pushing." Sistan lowered the side rail on the bed and while bent, unplugged the med

105

pump. He folded the air hose away from Jaima's face, laying it on the pillow. Jaima tossed the blankets aside, grabbing the other rail to help him sit up. Sliding his legs over the edge of the bed, he scooted his ass to the edge. "Wait a moment," the physician told him, his hand going inside the hospital gown. He gently pulled the cardiac electrodes off Jaima's chest and out from the gown. With a hand around his back, Sistan steadied the injured man as he stood, swaying slightly. "Grab the pole," Sistan instructed, "it goes with us."

They'd picked this room for Jaima because of the private adjoining bath. Rolling the pole along the floor, Sistan guided Jaima to the bathroom and kept a hand on him until he saw that he was able to keep vertical. "I'll wait right here," he told him, going to the doorway and leaning against the frame, his back turned.

Flipping the lid on the toilet, Jaima braced a hand on the wall, spread his legs and held his shaft with his other hand. "Gods' rods," he cried as a stream began, "that stings!" He heard Sistan snicker. Jo had warned him he would feel a sting the first time, but he gritted his teeth and hissed through it until he'd emptied himself. He shook, wiped, flushed, then washed and dried his hands, grabbing the pole again for balance. "I'm done," he announced.

Sky Clad Jaima

"Do I need these?" he asked once back in bed, indicating the medicines and tubing that connected him to them.

Sistan nodded. "You are less than a day from a fever. If the meds are stopped now, it might return. Does your arm hurt?" he continued, looking at the catheters on the inside of Jaima's arm below his elbow. There was no swelling or redness to indicate that the site had blown, the word Jo had used to describe an old, overused insertion site.

"No, it does not," he answered.

"Good. Perhaps another two days. I will ask Jo when she wakes what she thinks. You also need to eat and drink more to keep your body hydrated. The fever took a lot out of you, as fevers do."

"I am bored," he complained.

"There is a thing in the room I am using called a television. I do not understand the fascination with it, but perhaps we can move it in here to keep you occupied."

"What does it do?"

"It depicts life here on Earth. These people have thousands of things that they do. I watched a few of these depictions, one woman was having the child of her husband's brother while he was sharing nadryl with his clerk. Another had a man talking about who the father was of one woman and two men were fighting over the results of a test she had taken. There was another thing called a news rebroadcast of the king and queen when they first arrived here. Very strange."

"I would be interested in seeing this television then," Jaima decided.

"Let me speak with the queen. Since she lived here, she should know more about it. When dinner is ready will you be able to eat?"

"If it is not broth, I will eat."

"I will bring some in when it is ready. Patience, Lord Jaima. It will be over soon enough."

Not soon enough for Jaima, he was afraid. His side still ached, and when he moved, it pained him, but that was to be expected. Yet a soldier was expected to fight through such things because his life could depend on it, especially in battle. There was no time for indulging in lying about when someone was coming at you to kill you simply because you were the opposition. So Jaima would push as much as he could to get out of bed and back on his feet, for even injured, he was bound to protect his queen and the Earth woman who had placed herself in danger for him. Sistan, he knew had some training, but whether or not he'd kept his skills sharp made no difference. Jaima knew *he* had the skills and use them he would.

Jo occupied his thoughts far more than any other woman before. His dream came back to him, in vivid color and he saw her again, naked and beautiful on his bed in his chambers in the palace. Her hair would be spread out across the pillows, soft and curled, shining in the light from the bedside lamps.

Her skin would be bathed in warm light, perfect, without blemish. On her chest, she would have two of the most luscious breasts, round and full, more than enough to fill his hands or cushion his head. They would shiver in anticipation as she waited for him. Tipped with turgid nipples, he would take her invitation to suckle on each one and they would be sweet as summer berries ripe with flavor. Like a child starving, he would feed at her nipples, turgid peaks, reddened by the gentle bites he would give her that he would soothe with his tongue. As a connoisseur of female flesh, he would worship her breasts, exploring every curve and inch until they were as much a part of him as they were of her.

Once he'd spent a good half hour or more at her breasts, he would move down her body, tasting the skin of her arms, her waist, her hips. Each lick, every nibble, would be delicious, a morsel from the Gods, and he was their acolyte, made to worship at the altar. Each finger would be treated as if a gourmet treat made by the best chef on Taburon, her toes a delicate dessert.

But her pussy would be his ultimate goal, that sweet center of her womanhood, embraced by two flower petals of the most delicate hue, inviting the explorer to search for the treasure hidden within them. She would open to his gaze, warmed and wetted, shining with dew, salty like the sea, sweet as a piece of *trewen* candy. Her clit would be exposed, throbbing, pulsing in time to her heartbeat and his mouth would close over it firmly, pulling it inside to taste and play with. Her hips would thrust, wanting more, begging for more, but he would not give it to her until she was mindless with want, desperate with need, screaming in unfulfilled fervor.

He would bring her close, so very close, teasing her with impending orgasm, then let her come down. Again and again, he would bring her close to the heights of ecstasy only to deny her until she flooded with moisture, wetting the bed beneath, her pussy pulsing open and closed. Then, only then, would he press his cock to the entrance to her body and slowly, very slowly, sink inside, her sheath tight, until he was totally encased in her velvet warmth. Reveling in the exquisite feeling of the glove of her pussy around him, he would start a steady rhythm, in no hurry, enjoying his time inside her. She would scream to him to move faster, go deeper, but he would keep her on edge. She would lift her legs and wrap them around his hips, trying to pull him into her body faster, but he was stronger and would control their nadryl.

Until the feeling in his balls became so overpowering that he had no choice but to speed up his thrusts, pounding into her time and time again, kissing her cervix with the head of his cock. His balls would tighten impossibly high, his body would quake, seed would rush from his balls through his cock and he would explode, bathing her in burst after burst of his seed. It would set her sheath to fluttering around him as she came, squeezing him, forcing him to spend himself completely until he was thoroughly drained and exhausted.

Panting, he would roll, still embedded within her, turning her with him, embracing her with his arms and body, holding her close as they both descended from the high of orgasm, cuddling, kissing, soothing, waiting for the time when they start again.

The abrasion of the hospital gown against his now rigid cock brought him out of his fantasy and he glanced down. Tented between his legs, he was fully engorged and heavy, and uncomfortable. Rarely had any imagery had such an effect on him. He could joke and parry about sexual matters with the best of his men and not find himself in such an embarrassing state. He didn't dare to relieve himself. If passing urine had stung, what would it feel like to spend himself into his hand? Quite frankly, he wasn't interested in finding out, no matter the condition of his wayward body part.

He wanted Jo. It was as simple as that. But for what? He had been contemplating finding a woman and settling down. Would she...could she be the one he needed...wanted? He was a happy bachelor, able to take off at a moment's notice to wherever the king needed him, or join his troops in a rowdy drinking and debauchery escapade, indulging in occasional nadryl as the mood hit. But was he truly ready to give up his carefree days, or was it that he wanted something someone else had that he wished for himself?

He envied the king and queen. What they shared was special, only between them and he unreasonably felt left out for the first time in his life. Even as a child, being raised alongside of Radine, he had been included in all of the family events. They celebrated his birthday with as much enthusiasm as they did for their natural son, gifting him beyond his wildest dreams. Their greatest gift had been to allow him to call them *anmother* and *anfather*, parents by name if not by blood. And though he had estates in his own right, the position he held as the commander of the armies and guards he had earned.

To watch the love Radine and McKenna shared made him feel empty and hollow, unfulfilled despite all that he had. There were several women he could take for wife, well-bred and comely, but right now, not a single one of them sparked his interest in sharing not only his position but his bed. Only Jo filled his thoughts.

However, just because McKenna took to living on Taburon, could Jo? From what the queen had relayed in one of their many evenings dining together, the king had met with her when she had no other prospects for the future, her job gone, no family, and little chance of finding future employment, since her boss had attacked her at her apartment the morning after Radine and she had met.

Jo had a position she liked helping others. And after the furor died down over the Taburons visit, she would be able to return to it without fear. Taburon could always use more physicians, and the knowledge she would bring about methods they did not use but could employ for the betterment of Taburons would be welcomed. Was that enough though?

As on Earth, there were those in Taburon who weren't completely happy about the intrusion of humans, especially when they were finding positions with the highest ranking people on the planet. Espis had kidnapped McKenna because she felt a human was not worthy of the king as wife and queen. Jaima, with his position and titles, was considered as near a worthy husband as the king. He had not been blind to the looks he garnered wherever he went, even when in the company of the king. Many women, recognizing they had little to no chance at winning a crown, set their sights on the next best thing, the man who had the king's ear, position in the palace, and titles and estates worth nearly as much as the king's. Women pined and sighed after Jaima, mother's steered their daughters his way at gatherings, and fathers sought him out to discern if he was open to negotiating a contract of marriage, if for no other reason than to get his persistent wife and daughter off his back. Jaima dodged each of them with the dexterity of a dancer, yet kept them dangling on a thread every time he tossed a smile, kind word, or salute their way.

For Taburons to hold such anxiety for humans seemed out of character. They'd had experience with peoples from other worlds and dealt with them on a regular basis. So far, all of their dealings had been equitable and prosperous. Taburons were encouraged to talk out their disagreements, seek acceptable solutions, and deal with whatever the answers were, whether for or against their best interests.

As long as Radine was king, no human would have to face what he had here on Earth, at least not for the reasons he had. Jaima would discount the mad Espis, who'd kidnapped McKenna in order to torture her and kill her for the simple reason that the human woman had caught the eye - and the love - of the king. Espis had thought that position reserved for herself. It had been possible that any woman, Taburon or human, would have suffered the mad woman's wrath.

The dimming of the light in the room caught his attention. Unable to reach the lamps, he slowly and steadily scooted from the bed to wobble to the nearest lamp to turn it on. Going to the window, he folded back the curtain to peer outside. Though an Earth version, the street reminded him of any he might find back home. The houses appeared well cared for, trees lining the street, lawns kept and flowers blooming in the rising late spring sun. Lights twinkled in the windows of the houses as people were relaxing from the exertions of their day. The sound of footfalls behind him, firm but delicate, identified the person who entered the room and saved him from turning too fast to greet his visitor.

"Your arse is quite spectacular," McKenna observed, "but it should be in that bed. Not hanging out for all and sundry to see."

He turned back to the bed and hobbled over, sitting on the edge. "I had thought myself forgotten. It was getting darker in here."

"I was coming in to get the lights for you, and tell you Sistan will be in in about ten minutes with dinner. He also told me you are bored, so we're going to move the television in later in the morning. I don't think you'll find it dull."

"Is Jo still sleeping?" Following her hand order, he settled onto the mattress, sliding his legs under the blankets.

"She got up a little bit ago."

There was the slightest hint of a whine in his voice, though it mostly held annoyance. "She did not come in to see me."

"It's unbecoming to pout," McKenna scolded. Straightening the covers, she tucked the edges of the blankets under the mattress. "She's confused, Jaima. She's a professional and it's against her oaths as a nurse to become involved with a patient. As a woman, she's very tempted to see what can happen between the two of you."

"If I asked her to go with us back to Taburon, would you approve?"

"Are you asking me as your friend or your queen?"

"Both."

"And are you taking her as a lover, or a wife?"

Jaima grew thoughtful. "I do not know for sure."

"When you know, ask me again," she ordered. "But when you do ask her, be sure of your motives, Jaima. She's been hurt, how exactly, I don't know. She was married and her husband divorced her, something too easily done here, as you well know. She doesn't need to be hurt again, and I will never forgive you if you do."

Chapter Ten

Her bumping the bed slightly as she checked the monitors woke Jaima from a light sleep. The room was dimly lighted, the curtains pulled, allowing only enough light to see by. It was full dark outside, the birds silenced, the street noises of people ending their day now quieted. He stared at her as she read the windows of the machines, writing in the log she kept of his vitals.

Her hair had been pulled back into a single braid that hung half-way down her back, tendrils escaping along her temple to gently caress her throat and cheek. Her face was set, expressionless, her work demeanor in full force. She wore a simple shirt and skirt, non-descript and loose. As Jaima watched, she reached for his arm to check the iv catheter, but he grabbed her arm gently. She jumped, looking at her arm first then to his face.

"Where have you been?" he asked. She'd avoided him night the previous night, directing his care from another part of the house, but not stepping into the room with him. Sistan and McKenna had taken the initial readings and written on the charts.

"I was tired. I needed rest."

"A lie is not becoming, Jo. You are avoiding me."

"It's best we not get involved," she explained, finally deciding to be frank and upfront with him. "I've thought it over and you're just not the kind of man I can spend a few days with, and expect to forget. It's better if we don't start anything one of us might come to regret."

Sky Clad Jaima

With the rail on the side of the bed by which she stood down, it was easy for him to grab her and haul her onto the mattress, where as he twisted he partially covered her body with his. "I do not agree with you," he murmured right before he kissed her, holding her still in his grip.

She fought him at first, her tablet clattering to the floor, forgotten, but the power of his kiss and the strength of his hold was too much for her. Within a moment she melted, letting her body relax into the mattress and savoring the feel of his lips on hers, even giving back touch for touch, a soft sigh escaping. His cock was hard and heavy, poking into her side as he leaned more firmly into her, his hips pumping reflexively in imitation of the sex he would give her if only she would allow it.

His hand crept down her body, enclosing her breast in his palm and he squeezed. He'd been right, she filled his hand completely. Her nipple tightened into a hard bud that pressed against her shirt, he could feel it through the material of her bra. Yes, he knew about bras – Radine had told him about the sling like garment Earth women wore to encase their breasts, even showing him the one he'd pulled from McKenna their first nadryl and stored away. He pinched the little peak hard with his thumb and forefinger, making her groan into his mouth. Moving to her other breast, he treated it with the same reverence.

After teasing her to restlessness, her body hot for whatever he wanted, his hand slid down to grab the hem of her skirt, lifting it. Settling it above her hips, he delved between her legs, rubbing against the satin covering her pussy. She was wet there, wet and warm. Her pussy was full, engorged, the lips flushed with want, pressing outward towards the material of her panties. He could feel her clit as it burgeoned and rose from under its protective hood, seeking more attention from his knowing fingers. Her hips lifted, her legs opened more for him, for his questing hand.

Jaima was about to give her the best orgasm she'd ever had in her life, spectacular in its entirety, fireworks on the Fourth astounding and she'd not even undressed. This small bit of magic just from some high-handed heavy petting proved that if she ever gave in and seriously indulged in sex with Jaima, she would never emerge from the encounter the same woman. If her ex had ever had even a touch of the magic Jaima had in his kiss and hand…

Like a douse of cold water, her better senses took over and she shoved against his chest, clamping her thighs together to trap his hand, stopping him. "Please, Jaima, don't," she pleaded. "I don't want to have to leave yet, but I will if you don't stop."

He lifted, his hand and his body, letting her slide from his grasp as she scrambled off of the bed. They were both panting heavily, her face still flushed with arousal. Straightening her clothes, she picked up her clipboard, righting the pages. "Why?" he asked.

"I already explained. I'm afraid I'll give in, and I'll be the one who ends up with the broken heart. I can't take that again."

"He hurt you that badly?"

She moved to the end of the bed, putting distance between her and temptation. "He wanted children, it was the only reason he married me. And when I couldn't have any with him, he invited his friends to try and see if one of them could get me pregnant. He was ready to whore me out to his friends to fuck to get a child on me, no matter how long or how many it took. It never occurred to him the problem may have been his, though I last heard he had remarried and has children now. So I guess the problem was mine in the long run. You're young and healthy, and obviously very virile.

You're also titled. I may not be the smartest person on the block, but I do know that a titled person wants to have an heir. I don't know if I can do that for you.

"If I give in, it'll involve my heart. I can't have sex – share nadryl – without loving you. And I can't love you if I have to give you up."

She swiped at the tears that were forming in her eyes. "So, please, just let me do my job. Get better. That's all I want from you."

Jaima laid still, staring at her first with disbelief, then acceptance. Acceptance that he didn't want to make, but he didn't want to be the cause of any pain for Joanna. Flinging his arm over his eyes, he cut her out so he didn't have to watch as she went back to finishing what she had been doing when he interrupted, willing his cock to desist. Maybe in the morning it would be easier to face her, but for now, he couldn't stand the sight of her, the sound of her, the smell of the perfume she wore. The sooner she left, the better. He hoped Inoa was in good hands and that Radine was already heading back to Earth. He couldn't wait to return home.

He promised himself that as soon as he was better, once they were home, he would seek out his favorite *skala* and spend an entire three days using her body in order to forget Jo. She was skilled, this *skala*, she could do things that made him beg for mercy and still come back for more. She cost, but every coin would be worth it, if it made him forget, even for a few hours.

Jaima liked sex, loved sex in fact, and had ever since the first time when he lost his virginity. He and Radine had come of age, though Radine was a year older and had waited for his brother, and together they enlisted into the Taburon army to do their duty.

The boys had been getting into trouble for several years, doing what curious boys have done throughout the ages, peeking in windows, surreptitiously discovering the charms of women. Not many, mind you, but enough times to get them caught at least once and as punishment assigned prior to their enlistment to cleaning the stables and ancient privies for a month.

They had, at the ages of twelve and thirteen respectively, discovered masturbation and how good it felt to rub their cocks until they'd spent. So, naturally, a year or three later, when they heard sounds one day coming from a stable loft and went to investigate, and saw two of the servants engaged in nadryl, and their cocks responded in like fashion, they made a pact to see as much nadryl as they could. The fourth time they peeped, and were consequently caught, they were hauled in front of the king and queen, Radine's parents, and punished. Later the king would sit the boys down and explain some of the facts of life, including sex and how wrong it was to peek on others.

They hadn't really learned their lesson. Laughter and comraderies from the barracks on the palace grounds had them looking into a window one night just prior to their first day of training to find the soldiers enjoying an unusual night off. They were lounging in various states of undress, from totally clothed to totally nude, teasing each other, slapping arses, snapping wet towels at unsuspecting victims. The conversation was bawdy and very sexual, comparing the various attributes of women and what they would do. The boys had not realized they had not gone unnoticed. That the conversation in the barracks had become even more audacious had been lost on the young, virginal boys.

So, their first night in the barracks, they found themselves alone, the other enlistees gone to who knew where. At eighteen and nineteen, they were full grown men, but had not yet gained the muscle and mass so typical of their

126

race. Training would do that for them over the next four years or so. They rested on their bunks, relaxed, talking quietly about what their futures might hold. When the door opened and their drill instructor entered with two women, their interest perked up exponentially. The instructor kissed each woman on the cheek and pushed them towards the boys with an "Enjoy, fellas." He laughed as he left.

To say the boys didn't have a wonderful night would be a lie. The women, experienced *skalas,* took the boys every which they could until the boys and their cocks dropped from exhaustion and begged to be left alone. The *skalas* kissed the boys before leaving, promising that if they ever wanted to visit with them, they were more than welcome.

From that day on, when he had time and the coin, Jaima took the one woman up on her offer several times over the next few years. He enjoyed the woman's body, but he learned from her as well, what pleased a woman, how to bring her to completion with parts of his body other than just his cock, and that a woman liked to be considered as more than a convenient pussy in which to expend his cock. Jaima was discreet about his dalliances, never leaving a woman wanting, but never expecting more than he gave her in the space of a few nights.

127

Sky Clad Jaima

And he discovered that it was more than the relief to
his cock that he liked about being with a woman. If that's all
he wanted, he could have pleasured himself without
emotional entanglement. It was the holding after, the
gentling of emotions and bodies that had climbed a pinnacle
so high that it took lots of time to come back down. It was
the cuddling, the light kisses, the smooth touch over heated
skin and the soft breath against her hair as she slept that he
loved the most. He was not a love 'em and leave 'em man.
He made each one feel special, took time with each,
spending the night with most after intense nadryl to
sometimes wake them with gentle loving before rising
himself to depart. Each woman was smiling when he closed
the door. And Jaima's reputation as a considerate and
desirable lover followed him all over Taburon.

It wasn't just the afterglow of sex he loved either. He
actually loved women, all kinds of them – tall, short, perfect
weight or with extra pounds. Really thin women didn't do
too much for him, their boney bodies could hurt during
vigorous nadryl. But those with flesh on their bodies gave
him something into which he could lose himself exploring,
teasing, touching, loving. He found each one different and
fascinating. Their skin under his hard fingers. The smell of

them, from their hair to their feet and especially their pussies. Their taste, their mouths and juices. Small breasted or large breasted, well experienced or somewhat untutored, he loved them all and let each one know that she was the most beautiful woman he'd ever been with.

He knew he could please Jo, if she would ever give him the chance. He would not just dip his wick and run, but show her what her body could experience at his hands. To worship a woman was his greatest pleasure and he would prove that she could come many times in many ways in one night, no matter what she believed about herself. Jo was scared of what he could do for her, of what sharing nadryl could mean for herself, and what she might read into spending the night with him, what she might expect from him in the aftermath of the nadryl. Her past clouded her life. Her husband still had such a tight hold on her that she was running the other way when he wanted to help free her from the ties her ex had placed around her. Jaima knew the best way to expunge one's self from an old lover was to take another. He was offering himself as the cure.

If only Jo would give herself – them – a chance. They only had a few days to spend together, but he could make them memorable for the rest of her life. She was concerned for his injury, yet he'd been injured before and knew ways to get past that to take her to places she'd never thought possible. A warrior got passed his disabilities any way he could, and carried on, any way he could.

But he was stuck with these barriers between them. In the past he had learned that hard work and a good opponent could drive demons from his mind. His men were in for the workout of their lives. It was time he paid a visit to some of the other garrisons on Taburon, see how well the men were trained and perhaps even stay for a while to assure they came up to par. It would get him out of the range of the king and queen and their ongoing, very visible and very expressive love affair. It would give him some peace, maybe.

Maybe then he'd find a biddable woman willing to trade her freedom for a title, marry her and set her up on one of his estates. He'd take time from his duties to visit every so often to ease his cock. Maybe get an heir or two on her. He'd only ask her to remain faithful, as he would, since he took his vows to anything seriously and he'd tolerate no bastards. If she would provide him with his heirs, he'd give her a life of luxury for the rest of her life.

He waited until Jo had left before he uncovered his eyes. For the rest of the night he would seclude himself in the room, refusing the offer of the television in the morning. Call it pouting, he didn't care a wit. He would get away with it, claiming not feeling well and wanting to sleep. Tomorrow he would force himself to get out of bed and stay out for as long as possible. He would push his body, make himself better through sheer willpower if that was all he had, cut down on the amount of time she had to spend taking care of him. She would leave when she saw he was capable of handling his own needs and Sistan taking care of the medical. He would care for himself, even if it killed him. McKenna and Sistan would argue with him, but he was a warrior first and they held no hold over him in that regard. All he needed were clothes, and he would prove he was good on his own.

Chapter Eleven

In the year twenty forty-five, the United States, in coalition with countries around the world, started an initiative to kill or seriously curtail illegal drugs. The cost was unimportant because the costs of allowing the trade in illegal drugs had become unbearable for law enforcement and the health care industry. Those who'd believed legalization of marijuana would cut down on costs had not taken into consideration that once a person had reached the highest they could get with marijuana they then went in search of a higher high through the more potent drugs. Legalizing marijuana for medical use had proven a joke as it became easily the most available drug on the market and people made fortunes selling fake prescriptions and providing the drug to fake patients.

So with the aid of militaries from around the world, each well-known illegal drug center was raided, its 'lords,' seconds-in-command, and thirds-in-command were either arrested or killed and product burned.

This initiative left the world with a huge hole in available drugs and a fabulous opportunity for any entrepreneur with enough money to set up a legal business to develop and manufacture drugs approved by the government to fill the void with drugs that would produce the same effect. Into this environment, George Raymond set up his company to develop and manufacture approved drugs and started to make a fortune, especially after the war of twenty fifty-five. With the sons of his rivals dead because of the war, he moved in and bought up their businesses, expanding his investment and deepening his pockets.

With his new found wealth and ties to the government, he was able to work on certain drugs without oversight – drugs that otherwise would have never passed approval and were created for nefarious purposes. So while he provided legitimate drugs for the public, he also kept a pharmacopoeia of drugs that for the right price, with the right guarantees of silence, and the right connections, were available to make even the most reluctant person compliant or cooperative for whatever the user wanted.

Because he had the largest such company in the southern United States, he also had the largest ego, thinking he was God's gift to women. With men at a premium after the war, women found themselves in a tenuous situation. They were able to take over where men had led prior to the war, but where men still had control, they held it with cemented hands. Men also had the option to discard women at will – if for any reason a man tired of the woman he was with, he was permitted to leave/discard/dump her and take another with little recrimination. So George Raymond, though he was married, had no problem cutting a swath through his female employees in search of sexual gratification, threatening their jobs for noncompliance. His wife ignored his liaisons and kept her peace about his secrets as long as he stayed married to her and provided for her wants.

Until he'd gone after McKenna Primm, one of his clerks. His campaign to get into her panties had taken six months until the day he made an overt and unmistakable pass. She'd quit on the spot, leaving her desk and job immediately. On the way home she'd run into Radine, the king of Taburon, who'd come to Earth in search of a wife and queen, if for no other reason than to get his mother off his back about getting both. When Raymond had shown up at McKenna's apartment the day after she'd quit, and attacked her, Radine had beat him soundly, leaving him bleeding on the floor as they made their way to his ship to return to Taburon.

For two years Raymond had harbored a boiling hatred for the woman, the one that got away, the one he'd had planned to set up as his mistress. The one that had cost him dearly in the divorce settlement he'd had to make to keep Mrs. Raymond from talking. Now he'd discovered exactly what had happened to her and that she'd come back to Earth. That she'd done so well, married a king to become his queen and bore a child, grated on him more than anything thing he'd ever endured in his life, times ten. After seeing the news reports of her arrival back on Earth, and the ensuing incident, Raymond had set his mind to darker things. And he began to make plans to kidnap her, take her to an isolated cabin, and do what he willed to her body and mind. Whether or not he killed her after, he'd not decided. She could probably bring a nice price if he sold her to someone interested in continuing her torture or turning her into a sex slave for their enjoyment and profit.

How fortunate that big Taburon bastard – though not the one he'd have preferred - had been shot. Raymond drove to the capitol as soon as he'd seen the footage of the arrival of the Taburons and the ensuing attempt to kill either all of them or the President of the United States for hosting the aliens. He began to hang out at the hospital, just one of the crowd, watching the comings and goings with insidious intent. He'd seen the fake McKennas entering the hospital, figured they were about to move the injured the alien and staked out the least likely spots for his leaving. And he'd been right – they'd left from the loading dock via a van. Following, he'd discovered their whereabouts and started the ball rolling in his plans to take the bitch who thought she was something special because she'd married a king and spawned a mixed blood brat.

Sky Clad Jaima

He would take his time, since he had all the time in the world right now. Things had to go right, had to be precise in order for him to carry this off. He had to get in, get McKenna, then get out without having to run afoul of any of the others in the house with her. He had no problem with shooting any of them, if he had to, but that meant noise and that meant his time would have been limited, especially if there were nosy neighbors. So he bided his time and waited.

But now that all of his plans were set, he was ready to move tonight. In his hotel room, anxiety and excitement building, images filling his brain of the things he would do, the things he would relish as he worked over her body, he dropped his trousers and shorts and masturbated furiously, images of McKenna's naked and bound body quaking in terror as he enacted his revenge fulfilling his fantasy until he came more powerfully than ever before, slumping exhausted into the sheets.

Sky Clad Jaima

Chapter Twelve

Jaima woke the next morning with his normal
morning erection and a desperate need to empty his bladder.
Not wanting to disturb anyone - though he wouldn't have
minded if Jo had come in to find him impressively erect - but
not sure if anyone was awake yet, he slipped over the edge
of the bed, grabbing the medicine pole at the same time and
gingerly made his way to the bathroom. Keeping himself
upright without having to hold onto something, for which he
was quite pleased, he took care of his business. Once back in

the bedroom, he perched on the edge of the bed, waiting for another of his housemates to rise, considering his options for the next few days.

First, he needed the tubes taken from his arm so he could have the freedom of getting around without his metal dance partner. He felt fine, no matter that he'd been unconscious and feverish just two days ago. Surely Sistan had something that he could consume to continue his recovery without the human created intervention. And since he was up now, awake, and eating he could make sure he drank enough to keep his fluid levels acceptable.

Second, he needed clothes. It was downright embarrassing to be wearing this flimsy covering that barely reached his thighs and left his arse on display. Besides, it was cold in the garment, and he was tired of feeling cold.

Third, he was hungry, a sure sign that he was well on the road to recovery. His stomach rumbled loudly and he chuckled softly. For a man his size, he required a great deal of fuel and there was little he refused to eat. He always worked it off on the training field or keeping occupied with his other duties, but when it came time to eat, he did it heartily and well.

He would have preferred a decent bed. He was a big man and he liked to sprawl. The bed he was in now was too confining and narrow. He'd awoken more than once since regaining consciousness to find his feet hanging off the end or he too close to the edge. If not for the rails, he most likely would have rolled right over the edge.

Finally, he would have appreciated a good nadryl, but with Jo's refusal to share with him, that, he knew, had to wait until he returned to Taburon to find a willing *skala*. He would hope to keep the fire stoked and smoldering until then, and there was always self-gratification if necessary to take off the edge.

Sistan was the first person to come in to check on their patient, surprised to see him standing…leaning… against the edge of the bed, impatience on his face. A raised eyebrow was the only scolding Sistan was going to offer, since Jaima's lordly and stern expression dared him to try anything else. Though that had never worked on the physician ever before anyway.

"Good morning, Lord Jaima," he greeted. "I assume you're ready to get out of bed."

"If you will take these things out of my arm and get me some clothing, yes."

"Have a seat," Sistan indicated, pointing to the chair. Spinning on his heel, Jaima plopped himself down as Sistan gathered materials. Gloving his hands, he bent over the arm, peeling up an edge of the tape over the catheter. Gently pulling, he removed the tape, setting it aside. With a gauze pad, he covered the actual catheter and pulled the device gently from the skin, folded the gauze and then the arm to apply pressure. Discarding the soiled materials, Sistan opened a bandage and taped it over gauze, holding it in place. "If you wish to clean yourself, you will need that covered, unless you wait for an hour or so. Let the wound close over first."

"I will wait. Are there clothes for me?"

Sistan went to the dresser where there was a pile of material. "I believe so," he answered as he rooted through the pile. Taking out a pair of surgical pants, he shook it out and passed it to Jaima. "Those might be a bit tight, but they'll cover the essentials." He pawed through the pile again, passing over socks. "Sorry, there're aren't any shirts large enough for you, and you and I are not the same size, otherwise I would loan you something of mine. We can turn up the house temperature if you find yourself feeling cold."

Standing, Jaima pulled the gown off to drop to the floor, his arse and thighs braced against the edge of the bed. Sistan was a physician. If he couldn't tolerate sight of a naked man, he could turn his back. Bending, he shoved one leg into the pants, then the other, pulling them over his hips and settling them at his waist. The hems ended just above his ankles. Jaima tightened the string and tied it off. He donned the socks, and then threw the blanket from the bed over his shoulders for a shirt.

"Hungry?"

"I feel as though my throat has been cut. Yes, I am starving."

"They make a drink here called coffee. You may like it." Sistan directed the way, following closely with an eye on the injured man in case.

In the kitchen, they found Jo at a counter, cutting vegetables to make an omelet. "Good morning, Joanna," Sistan greeted. Jaima kept silent, wanting to see her reaction at finding him vertical and intruding on her space. Sistan pointed to the chair at the edge of the counter, indicating for the man to sit.

Jo glanced up and the knife slipped slightly, a frown crossing her features. Jaima quickly disguised the satisfied smile that crossed his face, perching a hip on the stool and settling in to watch with pleasure just how much he could disconcert her with only his presence. Quickly recovering, glad she hadn't cut her fingers in surprise, Jo kept her gaze on her task, slicing the vegetables with a vengeance. "Morning," she replied. She didn't fail to notice the long thick outline of his cock down the inside of his thigh under the material of his pants. She felt her blood rush through her with an electric zing.

"Is the queen up yet?" Sistan asked as he took cups from a cupboard to take to the pot of coffee nearby.

"She's sleeping in a little longer."

"Is she all right?" he asked as he poured. He slid a cup to Jaima, who picked it up to stare at it with suspicion.

"Just tired. She's pregnant. It's to be expected for a while yet."

Sky Clad Jaima

Jaima sipped at the hot brew delicately, a brow rising in surprise. "Told you," Sistan said smugly. "If it's too bitter, there is sweetener." Jaima shook his head, he found the brew acceptable.

"I'll have breakfast ready in about a half hour. Why don't you go sit in the living room until I call you?" Sistan plucked at the blanket Jaima wore until he got the other's attention and with a tilt of his head, led the man out of the room. Jaima followed only after sliding his glance once over his shoulder to toss her a meaningful look. He had been very much aware of her reaction to him and was pleased. Jo sighed in relief, hunching over the counter a second before going back to her task. God save her, she thought, from pig-headed and unbearably handsome, virile men that set her heart racing. Her shoulders shook with repressed laughter at her reaction as she went back to slicing.

Sistan showed Jaima to a couch and took a seat himself, finding the television control remote and turning on the television as he made himself comfortable.

Jaima jumped when the picture came on, nearly spitting out the mouthful of coffee he had just taken as he watched with fascination the three people on the screen talking about things of which he had no idea. When a picture of the president came on, he sat forward to listen intently, and his breath caught in his chest when a video of the arrival of the king, queen and himself on the planet and their descent down the gangplank was played. And he peered even more intently when they showed the incident in front of the White House, the cars pulling to a stop, the people exiting, and the shooting that occurred, even to Jaima collapsing after. The commentator spoke about how the man behind the shooting was part of a group of xenophobes and the whereabouts of the Taburons was still unknown, though it was confirmed that the injured man was no longer in the hospital.

"They were able to record that?" he asked with shock.

"It seems that anything that happens of importance on this planet is recorded and replayed time and time again for the people around the world."

Jaima shuddered watching the recording, remembering when the bullets hit him, the burning pain in his side and the loss of blood. He remembered the sadness on Radine's face, clutching at his friend, trying to stop the bleeding, tears filling his eyes. A cold shiver raced through him, his heart beating furiously in his chest. If he lived a thousand Taburon years, Jaima would never forget the pain, the burning, and especially the tears in Radine's eyes as he drifted into unconsciousness. It would take him a while to calm just from seeing the video.

He finished the coffee and sat, his eyes on the television, but his mind elsewhere. This was a strange place, where a person's life was news for everyone, no matter who they were. Yes, Radine was constantly being surrounded by people wanting to know what he was doing, but as the king, he could control what was disclosed and to whom, for some part. In a way, he, Jaima, was also a person of interest on Taburon, since he was so close to the king and a warrior of some renown, but he also had some control over who knew what and when. Their day to day lives were theirs to live – only the important things, like marriage, births and deaths were recorded for the people of the planet. New laws were transmitted by word of mouth or proclamation, handed down from the king's representatives to the people.

Not that the people did not have a say in their government. Every one of them could contact their king through channels and voice their opinion, ask a question, request a favor, or make an announcement, such as a marriage, birth or death. And the king made sure that every request was heard or read, if not by himself, then by one of his close advisors, who then assured that the king was kept apprised of what was going on in his kingdom. It was time consuming, yes, but Radine was a people's king. He lived the title fully. Taking McKenna for a wife only enhanced his reputation, since she was just as people orientated as the king, jumping in to help where she could. They lived and worked for the betterment of the people.

"Jaima," Jo called again. He'd been so inattentive that he'd not heard her call the first time, but his head swiveled her way. She stood in the doorway to the living room. "Breakfast," she invited. He rose, and swayed, reaching out with a hand, Jo rushing over to slip an arm under his uninjured side for support. Jaima tightened at her touch, so close, so sweet smelling, his body's reaction to her nearness out of his control as his cock filled, pressing outward into the thin material of the pants. He stumbled once when her hand went to his waist, his body tensing and the visible outline of his stiffened cock could be seen laying along his right thigh, but he caught himself before he could fall and walked gingerly in the direction she steered.

"You're not ready to be out of bed," she murmured as he settled onto a chair with a sigh. "You're pushing and might only make things worse if you aren't careful."

"I am fine," he retorted with annoyance.

Jo stared at him with her best 'I know better because I'm the nurse' look, but he pointedly ignored her by turning away from her face, concentrating on the table top before him. He was being not only stubborn, but stupid, and so very typical of a male. Joanna sighed and shrugged reaching for the dishes of food. She set a large dish of scrambled eggs and veggies on the table between the two men, dropped a plate of buttered toast nearby, then brought the coffee pot back to place it near as well. With her own dish in hand, she spooned a portion onto the dish for herself, set two pieces of toast next to the eggs, filled a cup and carried everything into the living room. Jaima followed her with hooded eyes. He could be obtuse as well.

"Don't take too much," Sistan requested after serving himself. "You've been without solid food for a few days. Too much and you may get sick." He pushed the dish across the table top. "When you're done, you should be able to shower if you wish and we'll move the television into your room then."

Jaima decided that if she could be obstinate, then he could as well. The small bit of glee he felt at becoming a thorn in her side he'd relish as he ate, his eyes never straying far from the sight of her back, which she had turned to the two men. "No," he replied loud enough to carry, "I am tired of that room. I will stay out here for as long as I can. The couch is comfortable."

Jo visibly tensed, overhearing the conversation. So he was going to be a prick, was he? She wouldn't give him the satisfaction, since she'd decided to return to her room to spend the day until he'd opened his mouth. If he was going to pout, he could do it wherever he wished, but she wasn't going to give him the first point by caving. In fact... "When did he get his last antibiotic?" she asked loud enough for both men to hear.

Sistan thought for a moment. "Last night."

"Then he'll be due as soon as he's finished eating," she determined. Neither could see the smile on her face.

She passed McKenna in the hallway a half hour later, the queen going to the kitchen area and the nurse heading for Jaima's bedroom where the meds were still kept. "Morning," she greeted, her training coming to the fore as she considered McKenna's shadowed eyes. "Are you all right?"

"Just tired, and missing my family."

"There's an omelet keeping warm in the oven for you and a fresh pot of coffee. I should warn you, Jaima is on the sofa and he's in a snit."

McKenna combed her hair from her face, a puzzled look crossing her features, wrapping her tresses with a scrunchie. "What's he in a snit about?"

"He's male. What isn't he in a snit about?" Jo replied sarcastically as she continued down the hall. Shaking her head, McKenna's stomach rumbling, she found the food and loading a plate, perched on one of the chairs at the table.

Sistan had discovered the delicious flavor of orange juice and was nursing a glass. "What's up with Jaima?" McKenna asked, pouring herself a cup of coffee.

"I am not sure. He appears particularly annoyed, and annoying."

"Seems Jo is, too." McKenna forked a mouthful of food, chewed. "I know he asked her to share nadryl. Maybe they haven't gotten to it yet and he's a little...stressed."

"I believe you humans call it blue balls," Sistan corrected.

McKenna chuckled. "Yeah, I believe that's what it's called. And Radine can get that way after about three days without sex."

"He is a healthy male," Sistan commented.

"They're both walking sex machines and pitiful puppies when they don't get any."

"A consistent release of sexual energy helps to keep a man focused."

The look she shot him was utter disbelief – that he'd said that, that he most likely believed it, that he probably spouted it off to other Taburon males. "And your excuse is?" she asked remembering that he'd said that he didn't want a wife, being ship bound.

"I did not say that I do not follow my own advice."

"You dog!" she exclaimed lasciviously, lightly punching at his shoulder. Sistan started to reply, but silenced when she, noticing Jo come into the living room with a needle in hand, dropped her hand to tap him on the arm. "This is going to be interesting," she whispered with a nod of her head.

Jo stood next to the sofa, waiting, until Jaima drew his gaze away from the television. He was watching one of those programs where the people were arguing over who was the father of one woman's baby. It was disturbing yet he couldn't take his eyes off of it. "What?" he finally asked.

"Your medicine," she said, showing him the needle.

"The tubes have been removed," he reminded her.

"It doesn't always need to go through an iv. Roll over some and show me the top of your ass." When he didn't immediately comply, she scowled again with her 'I'm in charge and the nurse' face. "You still need the antibiotic," she insisted.

He didn't trust her, but he loosened the ties, pulling them free, rolled his hips, and leaned onto the cushions with his elbows as she dragged the top of the pants down far enough to expose the top of his right cheek. Wiping the area with a wetted cotton ball, she took aim and jabbed.

"Gods' rods, woman!" he yelled. "That hurt!"

"Sorry," she said, none too regretfully. She depressed the plunger. "I may have been a little too rough. I'll try to be more gentle next time." Removing the needle, she rubbed, rather forcefully, at the spot. "Leave off!" he commanded, straightening abruptly, his hand going to the spot to rub tenderly.

"You'll need another in four hours. Don't go anywhere," she instructed as she left to dispose of the used needle. She smiled sweetly at McKenna and Sistan as she passed them, holding the needle up and blowing at it like she was blowing smoke from the barrel of a gun.

"Gods be damned you'll do it again in four hours," Jaima grumbled, glaring after her. His arse still hurt.

McKenna burst into laughter.

Sky Clad Jaima

Chapter Thirteen

"What is wrong these people? Do they not see the tree behind them?" Jaima asked. "The leaves can be braided to make rope. If they strip the bark from the tree, it will make string for a bow. Then all they need is a sapling, and there should be plenty of those on that island. Do these people not have any skills?"

McKenna peered over the magazine she was reading to watch the television show currently airing and giggled. It was one of those survival type shows, where people were dropped into a remote area with little equipment and expected to remain for at least a week, surviving off of the land and what they could find. Jaima had been intently watching, and commenting frequently on the lack of intelligence of the participants, as if they could actually hear him. "It's a program, Jaima, they're supposed to act like they don't know how to do things since it increases the audience's connection to the program and the people on it." She chuckled. "Gives the viewers a chance to call out suggestions even though they can't be heard," she added pointedly. "It also makes the viewers feel more superior, since they can see obvious answers that the contestants can't."

Jaima scowled, ignoring her jibe. "How do they survive?"

"They don't have to. If anything serious were to happen there are people who step in to make sure there are no injuries."

"But they said that one man was sick from drinking the water."

"And if he became so sick that he was in real danger of dying, they would have taken him off the island and to a hospital. It's for entertainment, Jaima. It really is just choreographed to make you get more involved."

"Why do people watch such things if they are not real?"

"Some people need to empathize with the people on a program. They live vicariously through their struggles and it often makes them feel superior if their lives are better."

Jaima frowned. "Humans are strange. That they would voluntarily do this to themselves is not sensible."

"No, it's not."

"And the show where they recorded a group of people sharing nadryl, is that normal as well?" While flipping through the channels, he had come across an adult movie program and watched with fascination until he'd become disgusted with the obvious fallacy and changed the station.

"It's called pornography, or porn. Again, it's so people might live vicariously through the actors on the screen."

"It is disturbing that people would allow themselves to be recorded sharing nadryl."

"Did you not have a reaction to what you saw?"

Jaima flushed slightly. His cock had begun to engorge as he'd watched the couples on the screen sharing nadryl, but he had quickly taken it under control, which told him that while such a program might have gotten things started, he still would have had control over his cock. Sharing nadryl with the right woman was supposed to involve unquenchable desires. Grunts and groans of faked passion held little interest for him. "Yes, but sharing nadryl with a live woman is much more preferable," he said, "and not with so many men."

"But there are people who believe they need that kind of stimulation in order to have nadryl."

"They are very sad men, to not be able to find something in their woman worth raising their cock to share nadryl."

McKenna smiled. "You're such a romantic," she said.

He scoffed and turned back to the television, not so interested now because he knew it was fake. He'd watched several programs through the day, fascinated by the fare, amazed at the variety. He could understand how humans could become addicted to this television and was glad they would soon be returning to Taburon. Too much more time with nothing to do except watch these programs and he would begin to grow fat and lazy. He was already concerned that he had lost muscle tone. And McKenna, Sistan, and Jo would not allow him to try any exercising to begin bringing it back, as though there was anything here in this house that he could have used. Yes, his sword was near, but there was nothing he could swing it against to practice and he was sure, no opponent with whom to spar. Every day that passed set him back more, which meant more time he would have to spend once they returned to Taburon.

From the corner of his eye he spied Jo walking across the house, her back straight, her hair pulled back into one of those things a woman called a ponytail. Why they would want something sticking out of the back of their head that resembled the back end of a *crufa*, he didn't know. After giving him the shot this morning, she returned to the bedroom, where she could be heard banging things around and making a lot of noise. Obviously she was angry, but really, he thought, she'd brought it on herself. He'd made the offer and she had turned him down. And now it appeared that she was regretting her decision. She'd come at him again with a needle twice since the first time. Despite being ill, he reminded her with a soft growl that he was stronger than she and she gave him the injections with much more care.

Of course he had no part in her becoming angry. He really was bored in the bedroom and feeling closed in. Plus, there had been no reason to bring a television into his room when he was capable of coming to the one here, his little snit notwithstanding. And after watching this one for the better part of a day, he would have requested the one in his room be removed, especially now that he knew the programs were faked. There was no enjoyment in watching people do things that were staged for the sole purpose of making viewers more involved.

Jaima shifted on the couch, pulling the edges of the blanket that had drooped higher across his shoulders. The room was starting to chill as the sun began to set, it was getting dark outside. His stomach grumbled.

"Hungry?" McKenna asked.

"Yes."

She stood, setting her magazine aside on a table. Reaching for the lamp, she turned on the light, casting the room in a soft yellow glow. "Let me see…"

From the front of the house, the doorbell sounded. McKenna looked towards the entry, Jo came out of the kitchen, Sistan on her heels. There was no reason for anyone to be visiting, but they had agreed that if anyone did come to the house, Jo would answer the door because she was the only one who'd not been part of the chaos surrounding the Taburons and would most likely not be recognized. "Let me get the weapon," McKenna whispered, fleeing to the room she shared with Jo. She was back in seconds, a laser weapon in hand, then nodded to Jo as she took a position near the door, but out of sight. The bell sounded again.

Jaima and Sistan had both risen and stood near, but out of sight, the physician's hand on the arm of the injured man, keeping him from moving closer to the door. No matter how much he felt obliged to protect the women, he was still too weak to be of any use if it came right down to it. The laser weapon would be much more effective if needed.

Jo peeked through the spy hole in the door to see who had arrived. They were supposed to be incognito in the house, but obviously their quiet activity, lights coming on at night, had attracted some attention.

A man stood on the stoop, dishes in his hand. He was on the portly side with a slight paunch and jowls that someday would hide his neck if he didn't take control of his weight. A pair of thick rimmed glasses sat low on his nose. He wore a crumpled suit that needed ironing, his tie was askew, his dull brown greyish tinted hair windblown, though there was no wind. He looked up at the door again and reached for the bell, but Jo opened the door, leaning on the edge.

The man smiled wanly, obviously uncomfortable. "Hey," he said, "ah, hi. I'm Bert, Bert Sockoff, I live just down the street. My wife, uh, Jeanne, uh, she's the one in charge of the, um, Welcome Wagon for the neighborhood. She noticed you folks had moved in, but one of our kids has the flu, so she asked me to pick up something from the grocery to send over. So I uh, stopped off despite my feet killing me like crazy and got this, uh, lasagna and brownies. You just need to heat it up." He pushed the two dishes in his hands forward into Jo's hands. "She said that she, uh, will try to get over later next week as soon as the kid stops barfing and is feeling better."

Jo glanced at the items she'd been given, then back to the man. He smiled again wanly, pushing up the glasses with a finger. "Thanks," she stammered, "it looks good." Both packages were wrapped in clear wrap, as though someone didn't want to admit it was store bought, but he'd said he'd bought it at the store. "I was just trying to decide what to have for dinner. Tell your wife thank you, but I just got in from work and I've got a bath running and need to go turn off the water before it overruns the tub." She started to step back, her hand on the door as she began to close it.

"She'll stop by later," the man reminded Jo loudly as she got the door halfway closed.

"Thank you," Jo yelled back, shutting the door completely. McKenna lowered the laser weapon with a sigh. Jo took the dishes to the kitchen, setting them on the counter separately. Underneath she found price tags from a well-known local grocery chain. Taking the covering from the larger dish, the scent of the lasagna wafted from the dish.

"Smells good," Jo commented.

"Yeah," McKenna agreed. "I haven't had lasagna in years." She turned on the oven and placed the dish inside. "Should be ready in about twenty minutes." McKenna lifted

162

the cover from the brownies and sniffed, sighing in undisguised near orgasmic ecstasy. Chocolate didn't exist on Taburon.

"Good, that'll give me time to finish straightening the med box. It's gotten kind of disorganized today." McKenna shot her a 'ya think?' look. Jo flushed but hurried away.

She'd been angry, she knew they'd heard her clomping around in Jaima's room. The man was irritating beyond belief. As long as he'd stayed in the bedroom, she had had the freedom of the house, and could walk away from the annoying injured man no matter how handsome he looked and how much he got her engine revving. The first time she'd given him the shot, she had been rough to get even, and instantly regretted her show of pique. It was unprofessional of her to let her emotions take over, especially when she was the one at fault. It had been her decision, she shouldn't be taking it out on her patient, causing him unnecessary pain.

But really, why, oh why did he have to be the most handsome man she'd ever seen? She'd actually enjoyed touching him while he'd been hospitalized, his skin warm and smooth, the muscles underneath firm with years of training. His sex appeal was off the charts, his voice was bedroom quality times ten, and she had had to fight herself to keep from drooling over his physical attributes, his chest, his arms…hell, his cock, wondering what he could do with that piece of man flesh that would rock her world. Her ex had been average-sized and not very concerned for her pleasure when between her legs. His pleasure came first and foremost, rutting until he'd come, playing with her clit for a few seconds until she groaned to let him know she'd orgasmed, never realizing she'd faked it.

After a year, when she'd not become pregnant, he'd suggested she let a group of his friends screw her for a month or two and see what happened. That was when she'd put her foot down and slept in another room that night. The next day, while she was at work, he'd packed up her things and put them outside in the yard. He'd changed the locks on the doors and the phone numbers for both the house and his cell. She'd dragged what she could to her car – at least it was in her name – and spent the next few nights at a motel. Two weeks later, he'd had the divorce papers delivered to her at her job, instructing the deliverer to loudly announce his reason for being there so that she might suffer that much more humiliation at his hands. She'd considered taking the rest of the day off, but her pride wouldn't let her give in and allow him to humiliate her further. He may have won the war, but she at least could claim victory in that particular battle.

Her emotions after…..

By the time she'd finished straightening the med box, the smell of the warmed lasagna had filled the house with its spicy aroma, drawing her to it like a moth to a flame. The men had already claimed their portions, the dish something neither Jaima nor Sistan had ever had before, the looks of culinary ecstasy apparent on their faces. McKenna had made a pitcher of iced tea and was pouring tall glasses for everyone when she entered.

But damn, that Jaima made eating a sensual experience. Taking a forkful of food, he placed the fork in his mouth, biting with his teeth to then slide the fork slowly out, closing his lips around the food, humming softly in delight as he chewed, his jaw working forcefully. She reddened again, yet after making sure he was watching, forked up her own portion, reproducing his action, but adding a slow, tantalizing lick of her lips with just the tip of her tongue after she'd taken the fork out, making sure she touched every part of her mouth. Jaima nearly choked as he swallowed, stabbing at his next bite with the fork with annoyance, so hard he might have broken the plate had he attacked it any harder. McKenna and Sistan both snorted at the children but kept their silence, steering the conversation, what little there had been, away from the heat simmering between the two. Too much longer and Jo and Jaima would burst into flame, and Sistan and McKenna both hoped they were far enough away so they wouldn't get scorched.

Sky Clad Jaima

Chapter Fourteen

Jo carried her piece of brownie into the room she shared with McKenna, setting it down on the dresser for a moment. From a suitcase she'd been allowed to bring, she pulled clean underwear, a pair of sweat pants and a loose t-shirt. Picking up the brownie, she went into the bathroom, placing the garments on one side of the sink and the brownie on the other.

With her brush, she loosened the ponytail and brushed out her hair until all of the knots were untangled, letting he strands hang down her back in gentle waves. Her shirt and work pants were dropped to the floor and kicked gently to the side. From behind, she unhooked her bra and added it to the pile of outer clothes, then slid her panties down her legs, dropping them on top of everything with her foot.

Jo took a hefty bite from the brownie, chewing as she reached into the shower and turned on the water, adjusting the spray so it would hit where she wanted and not directly into her face. As she hooked a towel from the bar to sling over the stall door, she caught a glimpse of herself in the full length mirror and stopped to stare for a moment.

She wasn't that bad, she decided, her figure acceptable to most males. Her neck was long and set dead center of her shoulders, the pulse beat strongly, her shoulders spread out from there in gentle curves. There was a deep cleft at the base of her throat, her collar bones were well defined.

Her breasts were still firm for the most part, standing fairly high on her chest, full globes of peach-toned flesh, rounded on the bottom, peaked by pert, brownish pink nipples which were surrounded by deep rouge-brown areola. They were very responsive to the right touch, as proven earlier by Jaima, tightening into hard buds that stood proud and demanding when stimulated. Her ex had, in the beginning of their marriage, given her breasts plenty of attention, if it got her to the point where he could thrust into her without having to use any sort of lubricant to ease his passage. As they got closer to the end, he would barely even acknowledge that she had breasts, let alone play with them to excite her. Only one of her subsequent lovers, and there had only been two, paid any amount of time above her waist before taking care of his own needs, leaving her not high and dry, but high and wet and wanting.

Her waist was trim, there was no excess bulge, no spare tire flesh there, but it was no longer rail thin as it had been when she'd been a young woman. Maturity had filled her out some, adding weight that didn't detract, but made her look like a woman a man could hold onto during sex. Below, her belly had lost the concave teenager flatness and rounded ever so much, again maturity giving her a more womanly look. Her hips flared from each side of her abdomen, well-defined, and tapered down to thighs that had not gained any weight over the years and did not jiggle when she walked.

Between her legs, her mound of Venus was lightly furred, the curls a darker blonde than that on her head, disappearing between her legs to hide her feminine treasures. She knew she had a sensitive pussy, her own explorations had confirmed it. Her clit would swell when stimulated, rising from its fleshy cave full and turgid, pulsing with need. She'd discovered that rubbing her slit from the top to the entrance of her body on either side of her clit could make her come and come hard, her clit would throb for minutes after until it settled on its own. Nothing was quite like the feel of a man rutting between her legs, but for the right reasons, not the ones she'd been subjected to in the past.

If Jaima wanted a bed partner, she wasn't sure if she could give him what he sought, no matter the desires of her body. If the small examples he given to her were any indication, sex with him would be mind-blowingly wonderful, something to remember for the rest of her life, something to write home about, if she'd had someone to write home and cared to share such intimacies. He proven with his kiss that he knew something about making love to a woman, his hand had closed around her breast with confidence and promise.

But she couldn't give in to it – to her desires, to his wants, to her needs. He would get better soon and be gone and she would be left wanting – again, filled with memories and regrets.

Giving herself a full body shake to dispel her rambling thoughts and critiques, she swung the towels over the shower stall door and stepped into the water.

Letting the warmth flow over her, tilting her head back to thoroughly soak her hair, Jo squirted a dollop of shampoo into the palm of her hand then spread between her two hands after replacing the bottle on the shelf. Working the suds through her hair, she washed it completely and rinsed, then washed it again. The long tresses tended to hold small particles of dirt deep inside and usually required a second wash.

After rinsing a second time, she reached for the conditioner, flattening her palm against the wall of the shower as a wave of dizziness washed through her head. Shaking it off, she applied the cream, twisting her hair into a loose knot and piling it on top of her head, securing it with a clip she took from the same shelf.

Her soap was creamy and lightly scented with patchouli, imported from an Eastern market. Pouring some onto a loofa sponge, she cleansed her body gently, drifting in a sort of drunken haze as the sponge slid across her skin. One she had cleaned herself, she released her hair and rinsed the conditioner from it, once more fighting a spell of dizziness as she leaned back to allow the spray full access to her hair.

Twisting the fall of her hair to squeeze out the moisture, Jo shut off the water and wrapped a towel around her hair turban style before grabbing another towel to dry her body. Pushing open the shower stall door, she had to grab for the edge of it as she started to step out, misjudging her step, nearly slipping as her foot touched the tile floor instead of the bath carpet.

Shaking it off again, she finished drying as quickly as possible, taking her robe from the hook on the back of the door where she'd left it that morning before getting dressed. With the towel around her tucked tightly over her left breast, she shouldered into the robe, her vision wavering.

Her nurse's training kicking in, Jo would have sworn she'd been drugged, but she knew she hadn't knowingly taken anything. Bracing herself on the counter top, she eyed the brownie warily. She'd only taken a bite, perhaps the size of a corner of a tic tac toe square, but had it poison enough to make her feel so woozy and disoriented? She didn't remember any off taste from the bite – usually there was some sort of difference - especially since the old tasteless drug rohypnol and other similar drugs had been banned from the market nearly a decade ago. Her nurse's education had taught her that new such drugs were now flavored in order to be recognizable. Plus she was fully cognizant of what was happening, something many of those earlier drugs took away.

She wasn't tired, sometimes exhaustion could make her feel out of sorts, and she hadn't had any alcohol of any kind for better than three weeks. The four of them were eating regularly, so a drop in her blood pressure due to hunger wasn't causing her to feel so lightheaded. Her gaze shifted to the brownie again.

Admittedly, the man who brought the treat was a stranger. But she was sure that they hadn't alerted any of the neighbors to exactly who had moved into the house, so there shouldn't have been any reason for someone to try to injure them – the Taburons – since no one knew they were there. But the possibility crossed her mind.

She needed to confer with McKenna and Sistan, see what they would recommend. Tying the robe closed, she staggered from the bathroom, keeping one hand on the wall of the hallway as she walked to keep herself from falling.

What greeted her as she entered the living room area turned her concern to outright fright. McKenna lay, sprawled over the coffee table as if she had stood and then every bone in her body had turned to mush. Her eyes were open, but unfocused until Jo entered into her realm of vision. They followed her as she groped her way around the furniture, using them as support before falling to her knees next to the stricken woman. The towel around her hair unraveled and she ignored it as it fell to the floor, her wet hair draping over her shoulders.

"My god," she murmured as she helped McKenna to lie flat. "Can you speak at all?" Her eyes wide with desperation, McKenna merely blinked, a tear forming in the corner of her eyes and building. Jo quickly checked her over, running her hands along McKenna's body to feel for any breaks or swellings and finding no reason for her not being able to move. "Lay still, I need to check on everyone else, then call for help. I'll be right back." Jo smoothed her hand down McKenna's face before standing, grabbing for the sofa to keep herself from falling as she rose. Putting a hand to her head, she blinked several times, shaking her head to dispel the fuzziness.

Once she felt steady, Jo went to the kitchen where she found Sistan, also slumped over, but half of his body was resting on the counter and his butt was on one of the bar stool chairs. He was slowly sliding off the chair and destined to injure himself. Wrapping her arms around his waist, Jo heaved the huge Taburon off the seat of the chair and lowered him to the floor, nearly dropping him and tumbling after. But with a huge sigh, she got him settled, sympathy in her expression for the look of bewilderment and silent pleading she saw in the eyes of the man who'd been so confident in his dealings with his injured companion. Her hand was warm as she touched his cheek.

"I'm so sorry," she whispered. "I'm going to try to get help, but whatever this is, I've got it too. Just hang in there. I need to check on Jaima."

She nearly didn't make it to the warrior's room, the condition worsening almost with every step until she felt as though she was near to passing out. But she struggled to remain upright and staggered to the room.

Sky Clad Jaima

The sound of glass breaking from behind her broke the silence as she entered the room and she startled, stopping in the doorway and turning to see what had happened. A creaking noise followed close on the heels of the glass shattering and she saw the back door at the rear of the kitchen opening to allow a shadowy figure enter the house. Stifling a cry of dismay and fear, she slipped quietly into Jaima's room, carefully and quietly pushing the door closed nearly completely.

Jaima gave her a bleary eyed look, seated in the chair, his hands hanging over the edges, his feet sprawled out in front of him. "Jo," he murmured as she entered.

Jo knelt next to him, keeping her voice low, barely above a whisper, leaning close to his ear. "Jaima, we've been poisoned somehow and someone has broken into the house. I didn't get a good look at him." She glanced around, her gaze falling on his slice of the brownie. There was only a medium sized bite taken from the confection. Convinced now that something had been put in the treat, she pushed herself up, heaving with the effort. Stumbling, she went to the meds container and lifted the lid. Moving the contents around one piece at a time to keep the noise down to a minimum, she finally found what she was looking for and withdrew a vial of clear liquid, a clean syringe and a sterilized needle. Going back to Jaima, she popped the top of the vial with one hand as she ripped open the needle with her teeth. Putting the vial on the arm of the chair, she assembled the syringe with its needle, upended the vial and shoved the needle in to draw out some of the fluid, explaining as best she could as she worked.

"I probably could lose my license over this, but I don't have time to ask permission. I'm going to give you a stimulant and hope it's enough to wake you up. I think the brownies had something put in them. I didn't eat much of mine, and it looks as though you didn't eat much either. You being non-human, you probably have a greater tolerance for whatever the drug is. That's why we're both more mobile. I suspect they both ate all of their pieces. Sistan is already totally under, as is McKenna, they know what's happening, but can't do anything for themselves." Having no time, she plunged the needle into his arm, checked quickly to make sure she hadn't hit a vein and pushed the plunger until all of the fluid was injected. "I'm sorry, Jaima, but we need your help." She tossed the now empty syringe to the side where it rolled under the bureau and was hidden. "I'll try to distract whoever it was that came in, give you time to absorb the stimulant. Please be careful." Rising to her feet, she kissed his lips and turned, going to the door.

Chapter Fifteen

Jaima sighed deeply watching her leave, the door being pulled almost all of the way closed behind her to give him some privacy and a chance to hide the effects of the drug if it worked. He'd wanted to reach out to her, to take her in his arms and hold her, to ease the fear in her eyes, his own fear rising with her words.

The brownie he'd found to be too sweet for his tastes. He liked chocolate, snitching from McKenna whenever she had some handy and he was nearby. During her pregnancy with RaKenn, in her seventh month, she's had what she'd called a craving fit and raided the pantry in the palace, dragging out ingredient after ingredient. Rousing the head cook, they'd spent the night mixing and cooking until, on the eleventh try she'd declared the concoction as near to Earth chocolate as possible and ate her fill. The cook had been none too happy with the mess left behind, grumbling the entire time he spent cleaning up, since McKenna had dropped off to sleep soon after her spree. Later, she spread the confection around, winning over most of the palace females and many of the males, including Jaima.

But this treat had been too sweet and he had only swallowed the small bite he'd taken after stomping to the bedroom in a fit of disgust – disgust at Jo for her teasing him and at himself for reacting, both emotionally and physically to her teasing. He'd dropped into the chair with a snort and sat there for several minutes, deep in thought.

He wanted Jo more than anything else he could think of, more than getting physically well, more than getting back to Taburon, more than his next breath. And he was failing miserably at reaching his goal of getting her into his arms and bed. Or at least making sure there was a commitment that as soon as he felt a little better, she would join him in his bed for a little sport and a lot of nadryl. He was certain that with a little cooperation from her, he could please her thoroughly.

His side still hurt. Every time he strained to rise from the chair or bed, he felt a pull inside that ached. Once he settled in a chair or on the mattress, the ache eased tremendously. There were positions that would make sharing nadryl comfortable for him, as well as visually stimulating, especially with her on top of his body. He was certain the view, whether front or back, would be equally enticing. And every time he pictured them in his head, he had the same reaction he expected to have through the real thing. It was becoming annoying to have to restrain his wayward thoughts. He was running out of unpleasant images to quell his body's reaction and regain some semblance of control. Also, McKenna's snickers were grating on his nerves.

As he sat, he felt a lethargy overtake him, an unwillingness to move. Yet when he tried to rise, to lift his head from the back of the chair, he found it difficult to force his body into motion, to straighten his head, to pull one of his legs up and raise his hands to the arms of the chair.

Then Jo entered and dropped in front of him, her eyes glazed, her voice slurred and walking as though through water, fighting against the pressure to merely go from one small point to another. He was glad to see her, frightened by his inability to move, and scared beyond any amount of fright he'd ever felt before as he listened to her explanation. He'd wanted to take her hand, smooth along her cheek, assure her that all would be well, take her in his arms and hold her until the danger had passed, protecting her from harm. Instead, he'd sat and listened, impotent and stunned as she spoke, telling him that someone had poisoned them, McKenna and Sistan were helpless, someone had broken into the house, and she injected him with a stimulant. He'd wanted to press his own lips against hers when she kissed him, to warn her to be careful as she slipped from the room, pulling the door mostly closed behind her. He wanted to cry out in frustration. But all he could do was wait, wait to see if her medicine would do what she hoped, release him from this paralysis and allow him to save all of them from whatever nefarious purpose the stranger had planned.

Jaima took a deep breath and prayed to the gods harder than he'd ever prayed in his life.

Sky Clad Jaima

Chapter Sixteen

Jo pulled the door to Jaima's room partially closed behind her then leaned against the jamb to take a deep breath and gather herself, praying that the drug she'd just given Jaima would work in time to help them, that he wouldn't be discovered and that she could lie convincingly enough to keep the intruder from checking on the injured Taburon. Everything from this moment forward depended on her keeping the stranger occupied long enough for Jaima to recover and gain enough strength for a long enough period of time to rescue them. She knew that often stimulant drugs on top of sedative drugs could cause a user to crash completely. She crossed her fingers behind her back and took a stumbling step forward.

From the kitchen area, the stranger rose from a stooped position, his gaze still downward. He had been bent over Sistan, tying the physician with a heavy rope. He grinned with pleasure as he considered his victory over the large man, obviously one of those aliens that McKenna had taken up with all those years ago after denying him. But this one was not the one from the television videos, the one that had been shot in front of the White House, so he determined that he needed to continue to proceed with caution.

As he reached for the coils of rope he'd placed on the counter top in front of him, he caught movement out of the corner of his eye and turned abruptly to his left. The woman who had answered the door earlier when he'd dropped off the dishes of food stood braced against a partially closed door, her body lax against the frame, her expression wary.

He'd been surprised when she had been the one to answer the door, expecting McKenna to be the only female in the house. This one had been a pleasant surprise, and the thought had crossed his mind to take her as well. Then he discarded the idea, figuring that as long as she was also under the control of the drug, there would have been no resistance from her, and his goal had to remain his intended target. But now that she was awake and on her feet, and had gotten a good look at him without the disguise, he began to reconsider his plans.

Pulling a gun from a pocket, he held the ropes in his other hand as he went to stand directly in front of the woman. Her eyes widened and she tensed, but held her ground, her arms crossed over her waist. Shoving the gun under her throat, his expression changed to fury that one of his victims was still standing and mobile, fighting the effects of the drug he had laced into the frosting on the brownies. "What is your name, bitch?" he demanded.

Jo swallowed and blinked. Her body was beginning to sag. Only the force of the gun under her chin was holding her on her feet. She licked her lips. "Jo," she whispered.

"How come you're not out like the rest of them?"

"Didn't like the brownie. Only ate a little."

He smirked. "So you know it was the brownies, huh?"

"I'm a nurse," she croaked softly.

"Where's the other one? The bastard who was shot?"

"Inside here. He's asleep." The stranger reached for the door behind her but she stepped to the side slightly, blocking him. "I gave him his meds right before dinner and he almost fell asleep then. I was lucky to get him to bed before he passed out."

"Eat any of the brownie?"

Her nod was jerky. She wouldn't have to lie. "Yes."

The man lowered the gun and pocketed it. With a firm grip, he grabbed the front of her robe and dragged her forward into the living room area where McKenna still lay slumped on the floor. The prone woman's eyes watched as he tossed Jo heedlessly to fall onto the sofa.

In the process, the sides of her robe split to reveal her warm flesh, the curve of her breast, a long expanse of slim thigh and the man ripped her robe open further to find her clothed in only a towel. "Just out of the shower, eh?" he asked, digging a finger under the fold of the towel and tugging. The sides parted, falling open, her naked body exposed to his leery gaze. "Well, well, well," he mulled softly. "Two for the price of one." Jo tried to slap his hand away as he reached to palm her breast, but her heart rate had sped up, the drug coursing through her body and making it hard for her to lift her arm. Closing his hand around her flesh, he squeezed until her eyes closed in response to the pain he was inflicting. He twisted his hand before releasing her breast, leaving a red imprint of his fingers on her skin. Moving to her other breast, he pinched the nipple tightly, pulling on it until it extended a good inch further than normal, twisting the nub, watching her face for any reaction. Jo had closed her eyes, clenching them tightly, her brow furrowed as he abused her.

"Nice tits," he complimented, releasing her abruptly. "It'll be fun seeing how far I can take them, how much pain you can stand." He straightened, pulling her forward by the head with one hand as he yanked the robe down her back, pinning her arms. Folding back the towel completely, he gave her body a second perusal and nodded in pleasure. "Stay there for now," he instructed. "Got to take care of the whore first, then I'll get back to you."

"Who are you?" she whispered as he started to turn away.

The man chuckled evilly. "The one she thought would forget about her," he responded, stabbing a finger towards McKenna. "She'll find out soon enough just how forgettable I am," he promised.

Stooping next to McKenna, George Raymond's grin was malicious. "You won't need these," he murmured as he started to strip the prone woman of her clothes, not caring that he ripped her blouse in the process. McKenna, paralyzed by the drug, couldn't fight back, her only reaction to his manhandling the tears that pooled in her eyes and ran down her temples. Her breasts fell free of her bra. "Gorgeous, just like I imagined," he commented, encompassing her closest breast in his hand, squeezing to feel the fullness of the mound. He palmed the other breast, laying her flat onto her back in the process. With a sharp blow, he slapped both breasts, chuckling as they jiggled at the impact. His chuckle turned to an outright laugh as he repeated the slap, imaging how he was going to abuse her breasts and make her scream in retaliation for her mistreatment of him years ago. Clamps, bands, wires, and needles waited at the safe house he had purchased where he would torture her before he fucked her to his heart's content for as long as he desired. He pictured months of fun with her body, if she survived his plans.

Pulling her trousers from her legs, his smile widened at seeing her hair free pussy. "Beautiful" he complimented. "Never had a bald pussy, not even with all the women I've had from the office. It'll be like fucking a little girl." Raymond tossed McKenna's clothes far from where he knelt and slipped one hand between her legs. "Smooth as a baby's bottom," he declared, delving through her folds. Spreading her legs open, he leaned down to peek, opening her outer lips with his hands. Holding her open with one hand, he speared two fingers inside her body, jamming them in as deeply as possible, then thrusting in imitation of the sex act. "Tight still," he decided. "The big bastard hasn't ruined you after all."

Freeing his fingers, Raymond looked over the rest of her body, smoothing a hand down across her abdomen where her unborn child grew. He palmed her abdomen lovingly, as if he were responsible for her condition. His expression softened for a moment, then hardened as he remembered his plans. "I might let you carry to term, then sell the brat to the highest bidder, but only if you behave yourself," he threatened. "Otherwise, I'll make sure you abort it and toss the remains in the trash like so much garbage." A single sob broke through the drug and McKenna's tears flowed freely as Raymond turned her over, pulling her hands behind her back. Wrapping the rope around her wrists, he secured her hands, then anchored them against her sides. Bringing her legs together, he started the rope at her thighs and wound it down her legs until he knotted it at her ankles. Certain she was restrained and wouldn't cause problems, Raymond pinched her left nipple, twisting it cruelly before rising. "Going to enjoy you," he promised, "before I turn you into a high-class whore. You're going to regret what you did to me before and letting that big son of a bitch beat me up."

Turning his attention back to the woman on the sofa, Raymond stood in front of her for a moment to examine her again. She had a good shape, larger breasts with large deep pink nipples that would hold clamps well, small waist and hips wide enough to hold onto while fucking. With both hands, he pulled her down the seat of the sofa and spread her legs to examine between. Unlike McKenna, Jo sported a full covering of blonde hair and Raymond instantly decided he would remove it completely to leave her exposed to anyone who wanted to see. Separating the curls, he opened her folds and pressed back the hood covering her clit. The prominent bud stood out far enough for him to pinch it with two fingers. He could feel her body tense.

Raymond held her clit a moment longer, squeezing tighter until the blood had pooled in the tip, then releasing it with a sharp tug. His middle finger jammed inside her, finger fucking her, feeling inside her body to test her girth and depth. "Not a virgin," he discovered, "not loose either. Nice and tight." Withdrawing his finger, he added his index finger and shoved both back inside, pumping several times before adding a third finger, spreading the three to open her as wide as he could with only three fingers. "Might be able to get my whole fist inside, but it'll be painful the first few times. At least until you get used to it."

He freed his fingers and lifted one of her legs as high as her shoulder, exposing her rear. Spitting on his already soiled fingers, he circled her anal opening. Jo tensed even further. Even through her marriage, her ex had never used her in her ass, never suggested it, nor ever attempted to enter her there. This fingering of her ass now frightened her tremendously, scared her to the point of tears. What she would have to endure at the whims of this evil man if Jaima couldn't help them. "Even tighter. Bet you never had a cock up here. Be fun to bust your anal cherry. You'll learn to like it, I promise. Especially with a cock on your cunt and one in your ass." Raymond pulled his fingers clear. "It'll take a few weeks to train you, but after you'll be making me a fortune, with your mouth, pussy and ass. Turn you into as big a whore as the other one, but sooner, since I don't have score to settle with you."

Tugging, he pulled the tie from the robe and pushed Jo over onto her side, grabbing her hands to tie them together behind her back. "Don't want to alert anyone that something is going on here worth calling the cops about," he said as he tied her. "Saving the fun times for when I get you both to my place, where there's no one around for miles, when the drugs finally wear off and I can enjoy the sound of your screams."

From the direction of the bedrooms, Raymond heard a sound and his head shot up, a frown crossing his features. "What was that?" he asked, straightening.

Sky Clad Jaima

Sky Clad Jaima

Chapter Seventeen

Jaima was becoming impatient, afraid the shot Jo had given to him wasn't working and he would lose both her, Sistan, and McKenna to a stranger with unscrupulous intentions. Several times over the next few minutes after she'd left the room he tried to move, to lift a hand or move a foot – anything to get his body moving and do his duty to his friends and queen. Frustration roiled through his body.

He listened as Jo was accosted by the intruder, heard her soft squeal when he grabbed her by her robe and dragged her away from the door. Though the voices were muffled, he could hear them as they moved to the living room, the sound of something falling onto the sofa followed by silence.

Surprised, his hand jerked once, then twice and his head rolled to the other side to see if he could get movement from his other hand. Excitement stirred him as he actually lifted the appendage slightly, settling on the arm of the chair. Forcing himself to take deep breaths, he found more and more movement was returning to his body, but he still felt weakened, as though he would soon be able to move but only as if through a pool of mud.

He had to get himself going. He was sure there was nothing pleasant in the future of the two women, and the possibility of none for either himself or Sistan as well. He would never be able to face Radine if McKenna was kidnapped. For him to have to go through that again would break the king's heart, especially since they'd already experienced it once before, and was pregnant then as well, though neither one had known it at the time. And she was now carrying their next child. McKenna was Radine's life, his heart and soul. He would never recover from her loss.

Sky Clad Jaima

With the ability to move his head restored, Jaima glanced around the room to see what was at hand that he could use was a weapon. His laser weapon was missing, but standing against the wall between the door and the dresser was his sword in its scabbard. If he could only move…

Shaking as if with palsy, Jaima lifted his hands to his face to scrub downwards as he took a deep breath. His skin was clammy and slick, his touch almost unreal against cool stone, but he tried to stretch outwards, contracting his arm muscles then releasing them, waking up groggy tendons and joints. His feet moved, flexing his thighs, rotating his feet, though he didn't quite trust himself to rise quite yet. Not until he felt more like himself. But Jo's drug was working, counteracting the effects of the drug put in the brownies. A few more minutes and he would be mobile.

Jaima strained the entire time to hear what was going on in the other room as he regained his faculties, moving his body limb by limb, bit by bit, until he felt confident enough to attempt to rise. Bracing himself with the arms of the chair, he heaved upwards, nearly collapsing, but managing to remain upright. Leaning forward he grabbed the railings of the bed and held on for dear life. Bending at the knees, he flexed his legs again three times until he knew he could stand

and gingerly he released his hold on the bed to straighten. Taking a step forward, he almost stumbled, but caught himself, taking baby steps to the door to lean close, his eyes peering through.

Jo was on the sofa, her robe opened and towel spread. The top of the man's head could be seen over the edge of the arm of the sofa, he was on the floor to the side of the piece of furniture dealing with something there but Jaima's view was blocked by the couch. And despite recognizing the direness of their situation, Jaima couldn't help but notice the beauty of the body of the woman he wanted, exposed for any person who happened to take a look. She was perfection, perfect breasts, perfect form, perfect skin with a perfect cleft between her legs, though it was currently covered with feminine curls. He promised himself that he would increase his efforts to have her once they were safe.

As he watched, his anger rising, the intruder rose from his kneeling position and turned to Jo. Jaima watched as he folded the towel back further, then reached out to grab her legs and pull her down on the cushion. Spreading her legs, the man began to play with Jo's pussy, pinching her clit until Jo tensed. Jaima became furious that this man dared to touch what he considered his, and to touch her with evil in his heart and not the pleasure that Jaima would give her. His blood boiled when first one, then two, then three fingers were shoved into her body, and reached volcanic proportions as he lifted her leg and began to play with her arse. Jaima could see the tears flow down her cheeks.

Having seen enough, Jaima reached to the side to grab his sword, missing on the first try and knocking a small cup from the top of the dresser. It fell to the carpet with a soft clatter, loud enough to grab the attention of the man in the other room. Rising abruptly, he stared in the direction of the noise, his expression wary. "What was that?" he asked.

Grabbing his sword, Jaima edged away from the door and softly withdrew the blade from the scabbard, tossing the cover to the bed. Bracing his feet, he held the sword at the ready and bent slightly at the knees. A wave of dizziness passed over him, but he shook his head and prepared himself. His grip tightened on the pommel as he waited.

The door swung open slowly and a hand appeared, a weapon in it as the rest of the intruder's body followed. But he hadn't trained as Jaima had, his eyes searching the room before him, not realizing someone waited slightly behind the door for him to fully enter the room. And once he did turn slightly, catching sight of the standing warrior from the corner of his eyes, it was too late. Jaima grabbed the hand that held the weapon and pushed it down as he stepped up to the man.

Thrusting upwards, Jaima buried the sword in the other's body, piercing him through the stomach, pushing until the tip of the weapon appeared through the man's back, blood covered and dripping. Raymond's eyes bulged, his mouth opened in a scream, cut off as Jaima heaved, ripping his sword upwards to slice through internal organs, cutting the man open from gut to heart. Blood spurted out, a waterfall of red that flew forward, over Jaima and the floor. Dropping the gun, Raymond latched onto the arm of the man who'd just killed him, staring at him with disbelief in his eyes. His plans had gone so well, yet he'd made a fatal mistake of not checking and securing all of the occupants of the house before finishing with his plans to abscond with the women.

"You'll never again touch what doesn't belong to you," Jaima growled harshly, grunting and giving the blade one final heft. Raymond's eyes shut, his breath huffed out on a loud sigh, and he sagged, his grip easing, his body slumping over the sword. Jaima tilted the weapon down and allowed the body to slide from it to fall in a heap, a form without bones and now without life.

Jaima took a deep breath and leaned on the wall by the door as another wave of dizziness swept over him. He looked down at the body with disgust then wiped what he could of the blade on the dead man's clothes, cleaning it partially of blood. Keeping a hand on the door to brace himself, he stepped over the body. The others still needed his help.

With every step, he felt more in control of his body, his steps surer and his strength returning, though he was still far from completely recovered. His footfalls were heavy as he stumbled to the living room, dropping to his knees next to McKenna to check for a pulse, dropping his sword to the carpet.

"Thank the gods," he murmured, finding her alive. Carefully, he sliced through the ropes and eased her into a more comfortable position, laying her on her side, smoothing a hank of hair away from her face. "Hold on, McKenna, I'll get help." The relief in her eyes was obvious as fresh tears fell. His palm against her cheek was reassuring.

Turning, he went to Jo. He first pulled the tie loose, then folded the edges of the robe back over her body before cupping her cheek in his big hand. "Jo," he said tenderly, "thank you. You saved us. Hold on, I need to check Sistan, then go for help." She tried to nod, but it was only her expression that showed she agreed with him, that she would be fine until he returned with help. Jaima started to rise, but found himself mesmerized for the moment by her eyes. He smiled slightly. "You are beautiful, Jo," he whispered huskily, placing a kiss on her lips, much as she'd done before offering herself to Raymond as a distraction in order to give him time to recover from the drug. He would chide himself later for taking advantage and cherishing her lips on his. For now he simply enjoyed the kiss until she whimpered, bringing him back to himself and the task at hand.

There was a blanket across the back of the sofa that he grabbed as he stood, then leaned over to drape it around McKenna, tucking it gently around her. She would stay warm enough for the time being while he made whatever attempt he could to get help.

He was undecided about what to do. He seen Jo use the device she called a cell phone several times, but had no idea how the instrument worked. She opened it and pushed several buttons on its face, but which ones he needed in order to summon aid were beyond his knowledge. And she was in no condition to show him at this point. He felt his head swim as he tried to decide on a course of action.

Covered in blood, he could imagine the thoughts that would go through anyone's head should he simply knock on the door of any of the houses in the neighborhood. If they didn't outright slam the door in his face, they would certainly call for help in the long run.

But he wasn't sure if he could stand upright long enough to go from house to house until he found someone willing to either listen to him or panic at the sight of him. It was then he remembered the weapon that had dropped from Raymond's hand when he'd been skewered.

His steps faltered slightly as he went back to the room, sinking to his knees to roll the body off of the weapon beneath. The dead weight was heavy and flaccid, Raymond not in the best of physical shape and overweight. Jaima remembered Radine telling him when he'd fought with the man all those years ago, while the human had had a few pounds on the king, Radine was trained, in shape, and quick, easily avoiding the knife the human had wielded then.

Though the human had gotten in a lucky slice on the king's arm.

Grabbing the weapon, Jaima studied it for a moment. Built much the same as his laser weapon, he assumed the trigger worked the same, but instead of projecting a laser, small metal pieces Jo had called bullets came from the end of the barrel, bullets that could do extensive damage. He knew the weapon made a great deal of noise. And that should be enough to get attention to have someone call the authorities.

Night had fallen completely when he left the house, standing on the stoop in the cool air. Lights from street lamps cast the street in patches of brightness and darkness, stars twinkled brightly in the cloudless sky. The moon was full, but his Taburon eyesight was good enough that even without its light, he would have been able to see clearly. Along the street, the houses were lighted from inside. The neighbors were home and still awake.

Jaima sank to the bottom step, his body giving up the fight to stay upright. Goosebumps sprang up along his arms and legs, his feet, bare, absorbed the cold as if sucking it in with relish. The blood on his chest that had yet to dry was cooling, raising prickles on his flesh. He hung the weapon between his legs for a moment, searching for a safe direction in which to discharge the weapon where there would be no injury to any person or damage to anyone's home. There was a large tree at the edge of the yard of the house they were using, he felt confident the trunk would take the bullets and not allow any of them to pierce through.

Steadying his hand by holding it with the other, Jaima took aim and fired. The recoil from the weapon shook him, nearly knocking him over, but he braced himself again and fired several more times, each bullet hitting dead center of the trunk, splintering the wood and sending shards flying. The noise was near deafening to his ears.

Along the street, porch lights came on and doors opened as citizens began to peer out to see what was happening, several of them carrying weapons of their own as they stepped out from the houses, meeting on the sidewalks and congregating in small groups.

Jaima lowered he weapon, tossing it on the ground to the side of where he sat, well out of his reach. He didn't want to be shot again. "Here," he called, drawing attention to himself.

Two of the men met in front of one of the houses, one armed, staring across the street at the man sitting hunched over on the stoop of what they'd thought was an empty house. "John," the armed one asked, "who is that?"

"Don't know, never saw him before," the other replied as he made to cross the street. The armed man followed close on the first one's heels, his weapon held tightly and at waist level, ready for what might happen.

Jaima held his hands up to show he was unarmed. "I am unarmed. Help," he pleaded, starting to crash.

"Geez, Henry, it's one of those alien guys. You know, the ones they showed on the news, the one who was shot."

"He's covered in blood," Henry said, kneeling next to Jaima after tucking the gun at his back in the waistband of his pants. "Are you hurt?"

Jaima reached for the man's sleeve. "Drugged," he replied. "Others, inside. Need help."

Other people had started to approach the trio, cautiously at first, then with more assurance as they saw two of their neighbors standing over the hunched figure of a man who was trying to remain upright. Several had pulled their cell phones free and were recording what was happening, shifting their device from side to side before honing in on the injured alien. The man named John looked up to the crowd. "Sally, call the cops. This is one of those Taburon people and he says there are others inside the house." The woman he'd addressed nodded, grabbing her cell phone from a pocket and opening the device, putting it up to her ear. "Think we should go inside and check it out?" John asked of Henry.

The other shook his head. "No way. Someone's been hurt in there and we could get into trouble if we interfere, mess up evidence or something."

"Someone could be dying in there," John argued.

"They're alien. Why do we care?"

"They're people. Stay out here if you want, but I'm going inside to check it out."

Jaima groaned softly, gripping the man's sleeve tighter. "The brownies," he whispered. "Poisoned."

"Did you hear that?" Henry asked.

"Yeah, something about poisoned brownies. I'll see what's going on. Give me your gun," he ordered. Henry pulled the gun free and passed it over as another man slid his jacket off, covering Jaima with it. "Be right back." John disappeared inside the house, the door left open behind him. In the far distance, sirens could be heard, screeching through the silence of the night. Jaima, assured now that help was on the way, crumpled and let the darkness take him with a soft sigh.

Sky Clad Jaima

Chapter Eighteen

Jaima had taken a shower and was laying on top of the quilt in the room given to him by one of the staff in the White House. He wore only the white pair of what he'd been told were briefs, the cotton soft against his skin, but the garment confining over his hips and cock, he having to turn the organ up as opposed to the normal way he allowed it to lay down his leg. Folding his cock was disturbing, though he found the picture he presented when he looked at himself in a mirror - his cock and balls a thick heavy bulge at the bottom of the briefs - impressive. The plummed head nearly reached the top band of the garment. No matter, he'd decided, it was only for a day, until proper clothes could be provided. Besides, word had come that Radine was expected to arrive the next afternoon. He would soon be heading home.

No repercussions had come from him killing the man Raymond the previous night. His intent had been clear from the scene – four drugged people, two women, out cold, stripped of their clothing, roped and tied on the floor. Jaima had barely managed to regain consciousness when the police arrived, his speech slurred, his thoughts jumbled, as he tried to explain the events that had taken place, his primary concern for the woman, especially McKenna and her unborn child. Making sure to mention the dish of brownies, though he was once more near collapse himself, he'd finally lapsed into complete unconsciousness only to awaken a few hours later, once again in a hospital, hooked up to machines and tubes.

He'd sat up abruptly, his intent to go in search of the others, when handcuffs kept him from leaving the bed. "What is this?" he demanded, lifting his hand as far as the cuffs would allow, tugging ferociously. "Where am I?"

The nurse that had been assigned to remain with the injured man rose from her chair, fright in her expression that was eased only slightly because of the handcuffs. And, in being honest with herself, the fact that he was an alien scared her enough to be glad he wore the cuffs. As long as he'd remained unconscious, she had managed to keep calm. Her fear increased once she saw that he had awakened, unsure if the handcuffs would keep him tied to the bed. The Taburon had been brought in unconscious and a guard had been posted outside the door, mostly to keep unauthorized people out, but also to keep him from leaving once he awoke. "Sir," she said, "you're in the hospital," she explained as she placed a hand on his arm with a firm grip. "You can't get out of bed."

"I need to see to my people. Unchain me and set me free." Jaima rattled the cuffs again.

"I can't, I don't have the key."

"Then summon the person who does and get me released." He tossed the covers back with his free hand and twisted, swinging his legs over the edge of the bed. Cursing that he was once again dressed in nothing but a short hospital gown, he nonetheless reached under the neckline and pulled the leads to the heart monitor free, the machine immediately changing from the constant beep sound to a loud wail.

The door to the room flew open as the nurse raced around to the other side of the bed to switch off the monitor. Entering, a uniformed police officer came to the end of the bed, his hand on his still holstered gun, the strap unsnapped. "What's going on in here?" he demanded.

"The patient wants to leave," the nurse explained, gathering the wire leads and setting them aside.

Jaima rattled the chain. "Unchain me," he ordered.

"I'm afraid I'm not allowed to free you at this time."

"Then find the person who might."

The guard firmed his stance, loosening his hold on his gun. "Sir, you've been implicated in a murder. Until you are cleared by the authorities, you will remain here, handcuffed, and compliant."

Jaima growled softly and yanked on the handcuffs, growling even louder when the chain held and he remained locked to the bed rail. He shook the device in frustration, settling his arse on the mattress heavily.

"How are my companions?" he asked. "They are my responsibility. I have sworn an oath. I am the king's protector, as well as the protector of his family."

"I wouldn't know, sir, but I can tell you I've not heard any negative news, if that helps."

Jaima nodded once, disappointment obvious on his face which turned to curiosity when the door opened again to admit a white coated man. The newcomer flashed his identification badge at the police officer as he made his way around the officer to come to stand near Jaima.

He plastered a pleasant look on his face and held out his hand. "Jaima, isn't it? Dr. Martin Tripp. I took care of you when you were brought in before. It's nice to finally meet you."

Jaima stared at the hand, his glance sliding to the physician's face, then back to the hand, an eyebrow raising.

Tripp lowered his hand, suddenly realizing that the Taburon's right hand was the one handcuffed and unshakeable. "Guess shaking hands is unfamiliar to you. It's something we humans developed a very long ago as a way to show we meant no harm to others when meeting, since most humans are right handed and held their swords in that hand." Tripp shrugged slightly. "Anyway, you'll be glad to know that there shouldn't be any lasting after effects from the drug you were given..."

"The queen?" Jaima interrupted. "Her unborn child?"

"They're fine. We had one of our best ob's examine her and he's cleared both of them."

"I want to see them."

"I know you do, and I understand, but there's nothing I can do for you until the authorities finish their investigation and decide you're not going to be charged."

"I killed that man to protect the queen, Sistan, and Joanna. His intent was to kidnap the women. Who knows what his further intentions might have been? I had little choice in what to do to protect everyone and save us.'

Tripp shoved his hands into the pockets of his coat. "Those in charge have spoken with your queen and Joanna, and they confirm that Raymond – that's his name – did intend to take only the queen at first, since she'd once refused him before she married your king. He was out for revenge. Joanna just happened to be in the wrong place at the wrong time. He was going to torture both women and then turn them into prostitutes. I think your queen called them *skalas*?" Jaima nodded, Tripp had gotten the term correct, the Taburon word for whore. "We tested the brownies you told someone about. They contained a drug we've never seen before, but I think we'll not be seeing any more of it around. It appears Raymond developed it and sold it under the table – illegally. There will be a lot of people who will have a lot of explaining to do about that. I think the authorities will want to speak with you before you're allowed to visit with the queen, so it's probably best if you just try to relax and be patient. You've been through a lot in the last twelve hours, you should rest." A small device in the belt of the doctor's trousers binged twice and he pulled it free to look at it. "I need to take care of this. I'll see what I can do to speed things up for you, but the government runs at its own pace even in the best of times." He turned to leave, then swung back as a thought crossed his mind. The look on his face was one of pleasant curiosity. "I would like to know how you healed so fast. When you left here, you had a sizeable wound in your side that now looks as if it's weeks old. Perhaps you can explain that to me later?" He didn't wait for an answer but pulled the door open and walked out.

With a nod, satisfied, the guard followed the physician. With a huff of frustrated resignation, Jaima settled back onto the bed, his scowl enough to convince the nurse to keep her distance.

Tripp had followed through on his promise and soon after he'd left, five men, a combination of the governmental alphabet organizations, appeared, spending three hours going over what had happened until they were satisfied that Jaima had indeed acted to protect his people and would face no charges. His sword, which had been confiscated at the scene, would be returned to him when he was discharged from the hospital.

Released from the handcuffs and given an oversized robe to cover him, Jaima made a beeline for his people, checking on Sistan first, finding him sleeping soundly. Joanna was also asleep he discovered, hovering next to her bed and watching the gentle rise and fall of her chest. He wanted to crawl into the bed with her and enfold her in his arms, offer comfort as well as find it for himself, to just feel the warmth of her body against his. Instead, he settled for simply smoothing his hand down her cheek, the skin as soft and delicate as the wings of a *milia* insect. He was still under guard – a new one - but now for his own safety. She sighed slightly, mildly disturbed by his touch, turning her head in his direction until he pulled his hand back.

McKenna was laying on her side when he entered her room, her shoulders shaking as she softly sobbed into her pillow. Perching on the edge of the bed, he gathered her up into a tight embrace, her face buried into his shoulder. "It's okay," he soothed gently, "you're all right."

"I was so scared, and so helpless. I was afraid for the baby."

"As was I," he agreed. "But I was told you're both fine. Things can't be all bad then."

"I don't know how many more times I can handle someone trying to kidnap me."

"If I have any say in it, this was the very last. I'll protect you with my life, you know."

She glanced up to him, her eyes wetted with tears. "You nearly did a few days ago. But I don't want to lose you, Jaima."

With his thumb, Jaima swiped the tears from her cheeks. "Then I'd better learn how to duck faster," he mused facetiously for her benefit. She sighed, finding the strength to bring her crying under control if he felt a little lightheartedness was appropriate. He continued to hold her as she sniffed, taking deep breaths, releasing soft sighs, letting the strength and warmth of his big body comfort her in lieu of the man she loved and needed and wanted more than anything.

"I want Radine," she whispered. "I miss him so much."

"I know," he agreed. "I know I'm not him, but for now I'll have to do." His hand smoothed along her back. "He'll be here soon and then we can go home." He rocked her gently, murmuring softly until he felt her body relax and her sniffling ease. Realizing she'd nearly fallen to sleep, he laid her back onto her pillow, combing her hair away from her face as he rose.

"Jaima," she whispered, her eyes remaining closed as her head rested on one hand under her cheek. "I love you."

"I love you as well, little one."

She snorted. "Only Radine calls me little one," she scolded mildly.

He grinned. "Of course, Your Majesty," he concurred with a sassy bow. She would be fine if she could sass him. Of course, being back with Radine would help tremendously, going home to see her son would only aid in curing any mental wounds she might bring back to Taburon. They would deal with the fallout later. Now it only mattered that they moved someplace where they would be safe until Radine returned.

Sky Clad Jaima

Chapter Nineteen

To where was answered when the President offered rooms in the White House, perhaps the most secure building in the country, especially after what had happened twice now to the visitors from Taburon. McKenna had accepted on the condition that all of them, including Jo, were made the same offer. So they were settled in the guest wing, given fresh clothing, servants at their beck and call for whatever they might have wanted.

Sky Clad Jaima

Jaima was ready to call the whole thing quits. He'd had enough – more than enough. Shot, drugged, hiding out, and killing a second man – his first seven days on Earth had cured him of visiting this planet, for any reason, for the rest of his life. The news that Radine was coming tomorrow had made him happier than any other news he'd had for a long time.

Except he would be leaving Jo behind. The only dark spot in going home. His heart was heavy, a feeling with which he was not familiar. He wanted her, badly, but didn't know how he could get her to be with him. He couldn't say he loved her, he was unfamiliar with the emotion, but realized that they could share something exceptional for whatever time she would give him. He'd always been upfront with women, never leaving them wanting and never promising more than an excellent time while they were together.

Remembering the sight of Jo in the nude had not left his memory. She was perfect, her skin, her body beneath the clothes she wore. She was a vision he would never get out of his mind. Her nipples were the rosiest color, surrounded by a darker areola, both puckered from the chill in the house and fright at her captivity. She had a nipped in waist which flared to hips made to be held while sharing nadryl. And her pussy was trimmed, a very thin line of hair pointing to her secret treasures, shaven or creamed into control he did not know, but it would have been delightful to feel the warm wetness of the petals there against his fingers. The taste of her juices sweet against his tongue would have been a treat.

He'd been infuriated when Raymond had shoved his fingers inside Joanna, and blind with rage when he repeated the process with her anal passage. He'd been told that at least McKenna had been totally under the influence of the drug when Raymond accosted her, but Jo, fighting the drug and still awake, had winced and tensed, her eyes going wide in fright, her face turning red in anger as Raymond felt around inside her body. When he'd pinched her nipples, she'd whimpered out through her drugged state, jerking her body in an effort to get away, but there had been nothing she could do to stop him. Jaima had been glad when he'd run the man through with his sword.

But the memory of her luscious body had his cock hardening again, pulling the material of the briefs tighter as it pushed against the tight fit of the garment. He'd already wrapped his hand around his cock while in the shower, letting the water and slickness of the soap help the stimulation until he'd spewed onto the tile, bracing himself with one hand while the other worked himself until everything he had was spilled.

He was such a *tritio*, he decided as he'd dropped his head against the tiled wall, letting the water wash down his back, moving slightly to the side to let it clean his seed from the wall. Pitiful in the best sense of the word. He rarely had to masturbate, there was always a willing woman in which to spend himself, even for one night, to work the tension out of his system and the need from his body. Yet even after such a shameless display, his cock was still hard, still ached, still wanting for the warm wet flesh of a certain woman that his mind knew he would probably never have.

He draped his hand over his eyes, sighing deeply. Tomorrow he'd be gone, in three days he could seek out a *skala* and in four days he'd be back at his post, harassing his men to the point of exhaustion. They would hate him, he knew, but he would finally get a chance to work her out of his system for good. Such things drove a man, and he was bound and determined to be driven until he no longer felt these things that were proving unbearable.

There was knock on his bedroom door and he didn't bother to cover up. If whomever was out there was going to be offended by a near naked Taburon, then let them. He was too tired to care. "Come in," he called.

He did sit up though, when the door opened to reveal Jo, a thick robe around her shoulders, standing there, looking hesitant. "Jo?" he asked, searching her face. He thought he'd see her once more tomorrow, as they met the shuttle before going to the ship to go home - if she was brave enough to come with them to meet the shuttle. She looked absolutely fractured, her face pale, her hands clasping and unclasping, shaking, her breathing was harsh. "What is wrong?"

She stepped into the room warily as he stood. Oh, god, did he have to look so tempting, like a large piece of sweet that she hadn't had in a long time and desperately wanted more than her next breath. He was all but naked, his glorious body on display, nothing left to the imagination, especially the bulge in the briefs that grew larger as she walked into the room. He was so bad for her, like the candy, but the call of her body to his had been irresistible and coupled with what had happened, she found she had no choice but to seek him out. "I can't seem to stop shaking," she stuttered, her arms crossing under her breasts as if to hold herself together.

He moved fast for such a large man, springing forward to engulf her in his embrace, then pull her back towards the bed. Sitting, he made her sit next to him as he yanked the quilt from the top of the bed and wrapped it around both of them, tucking her tighter against his body. The warmth that radiated from him was like a furnace, enveloping her with its musky scented heat.

"Talk to me," he encouraged softly.

"I was okay when we left the hospital, but now I can't seem to stop shaking. Reaction, I guess, setting in."

"It is natural," he told her. "Warriors may get the shakes after the battle is over. I have seen seasoned soldiers take to their beds after a particularly harsh battle, suffering from the aftermath." Tucking a finger under her chin, he raised her head to look into her eyes. "Even Radine. He didn't come to his throne easily, though he inherited it from his father and it was his right to rule. He had to fight for it, his first real battle and after he killed the leader of the opposition, he promptly vomited. You shouldn't worry about how you feel."

"I know, I've read about it and been taught how to handle it…when it's someone else who's suffering. Never when it's me."

Jaima rubbed her arms firmly but gently. "It will pass, Jo. Give yourself time."

She began to settle, sinking into the warmth of the quilt and his touch. "I'm afraid," she whispered.

"Of what?"

"Of dying."

"As we all are, *Olana*," he murmured. "Even I."

She took a deep breath and tossed her hesitancy to the wind. She needed him more than ever now, and while she still believed with her head it was the wrong thing to do, her heart had been saying something else ever since she'd awakened in the hospital, the voice growing louder with every passing hour. "I'm afraid of dying," she repeated, "and never knowing the feel of loving a real man, of what he might do to me, for me, of what he could make me feel." She glanced up at him at her confession, afraid of what her confession, and subtle request, may mean to him. Jaima looked over her head, resting his chin on top of her soft hair and sighed. So, he didn't want to make love to her? She would accept it. After all, without a doubt, she'd turned him down enough times. She couldn't blame him if he wasn't willing to have sex with her now.

She couldn't prevent the soft whimper that escaped. With a single nod, she made to leave his embrace, but his hold tightened even as he continued to stare over her head. "Let me understand you," he mumbled. "You want to share nadryl with me." He took a deep breath. "Is it because you want me, or because you want to thank me for what happened, that I saved you?"

"Because I want to feel alive again, and the best way to do that is do something very much alive, because I never had that with my ex. I want to know what making love with you is like. I want a memory that is positive to have for the rest of my life, to erase what happened, and I want...I know you can give that to me."

With a finger, Jaima tipped her chin to gaze into her eyes. Such a beautiful brown color, like the fur of a pure bred crufa, so soft and warm. Tears hung from the corners, little jewels of moisture that glittered in the low light of the bedroom. Bending close, he touched his lips to the corner of each eye, taking in the wetness until his lips were moist with the salty liquid. Bending slightly, he placed his lips against her mouth letting her taste her own tears, his hand sliding to cup her cheek, then hold her still as the other hand rested against where her jaw and neck met.

He pressed tighter to her, scrubbing his mouth over hers, her lips warm and full, pouty, swelling as he explored, begging her to open for him. The tip of his tongue teased and tasted, prodding insistently until her lips parted and allowing him to dart inside to dance in her mouth, inviting her to dance with him. Tentatively, she reached out with her own tongue and touched his, getting a rumbling approval from him. Coaxing her tongue to follow his, he drew hers back into his mouth where he sucked on it, holding it still with his teeth until he'd thoroughly discovered each inch. "Sweet," he murmured against her mouth, "so sweet."

He pulled his mouth away to press kisses against her forehead, her eyelids, the sides of her eyes where moisture, salty and warm, still clung, the bridge of her nose, the tip of her nose. He nibbled his way along her jaw on the right, then on the left, nipping the skin between her neck and ear where her pulse beat at an accelerated rate. Lifting her hair he ran his tongue across the back of her neck.

His hands worked at the ties to her robe, pulling them free and opening the garment. He discovered with his hands that she wore only a pair of panties underneath as they slid up the robe to push it from her shoulders. With it went the quilt and he sat back to peruse her.

He was glad to see that his drugged memory was as accurate as he'd remembered. She was perfect. Her skin was soft and rosy, smooth as a baby's, unblemished. Except for one spot directly over her heart where a small mole challenged the perfection of her perked nipples.

She had a long neck that branched out to straight shoulders. Her arms looked strong, muscles apparent beneath her peach-toned skin. Her wrists were delicate, ending in hands with long, tapered fingers.

Her breasts were a little more than a handful, they would overflow when he held them in his palm. Firm, they sat high on her chest, peaked by tight nipples the color of ripe berries sun-kissed while on the vine. He would bet they tasted just as good. He watched as she shuddered, her breasts vibrating visibly, the tips tightening even more.

His chest filled and he groaned deeply, swooping down to claim her mouth again, stealing her breath before giving it back mingled with his own. She whimpered softly as he devastated her lips and plunged his tongue ruthlessly inside, tangling with her warm, wet interior. Jo's arm started to rise but he caught each wrist and held them by her side, breaking the kiss.

Jaima's lips didn't stray far, mouthing along her cheek to the left of her mouth, across her upper lip, then down the right side of her cheek. Her skin was softer than dew, his breath hotter than a fire. "No," he breathed, "keep your hands down by your sides," he whispered before claiming her mouth again on an inhaled breath. Sliding his hands around her back, he pulled her tightly against his chest, her breasts smashing into his hard planes.

Minutes that seemed endless passed before he'd had his fill of kissing her, drawing in a deep breath as he lifted his mouth from hers, his hands roaming along her spine until he met the dimples at the tops of her buttocks. Jaima leaned back, pleased at the sight of her reddened and swollen lips, her skin a warmed pink and her eyes glazed with passion. He softly chuckled. "Just the way I like it," he murmured, "dazed and passionate."

She had a waist that he would span with his hands, nipped in and smooth, no extra flesh there. From there her body flared to hips he could hold as he pummeled her relentlessly during nadryl. Her stomach had the slightest roundness to it, the sign of a mature woman and not the flat plane of youth edged by sharp bones. Her mound, shadowed between her legs, barely hidden by the sheer panties, was crested by curls the same color as the hair on her head.

Joanna flushed at his scrutiny. "Shameless," he grinningly commented, "but absolutely gorgeous." He palmed her breasts. "I hated it when he touched you. I would have killed him for that reason alone." She shuddered again through the memory, but he tightened his grip, letting her know it was him who held her in his hands and not that evil man. She had no reason to fear him, yet she took his wrists in her hands to hold on, to still him for a moment. Her head bent, her hair covering her face, as if ashamed of what had happened. "Jo," he said softly, "I'm not him. Don't shut me out. Watch me as I take you where you want to be so badly, where your body will scream." He kissed her. "Keep your eyes on me, Joanna." When her head lifted, she had tears in her eyes, but she sniffed and nodded once, tossing her hair back so there were no obstacles to him seeing her. "Better. Good girl."

Jaima scooted back to lean down and closed his mouth over the nipple of her left breast, holding the flesh in the cup of one hand. With just the tip of his tongue, he explored the areola until it beaded, peaked by the tight bud of her nipple, teasing her, denying her what she wanted most – his mouth on her nipple. Humming deeply, the vibration thrummed straight to her nipple. She answered with a sigh, arching her back to give him better access, a silent plea for him to readjust his mouth. He laughed again as he complied.

Licking it first, he sucked the little nubbin, closing his teeth around it to hold on once it had tightened into a tight, hard tip. With the tip of his tongue, he flipped the tip back and forth, squeezing her breast to make it more pointed, suckling deeply. Once he was satisfied with the one nipple, he switched to the other side and repeated the entire process on her right breast. Tilting away, he looked her over before placing a kiss on the tip of each breast.

Jo melted completely, sure her body was a pile of mush dribbling onto the floor at their feet. No one had ever paid as much attention to her breasts as this one, no one had brought her so close to crossing over into bliss as he did just by exploring her breasts with his mouth as this man. Her heart was beating so strongly she was sure he could see it just by looking, her skin felt hot, her body tight, on edge, and she knew her pussy was soaking the small scrap of material that still covered it.

He finished taking her robe from her, standing to toss the garment across the room. Pulling her to her feet, he shoved the blankets down the bed, lifted her and reverently set her in the middle of the bed on the cool sheets. He settled near her knees. "So these are panties," he discovered, hooking his fingers in the top of the satiny material. Sliding his hands along the top, he ran them from the front to each side, lifting the material. "McKenna wore them when she first came to Taburon. Radine threw them all out. Ripped them to shreds and tossed them." Jaima followed suit, grabbing the panties at the center over her belly and rending them in one swift tug. Holding them high, the stain was obvious, a large wet spot right where the material had covered her intimate secrets. Jo flushed with embarrassment when he brought them close to his face to sniff, inhaling deeply, sighing as though the scent were that of the most expensive perfume. He looked at her and grinned unabashedly, eyes dancing in mischief. He tossed the ripped garment off the bed. "He was right, they only get in the way," he declared, spreading her legs and laying on his belly between them.

He bent her legs and parted them wider, opening her up to his view, the petals of her pussy flowering open like a blossom in summer. She already glistened as if a soft rain had fallen on the flower of her intimate folds. "Lovely, beautiful, like a *garnia* flower, soft and dewy."

Sitting back on his heels, Jaima lifted one of her feet and rubbed the sole gently, each toe getting an individual massage, lick and kiss - her ankle, her calf, her thigh, rising up to nearly touching her where she wanted him the most, but he let her foot down to the bed to do the other foot, the same way; the same, slow way. Grabbing both legs, he made her flip and started over, exploring her body from her feet to her thighs until he came to the rounded globes of her ass.

A hand on each buttock, he squeezed tightly, the flesh yielding to his mastery, lifting, separating until he could see the rosebud of her anus, clenching and furrowing with his administration. Holding her open with his thumbs, he dipped a finger into the fluids at her pussy and brought it up to rim the entrance to her ass, drawing circles around the wrinkled hole, not dipping inside – that would be for later when they knew each other better. When the moisture began to dry, he rewetted his finger and continued until she lifted her hips, begging, swinging them from side to side with want and need. Jaima released his hold on her cheeks, watching as they snapped closed. He nipped each cheek, under it, on the side, at the top of the curve, leaving little indentations from his teeth which he soothed with kisses and licks.

"God, Jaima," she moaned, "please."

"Please, what, Jo?" he asked, continuing his slow nibbling exploration.

"I need you."

"You need me to do what? Tell me, Jo."

"I need you, inside me. Please, I'm so...Please, Jaima."

She couldn't see him shake his head. "Not yet, *Olana*, but soon. My cock is aching to sink into you, but you're not ready yet. I don't want to hurt you." His teeth sank gently into the flesh of her cheek again, biting until he left a mark. "Soon though."

His hands continued up her sides, thumbs sliding along her spine, finding and counting each vertebrae, crossing her shoulders as he pressed his full length over her, but held himself up so as to not smoother her. He gave her an entire body rub, up, then down, letting her feel the hard planes of his own body against the smoother ones of hers, his hardened cock slipping between the split of her buttocks, even through the cloth of the briefs he still wore.

From her shoulders, he worked his way back down her body, doing what he'd just done in reverse, until he reached her feet. Grabbing her calves, he flipped her back onto her back, spreading her legs so wide she feared she was going to split up the middle. Rising to his knees, he shucked the briefs, which had become way too tight to contain his cock, the shaft achy and needy, pulsing with strength, a velvety, flesh encased piece of steel. It sprang out and bobbed a few times, then pointed right at her, the bulbous head large and thick, the shaft deeply veined and throbbing. There was a drop of pre-cum at the tip, the deep slit there opened slightly. His balls swung underneath, large egg sized organs fully rounded and heavy.

Her eyes widened with surprise at his size, not having seen him fully engorged, knowing he was large even before that, but what she'd imagined never coming close to what she saw now in the flesh. He was so much bigger than any man she ever been with. She didn't know how she was going to take him inside, it had been so long since she'd had sex. With any luck, she'd remember what McKenna had told her about handling big Taburon men before she became mindless with the want he was creating in her.

Falling to his elbows, Jaima nestled at the junction of her thighs and spread her pussy open further. "I have never shared nadryl with a woman who had hair on her pussy. This will be interesting," he said right before he licked her from bottom to top, a full, unending, single lick until he reached her clit, hiding behind its hood. "Sweet, like honey, yet salty as if from the sea," he decided, delighted at her taste. At her pleasure bud he swirled his tongue around the nerve filled nub, coaxing it to come out to play. Pulling her clit free from its hood, he studied the little organ for a moment. It pulsed once, begging for attention, and he gave it. Closing his mouth over it, he sucked, hard, holding her writhing body still with his hands as he toyed with her clit. Looking up at her as he tormented her, he saw she was panting heavily, her back was arched, her breasts jiggling as she took each breath.

He stabbed into her with his tongue, but when he couldn't penetrate the way he wanted, he instead slid his middle finger inside, his pointer and ring fingers laying to the sides of her clit where he pressed and rubbed, his tongue concentrating on the clit that had poked its head out now. She was tight, so very tight, virginally tight (or so as he'd been led to believe virgins were, since he'd never had one). She would hold him like a glove that was a little too small, but eventually yield as his cock breached her. A woman's sheath was made to expand to give birth, it would expand to hold him, and it would be a glorious ride taming her pussy to his cock. Withdrawing one finger, he slid two into her, then three, mimicking intercourse, spearing into her, spreading her, getting her passage used to the penetration of something larger than she'd ever had inside her before. She lubricated freely and easily, coating his fingers thickly with dripping moisture.

Her hands grasped the sheets. "McKenna said," she panted, "McKenna said…"

"What?" he asked, releasing her clit, not withdrawing his fingers, but toying with her clit by twisting his hand to lay his thumb over her button, tapping it firmly.

"Take me, from behind, or let me ride you." She lifted her head. "Oh god, Jaima, that's so… oh my god!"

"Don't come, not yet. I want to feel you around me when you come." He pulled back and rose, tapping her hip. "Ride me. It will be most delightful to watch you, your face and your breasts as you ride me." He laid on his back on the bed and tapped his hips. "Up and over," he instructed.

Swinging one leg over him, she settled on his hips, her pussy inches from his goal, his cock kissing against her ass as she adjusted. Raising her ass, she looked between her legs to locate his cock and positioned herself over it. With his hand holding his cock firmly at the base, she let herself fit the tip just inside her pussy. The thick bulbous head split her open, but once the largest part was in, the rest would more easily follow.

"You are wet enough. Let your body drop you onto me."

"You're so big," she gasped as his cock spread her flesh. She rose up then sank back down again, inch by inch, a little more of his cock delving into her sheath with every dip of her hips.

"A baby comes out of here. I'll fit," he promised. Reaching up he plucked at her nipples to take her mind from his breaching, rolling the hardened tips, pulling until her breasts reshaped into a cone before releasing them with a pinch. Jo's eyes closed as she concentrated, half of her mind on his cock, half on his hands.

Slowly, ever so slowly, she allowed her body to slide down his cock, twisting a little from side to side to fit him within, his cock pressing through her tight sheath, spreading the flesh with unrelenting pressure. "Gods' rods, Jo, you're killing me," he groaned as she slowly fell, his hands on her thighs. She moaned.

"Oh. My. God!" she cried, her head tossed back, her eyes closed, wanting to get it done and over with. She shoved, seating him entirely inside her sheath, his cock head buried so deep she thought he might just easily jam in her throat.

He was home. He'd never felt that way before with any woman, but with Jo, he felt as though he had come home and never wanted to leave. His heart swelled with joy, his body shifted enough that he could feel his whole world upend and he sighed quietly. She was so much what he wanted, so warm, so wet, so tight, and so beautiful. His cock could happily stay right where it was right now and never tire.

Her body vibrated, her insides fluttered. Once again to take her mind from the fullness of his cock in her sheath, to keep her from coming too soon, he pinched her nipples tightly, rolling them between his fingers until she moaned and her hands rose to grab his wrists to stay him. He released her nipples to wrap around her wrists, bringing her hands close to place a kiss on the palm of each one.

"Relax a moment, let your body adjust."

"You're so big, I can feel you in every inch."

"And I can feel your every inch," he added, shifting slightly and sinking just a smidge further, fully seated now. She was the warmest, softest, and finest glove ever made and he reveled in the way she surrounded him, holding firmly, tightly, exquisitely.

She breathed deeply. He filled her to overflowing, like she'd known he would and it felt wonderful, like the most expensive hot chocolate on a cold day, fresh, rare flowers from a lover, a steeping bath after a long day at work.

The best present ever that any adult could ask for in history. Jo wiggled slightly, letting him touch all inside of her, her eyes still closed as she allowed her body to become used to his girth and length. Another hard pinch to both nipples had her head snap up to find him grinning at her like a Cheshire. He'd once again taken her mind from the absolute fullness in her pussy as he pressed just the smallest bit further, now fully embedded. When she took a shuddering breath, he tilted his hips a little, pushing her up from his cock, then feeling her slide back down, a gentle thrust. Her squeal told him that while it was still tight, she could handle him now. With his hands under her arse, he lifted her before letting her fall back as he thrust up. She grunted and her breasts bounced delightfully.

As she became more used to the movement, bouncing on top of him, he increased the pace and the depth of the thrusts until he could feel her tire. Muscles unused to sexual activity tired quickly. Rather than bouncing on him, he showed her how to ride him, sliding her hips back and forth across his groin, her moisture providing a natural lubricant. Either way, he got the best view of her breasts as she moved her body, the round full globes bouncing and swaying, enticing and keeping his cock filled. Exhausted even from this after a time, she fell forward onto his chest, breathing heavily. She would improve in time, he would make sure her sex muscles became firmed and stayed well-honed from constant use.

Jaima knew the time had come for him to take control. He wrapped his arms around her in a bear hug as he sat up then twisted, never breaking their connection, flipping her onto her back. They adjusted themselves more comfortably while he hovered over her, his arms bracing his body so he wouldn't squish her, thrusting gently, but unerringly.

Bracing his elbows on either side of her, his hands sought out her breasts, taking the flesh, covering her nipples between two fingers to pinch them as he mouth descended again to devour her lips in a searing kiss as his hips moved rhythmically, pumping in and out of her sweet body.

Bending her legs, she lifted them to his shoulder, opening her wider, letting him penetrate deeper with every thrust, the pace increasing as he pounded into her pussy. She creamed all around him, her body knowing what it needed to do in order to continue this joyous experience, her legs locking by themselves around his neck as she met him, thrust for thrust. Sliding one hand to her ass, he lifted her slightly, realigning his cock so he could hit that delicate spot inside that would send her flying. The head of his cock rubbed her g-spot as he pulled nearly all the way out, then slammed back in to be seated fully. She screamed as her orgasm hit, a keening sound that started as a soft wail then grew as electricity zinged through her body and centered in her pussy before exploding.

Her sheath fluttered and pulsed, wave after wave of flesh tightening up and down his cock, forcing him to tense, his balls drawn up into his body as seed rushed from them to the end of his cock to spurt hotly into her sheath, breathing hotly into the curve of her neck. Spurt after spurt, he bathed her cervix with his seed, his back straight and face flushed as he groaned deeply in his chest, his hands tight on her legs.

They both needed several minutes to catch their breaths, Jaima on his knees holding most of his body above her, Jo lying flat, but once he could move, he let her legs down his side, gently withdrew from her body, and fell to the side.

"Are you all right?" he asked.

"Wonderful," she breathed softly. Her breath hitched and he heard her sniff.

He rose to an elbow to face her. "Why do you cry?" he asked with concern. Had he injured her by being too rough or too big for her? There were tears in her eyes and rolling down her cheeks. She angrily swiped at them with a hand, not wanting to discourage or anger Jaima with a show of emotion. Her ex had hated it when she cried. But Jaima instead touched a tear by her eye with the tip of his finger.

"No one has ever been so gentle or loved me so well before. I've never had an orgasm."

"You've never come before?" His hand rested on her stomach, drawing circles on the skin.

"I learned to fake it to get him done and off me. When he bothered to try to make me come," she added abstractedly. Jo placed a hand over his, staying his wandering fingers. "Usually he never bothered."

"He should be hung by his balls and left," Jaima growled, angry for her.

She felt her insides shift. That this man, this wonderful man who was only days from being a total

244

stranger and now for this short time her lover, felt strong enough about her pleasure that he defended her and was willing to take retribution on her ex on her behalf. It was a shame that he was leaving to return to his planet and the chances that she'd see him again slim. But she was grateful for the expression, and for that she would be content. "It was long enough ago that it doesn't matter anymore."

"I am pleased I could be the one to show you what nadryl can be. But we're not through, not by a long shot. We have all night yet, and I want to be inside you many more times." He kissed her and rose.

"Where...?" she started to ask.

He padded barefoot and bare-assed to the bathroom to wring out a washcloth with hot water, giving her an eyeful of his firm, rounded butt cheeks as he walked. She flushed again at his beauty – no man should be as gorgeous from the back as he was from the front. But this one was. He was in perfect shape, despite his injury. There wasn't an ounce of fat on him, everything was tight and sat high on his hips. He was muscle and sinew, a walking wet dream. The front view was even more impressive.

Sky Clad Jaima

Sitting on the edge of the bed, he opened her legs and gently wiped between them, cleaning her of the overflow of seed and her own juices that leaked from her pussy lips. Finding a clean corner, he wiped himself as well then returned the cloth to the bathroom. When he returned, he stopped for a moment, puzzled at the look she was giving him. "What?" he questioned, a brow arched.

"You're beautiful," she murmured. "All muscle and sinew, firm and well-honed. You are a girl's wet dream."

He stretched out beside her, taking her into his arms as he pulled her against his body full length. "I am not beautiful," he corrected, "I am a warrior. Men are handsome."

"No," she argued, her hands braced against his chest, "You are beautiful. I wish I could sculpt or paint, for I would certainly love to commit you to something for everyone to see how gorgeous you are for all eternity."

"Such a compliment, my lady. I am flattered beyond all flattery."

"No, Lord Jaima, I am honored. You have treated me like no man ever has before." His arms tightened around her with her words. No man had ever been so considerate to clean his fluids from her, to wipe the sticky residue that she knew would eventually cool and turn tacky and uncomfortable. If only he would say the words she wanted him to say, that he loved her, she would follow him anywhere he asked, even if he never intended to marry her. She'd leave her life on Earth to sleep by his side, share his life, even have children for him, if he would only…

She sighed softly, soaking in the warmth of his body and the heady aroma of his skin.

"Jo?"

"Tired," she murmured, her nose buried in his chest. Nice to not have to worry about hair tickling her nose. These Taburons were worth their weight in gold, if all of them were anything like Jaima.

With his toes, he grabbed a corner of the quilt that had managed to remain on the bed and pulled it close, draping it over their bodies. "Sleep, *Olana*. You will need your strength for later."

Sky Clad Jaima

Chapter Twenty

The afterglow of satisfying sex was powerful, stripping Jo of all desire to move from the spot where she lay, her head resting on Jaima's shoulder, a hand tracing lazy patterns across his chest. She liked the fact that he had no chest hair, no little strands to catch her fingers, no loose hairs to tickle her lips when she explored his torso with her mouth, licking his nipples and trailing a moist line to his groin. She sighed softly.

Sky Clad Jaima

Jaima held her close, an arm wrapped around her to keep her pinned against his side, her breasts cupping him warmly. Somnolence was close, his body exhausted from loving her every which way he could, no energy left for further dalliance for a good number of hours. He didn't believe he had a single drop of seed left in him, all of it expended during the night and once just an hour or so ago. The arm upon which she rested drifted slowly up and down her back along her spine, dipping into the dimples at its base before sliding teasingly up to rub at her neck and repeat the journey going south. His other arm was braced under his head, fingers dug into his hair.

The room was warm enough, and Jaima exuded enough body heat that the sheet had only been drawn as far as their waists. The sweat they'd created in their enthusiasm had already evaporated leaving the area around their bodies perfumed with the scent of sex and sweat. Neither cared at the moment. Sunrise was on the horizon and soon they would have to part to make ready for the day.

"I like that you have no body hair," Jo said into the dimness of the room. "I noticed that about you in the hospital. Is it because you are a warrior, you shave it off?"

"It is because I am Taburon. On our heads and around our manhoods is the only place we have body hair. Unlike your human males, some of whom have a very thick pelt."

He could feel the slight nod of agreement of her head against his side as she softly chuckled. "Yeah, some of our men don't appear to have evolved past the Stone Age. It's rather nice to have you as you are, no loose hairs."

He huffed softly in response. "Unlike what I had to contend with," he reminded her.

"I never considered shaving down there. Never had a reason to."

"Perhaps you will think about it now."

"I like to think I'm open to suggestion." She fell silent. Would he make the suggestion, ask her to make a change for him? Give any indication that he wanted her? He remained quiet, his only indication of still being awake the deep breath he took and the slight tightening of his arm around her. She continued to twirl her fingers.

"What does it mean, that word you use...*olana*?"

His breath hitched for a heartbeat. Eyes popping open, he spent a moment staring into the dim light. "Sweet," he finally responded quietly. "It means sweet," he repeated. He didn't tell her he was lying, for the word actually meant dear one, a term he was willing to express in a language he knew she wouldn't understand. But he himself wasn't willing quite yet to be completely up front with her either.

Her voice was tinged with disappointment. "Oh," she whispered.

He lay silent a few more minutes, then pulled his arm free from under her and sat up, bending his leg, the sheet falling to his lap. Scrambling, suddenly embarrassed, Jo pulled her side of the sheet to her breasts, hiding them from him as he twisted to face her. "Jo, come with me to Taburon. You'll love my planet, it's so beautiful and peaceful. I would love to show it to you."

"How long are you talking about?"

"However long you wish to stay. I'll take you to every place you want to see and then some. We'll stay in all the best hostels, or palaces if there are any. I have that right as captain of the King's Guard, there are very few places denied to me. You will enjoy it, and we can be together."

Jo leaned over the side of the bed as she listened to his plans, grabbing her robe from the floor where it had been dropped. Sitting up, she drew it over her shoulders and slid from between the sheets, overlapping the sides and tying the belt tightly. Standing, she searched the floor for her panties in the dark, giving up when she couldn't locate them without making a fuss.

"Jo?" he asked when she didn't respond to his suggestion. He stood, leaving himself nude before her.

Swiping her hair away from her face and tucking it behind an ear, she glanced up at him. She could live without the panties and she buried the sense of embarrassment that swept through her at the possibility that whoever came to straighten the room after their departure would find them and know she'd spent at least some time with the Taburon. "What?" she asked.

"What do you think? Will you come to Taburon with me?"

Deliberately, she kept her eyes averted from below his waist. "I don't think I can, Jaima. I have a job, I have to work, and can't take that kind of time off without giving a lot of notice so someone can cover." She shrugged.

"McKenna...Queen McKenna," she corrected, backing away from him, "talked about it a little while we were in that house and it sounds like a very lovely place. Your invitation is really appreciated, but the timing isn't right now. Maybe some time in the future..." she concluded as she headed for the door.

He grabbed her arm. "Is something wrong? Did I do something to displease you?"

Her chin lifted slightly. She wouldn't allow herself to fall apart and appear needy. If a man could put sex into a neatly kept indifferent pigeon hole, then so could she. "No, not at all. It was a wonderful night."

"Then why are you running away?"

She gently pulled her arm free, taking a deep breath to harness her wayward emotions. "I'm not. It's just the sun will be up soon and you'll all be wanting to get ready for your trip. I need to go back to my apartment and change, get my things from the house, and arrange for the equipment and the meds to be returned to the hospital, then get my new schedule for work set up."

Sky Clad Jaima

Jaima pulled away. The rejection couldn't have been made any clearer if she had physically slapped him across the face. He crossed his arms over his chest, refusing to be forced into saying something he wasn't sure he was feeling. Last night had been the best nadryl he'd ever experienced, he'd felt a connection as never before. But to define it in terms that meant a permanent relationship was just something he wasn't ready to admit to at the moment. If she would only agree to come with him, perhaps in time they would find that deeper tie with which to create a life of forever, of marriage and children and happily ever after. If not, she could always return to Earth, or find a position on Taburon where her skills could be utilized and she would be useful. Sistan had indicated an interest in Earth medicine, she could help him to better understand its methods and intricacies.

Joanna blinked at his withdrawal. She had hoped for some sort of want from him besides a non-committal offer to take her on a tour of his planet. If she'd wanted a vacation, she certainly didn't have to go to another planet in order to have one. She'd never been to Europe, or Asia, or even the western United States with its mountains and vista views. A tropical beach sounded pleasant. At this particular moment, any place other than where she was right now sounded inviting.

But to go to Taburon required commitment in her mind, a long term kind of commitment that she needed that came from a place deep inside her. She'd already done the love 'em and leave 'em and she'd learned the hard way that promises men made weren't always made with forever in mind. There'd certainly been no indication of forever throughout the night, just a great deal of pleasure for the moment. Which meant that even were he to use words of love and forever, he didn't necessarily have to mean them. Only utter them to get her to do what he wanted. To go with him and be a convenient bed partner for however long he wanted her. Not again.

Stepping closer to the door, she reached for the handle. "Will you at least come with us when Radine arrives?" Jaima asked. "I'm sure he'd like to thank you for the sacrifices you've made these last days."

"I don't know, Jaima. I'll think about it. If there's time." His quick glance at the door handle gave her permission to leave, he wouldn't delay her or push her further. She nodded once, a bare movement of her head as the knob turned in her hand. "I guess I'll see you later," she murmured just before fleeing.

The door closed behind her with a soft snick. Jaima extended a hand to place against the door, the cool wood preventing him from touching her, his chest rising in a deep sigh. "I doubt it," he responded softly.

Chapter Twenty-One

King Radine's shuttle touched down in the same place it had all those days ago, and as before, the gangplank was fully extended as the guard marched smartly down to line the way for their king, standing at attention, their swords drawn and held up, points skyward. Waiting to the side along the edge of the landing area, three limos with their engines still running, had lined up, their passengers remaining inside until the king appeared. A large paneled truck also waited, its cargo items both Sistan and McKenna thought might be of use on Taburon, especially the medical supplies.

McKenna didn't hesitate. As soon as Radine appeared at the top of the gangplank, dressed in comfortable clothes instead of an official uniform, she threw open the door of the car and raced across the grass, up the gangplank, passed the guards and threw herself into his embrace. He caught her with an "oof," nearly losing his balance, but he braced himself, catching her and holding her tightly as she gave him a bruising kiss. Every man in the guard smiled, one even chuckled, but they held their position. They knew their king and queen were stupidly and deliriously in love.

"I assume you missed me," he said. Delight filled his expression and sparkled in his eyes. McKenna had fallen in love with his eyes the day she met him, and the joy he showed whenever she was near that shined and glittered through his eyes always pleased her. She wrapped her legs around his waist, her arms over his neck, covering his obvious reaction to her with the junction of her thighs and ass.

"You don't know the half of it," she replied, nibbling at the edges of his mouth. He dallied for a moment, luxuriating in having her back in his arms before reality hit with a thud. They were being watched, some with indulgence, some with amusement, and some he was sure with disgust.

"This is really not the time for you to crawl up me," he admonished softly, willing his erection away.

"I'd take you here if I could," she declared with mischief, wiggling her hips.

"Behave yourself," he replied, pinching one of her ass cheeks surreptitiously, "and you'll get plenty of chances to say hello in a more proper fashion." She pouted childishly but allowed him to set her on her feet. He turned to face the rest of his people who'd been left behind.

Sistan had waited until the couple had gotten through the more passionate part of their greeting before approaching them. Behind him two men carried a trunk which they set at the feet of the guards at the bottom of the gangplank. With a single motion of his hand, Sistan indicated for the guards to take the trunk and bring it on the shuttle. They passed the couple as they boarded.

Sistan bowed. "Your Majesty," he greeted, choosing to ignore their byplay.

"Sistan, welcome home." He smiled. "Thank you for your service to my wife and friend. What is in the trunk?"

"Medicine for Lord Jaima's continued recovery and supplies I believe might be of use on Taburon."

Radine nodded approval. "There is a promotion for you when we get home."

He showed surprise, but bowed again. "That is not necessary, but thank you, Your Majesty." He skirted the king and queen to make his way up the gangplank. He was extremely glad to going home, which for him was the ship in orbit in space right now. Sistan could be honest in that he'd had enough of Earth for the time being and wanted nothing more than to surround himself with everything Taburon. His first order of business would be to change into clothes that fit properly, then have one of his favorite foods as a treat. Radine watched the physician make his way up the gangplank before he turned forward.

Jaima had yet to leave the vehicles. Instead, he stood in the opened door on one side, looking over the roof of the car at the young woman standing on the other side. Her face was a study in sadness. Jaima held his hand out to her, asking. She shook her head no, her chin lifting slightly before disappearing back into the car, closing the door firmly.

Jaima's shoulders sagged for only a heartbeat or two, his hand clenched, then he straightened, stepping back and slamming the door with a thud loud enough to carry to the ship.

Radine leaned down. "What…?"

"They're in love with each other, but they're being stubborn. He wants her, she wants commitment, any kind, yet he won't give it. He won't tell her he loves her." They both watched Jaima approach, his back stiff, his face wiped of all emotion for the moment. He'd found clothes similar to his uniform, but his medals and epaulettes were in a pocket. His sword he carried, clenched tightly in his hand and held close to his waist.

Not until he came close to Radine did he let a small amount of emotion cross his expression. A sense of relief filled him, a weight lifted from his shoulders, though his heart was heavy. Stopping in front of the king, he went down on one knee, his sword in the ground, his head bent. "Your Majesty," he murmured.

Radine placed his hand on top of Jaima's head, his fingers digging in slightly. He'd really feared for his friend and brother, afraid that he'd never see him alive again. His joy was complete, his wife and best friend were well and coming home. "My brother," he said softly, "you never have need to bow to me."

"I failed your queen, Your Majesty. I will accept whatever you decide as a fitting punishment."

"How did you fail McKenna?" Radine asked, curious. "Little one?"

"My old boss tried to kidnap me, again. Jaima killed the bastard."

"Then you did what I would have done, had I been there at the time. You did not fail anyone, my friend."

McKenna piped up again, wanting her husband to understand just exactly how much danger they had been in and how much Jaima had endured in order to defend his people. "He was barely recovered from his wound," she added. "Plus, he was drugged at the time. He could barely function. He saved Sistan, me, and Jo."

"Jo?"

McKenna's head bobbed in the direction of the cars. "The nurse that took care of Jaima while he was ill, Joanna Simon. I'll tell you all about it when we're back on the ship."

"The babe?" he asked, his hand covering the spot where their child grew.

"Safe, husband."

"Will she not come forward so I might offer my gratitude?"

"She does not feel it necessary," Jaima replied, his voice flat and unemotional. He kept his expression controlled, but his eyes sparked with unrestrained anger.

Radine glanced from his wife to his friend, his brow furrowing in consternation and confusion and choosing to let the matter drop – for now. "Board, Lord Jaima. We'll talk later." With a second bow, Jaima boarded the shuttle.

The President, having waited his turn now stepped forward. "Your Majesty."

"Mr. President. I hope you will not feel insulted that we do not stay. I wish to get my wife and friends back to Taburon. Our son misses his mother."

"I understand, Your Majesty. I hope you might find a chance to return so we might redeem ourselves in your eyes."

"Sometime in the future, Mr. President. We will keep the lines of communication open in the meantime."

"We cannot expect anything more." He bowed to Radine first, then McKenna. "Have a safe trip home." He backed away, finally turning to go back to the limo. As the president's limo moved away, the truck backed up to the gangplank and parked. Jumping from the cab, the men from the truck enlisted several of the guards to help unload the truck until all of the three dozen or so crates were placed inside the shuttle. The other cars pulled away and no one save the driver of her vehicle was aware of Jo silently crying as the guards marched back onto the shuttle and the gangplank was withdrawn. The engines fired up and the shuttle began its ascent. The truck followed the limos and turned to head back to the city proper.

Sky Clad Jaima

Radine waited until he'd thoroughly welcomed McKenna home before meeting with his friend. Relaxed, in casual clothes, shirtless, socks on his feet, he invited the warrior into the sitting area of their quarters, pouring a glass of wine for the two of them. Jaima was dressed in his usual uniform, dark trousers, pale blue colored shirt, black boots, and a laser weapon hanging at his side. He'd tied his hair back with a length of leather.

"Want to tell me what happened?" the king asked, taking a seat. Jaima remained standing and refused the drink. Radine was totally unconcerned and carefree. Nadryl did that for a man. Draping a leg over the arm of the chair in which he sat, he waited for Jaima to speak.

"Our presence in the hospital was causing a problem and we had to move to a different location. I was still unconscious at the time. No one realized McKenna's ex-boss had been watching and knew where we had gone. He disguised himself and gave us a dish of something she called brownies, but he'd drugged them. Once he believed everyone to be unconscious, he entered the house. He intended to kidnap McKenna, and Jo, since she was there, take them to a secret hideaway, and torture them. I had not eaten much of the brownie, not caring for the taste, so I still had some ability, though Jo gave me a stimulant to revive me. Jo had also not eaten much of the treat, and she helped for as long as she could. She finally succumbed to the drug while trying to keep McKenna's ex-boss occupied until I had enough energy to be of any use. I put my sword through the man and went to find help. We were taken to the White House after we were cleared at the hospital and where we received word you were expected to arrive in the morning."

Radine swirled the wine in his glass, watching until the liquid had coated the inside of the vessel. "And the woman?" he finally asked.

Jaima frowned. "What about her?"

"You left her behind."

"She did not wish to come with me."

"Did you share nadryl with her?"

The other took a deep breath, his eyes straying to find a spot somewhere over Radine's head, lingering a moment before he decided on an answer. "It is not your concern, Radine, as my king, since she is not Taburon, nor my friend, since it is private. Even a brother does not have to know everything. She chose to stay on Earth. That is all you need to know."

Radine's brow furrowed. Over the years, even after his marriage, there hadn't been much the two of them couldn't discuss. From politics, to dreams, to bed partners, throughout their lives they'd covered the gambit of subjects, emotions and all. Yet Jaima's face was tight, his eyes shuttered, and Radine could see that he was holding himself stiff and closed off, as if greatly hurt.

He hadn't seen Jaima make a beeline to his own quarters as soon as the *Veleda* had been given the orders to make ready to leave Earth orbit for its return trip home. Once they'd left the solar system and everything was functioning normally, Jaima had peeled the clothing he'd been given from his body, tossing it into a heap in a corner. It had been uncomfortable, just that much too tight and binding, especially across his groin. But the choice had been something too tight or too loose, and he'd preferred his cock and balls contained instead of swinging free. The panties he'd found on the floor that morning and tucked in a pocket he placed deep in a drawer, a keepsake he would hide in his quarters once they arrived home, keeping the memories private for the time when he believed he might be ready to remember. For now, it was too soon and it hurt too much.

Taking a shower to rid himself of all traces of the scents of Earth, including the perfume of her body that skimmed along his skin, he'd then set an alarm and dropped onto his bed to sleep, knowing Radine would take several hours to reacquaint himself with his wife and that time for him was free. His sleep had been deep and dreamless, his mood as dour after waking as it had been before.

Joanna's refusal to join him had hurt. Yet he'd still been too stubborn to pull out and examine his emotions to deal with them, admitting that he might be falling in love with Joanna. Only the driver of their limo had seen the awkward exchanges between them, his questions polite and impersonal while her answers had been curt and monosyllabic. He'd carried it with him as they flew from the ground to the ship, stoic and unsociable, very unlike their amicable Jaima. That the man was unwilling to talk to Radine now. Keeping something of this import a secret was unusual for Jaima.

And that told Radine all he needed to know. Jaima had fallen in love, no matter how he perceived it at this time and was unwilling to admit to it. But his friend was a stubborn man, and until he realized what he needed to do, he would remain stubborn, and alone. Radine hoped it wouldn't take too long. They really couldn't keep traveling back and forth between Earth and Taburon so many times.

What Jaima had yet to realize, and would discover over the next few days and weeks, was that their decisions would affect him greatly. Being in the arms of his favorite *skala* would not ease the ache nor satisfy the hunger, there would be no peace in his sleep. And the love shared between McKenna and Radine, which flared to blazing because of their separation, because of what might have happened, because they were overjoyed with the impending birth, would drive Jaima to a kind of madness that he would only be able to escape by leaving the palace and their presence and eventually be forced to acknowledge and deal with. But for now, with his emotions in a turmoil and under the tightest control he'd ever exerted, he stood stiff and ill at ease in front of his king.

Jaima was ready to drop the subject, shifting from one foot to the other, clasping his hands behind his back. "When we get home, I will make out a schedule for the men for training. I have been too long without it and feel my body growing lax. I'll run it by you a day or so later, so you might approve it."

"Are you well enough?"

"I will not be if I do not get back to training."

Radine drained his cup. He was disappointed, with Jaima, with the man's stubbornness, with the whole episode that had turned disastrous when they'd had such high hopes. "Very well, then, Lord Jaima. Dismissed." Jaima bowed and backed away a few steps before he turned and exited. His attitude of high propriety – bowing to his king in private when he'd never needed to before - towards the man he knew as friend and brother irritated Radine as well. Draining the other cup, not willing to let good wine go to waste, he set it down with a distinct thud.

Radine went back to his wife. She was sprawled out on their bed like a *skala*, her body opened to whatever he wanted to do to her. She grinned at him as he dropped his trousers and threw himself onto the mattress, making her bounce. "Well?" she asked as he gathered her close, burying his nose in the junction of her neck and shoulder, covering half of her body with his own.

His sigh was resigned, rolling and dragging her along until she braced on his chest. He pinned her down with his arms crossed over her back. "You were right. And he's a stubborn man. It's not going to be pleasant until he realizes it."

McKenna lovingly cupped his face. "You'll handle it, as you always do." She bussed his lips briefly. "Tell me, what happened with your mother? You only hinted at it a little bit ago."

Folding her more tightly into his embrace, he rolled so they faced each other, their legs tangling, his amorous mood tamped down slightly with the memory. "My mother," he said, his hands gliding across her skin. "My mother was fine, more than fine. I harassed my pilot and crew, rushed home and dashed through the palace to her chambers to find her in the midst of sharing nadryl. Turns out she had suffered a few scrapes and bruises, but was fine."

"This is interesting. With whom was she in bed?"

"You'll never guess. Remember when you suggested I send a few of the guards her way, have them express an interest in her and she rebuffed every one of them?" McKenna nodded, drawing swirls with her fingers on his chest. "Turns out she already had a lover. And I caught them, his arse up, when I walked into her chambers. It was Pologa."

She raised up in surprise, her eyes going wide, her fingers digging into the flesh of his chest. "You're kidding!" she exclaimed.

He gently pried her fingers from his skin. "No, I am not, and that is a sight I wish I could erase from my memory. There are just some things a child, even an adult one, should never see his mother doing, and that is definitely one of them."

And the memory was still with him. He'd been worried sick the whole trip back, thinking the worse about his mother, hoping that she wasn't dying or dead, especially with Jaima lying unconscious in a hospital, his prognosis unknown. As soon as they'd docked, and his shuttle had taken him planet side, he'd rushed through the palace to her chambers, letting the nursemaids take charge of Rakenn. Throwing open the doors to her room, he stopped, nearly losing his balance as his feet rooted to the floor.

On the bed, a man's arse was heaving, vigorously pumping, his cock shuttling in and out of a woman's body, her legs draped over the hips of the man. He needed a moment to process the sight and for it to coalesce in his brain that he was seeing his mother in the throes of nadryl, her voice heavy with lust as she huskily and enthusiastically encouraged her lover to go faster, deeper, harder. Finally finding his body answering to his commands, without saying a word or making a sound, he backed away and spun on his heel and was leaving the room as the man grunted tightly with orgasm, the woman shouting as she joined him. Radine fled to his own chambers.

Inoa had breezed in an hour later, looking nothing like the wanton he'd caught recently, her hair perfect and her dress unwrinkled. It was the first time he'd truly noticed the flushed look of a satisfied woman on the face of his mother, though now that he remembered and considered it, he'd seen it before but had never made the connection. "Radine, I didn't..." she started to say stopping short almost as fast as he had upon finding her earlier.

He was sprawled over the most comfortable chair in the room, a leg over one of the arms, a large glass of wine in the other, a half empty carafe on a table nearby. He glanced at his mother with a bleary expression, lifted the glass and took a healthy gulp. Her eyebrows came together as her forehead creased. "Are you drinking this early in the day?"

"Yep."

"Are you drunk?"

Radine saluted her with the glass. "Not enough yet. Soon though." He took another deep pull.

Inoa looked around the room. "Where is McKenna? Rakenn?"

"Rakenn is in his nursery. McKenna is still on Earth."

Inoa panicked. "Did she leave you? What have you done?"

He raised the hand with the glass and pointed one of his fingers at her. "*I* didn't do anything. She, Sistan and Jaima are still on Earth because Jaima was shot, severely injured, was still unconscious when I left." He peered into his glass for a moment as though searching for a bug. Or trying to remember what he wanted to say. His head swayed with intoxication, but the look of accusation he shot at his mother was clear. "We were waiting for him to be declared well enough to travel before we headed home. He could be dead for all I know right now, but I came home because someone sent a message saying you'd been hurt in a fall."

Inoa sank into the chair nearest, fear in her eyes, despair in her heart. "Jaima shot? How?"

"With a thing the Earthers call a gun. An interesting piece of weaponry, it shoots a projectile of metal from the barrel that penetrates a body and causes all kinds of internal damage. He was injured protecting us. McKenna stayed to watch over him. I didn't want to leave Jaima, but you are my mother. Nor could I leave my kingdom in the hands of the Council, on the off chance you were incapacitated or Gods' forbid, dead, so I rushed home. Obviously the message was wrong." He drained half of the contents left in the cup.

"Obviously," Inoa agreed wryly.

"I made a decision I didn't want to make and left my wife on Earth. My best friend, my brother, is on Earth. And my mother…"

Her look became suspicious. "Your mother is what?"

He finished his drink in one gulp. "Who is he, Mother?" he asked as he took the stopper from the carafe and refilled the glass. "All I could see was his arse." He would have the gods be damned kind of headache in the morning, but he was angry and lonely and missing McKenna more than life itself. As he raised the refilled cup to his mouth, he shot his mother a dour look, daring her to argue with him or scold him for leaving his wife and best friend behind.

Inoa paled. So he'd seen her had he? That would explain a lot then. Taking a deep breath, Inoa stood, straightening her shoulders, her hands smoothing down the front of her dress along invisible wrinkles, as regal as she could get. "I'll be back to speak with you when you're sober," she announced and strode from the room, the door shutting firmly. Radine saluted her with his cup and drained it, then poured the rest of the wine from the carafe into the empty vessel, his hand swaying slightly.

McKenna began to laugh in delight. "Oh, your mother is so busted," she promised. "She is still slipping me dildos for when you go away for more than three days. As if anything like that could compare to having the real thing," she added meaningfully, cupping her hand over the real corresponding part between his thighs. Radine groaned when her fingers enclosed him tightly, spreading his legs slightly to allow her better access. He permitted her a moment to work his cock then twisted, pinning her under his body, seating himself between her splayed thighs. "Now, where were we?" she asked as he thrust forward.

Chapter Twenty-Two

Jo walked into the break room reserved for staff, dropped onto a chair and rested her head on the table top. She was so tired. She'd not been sleeping well since Jaima left, her nights plagued by two dreams.

The worst one involved Raymond, his body looming over hers, his eyes feral as he reached for her with a bloodied hand. He grinned viciously, touching her body painfully as it explored her curves, shoving inside her body, the feel like sandpaper on her sensitive flesh. Evil personified, he became vicious as he raped her, his manhood more weapon than flesh, ripping into her, tearing her apart from the inside as she screamed. She'd wake, shaking, covered in a cold sweat, realizing the screams she'd thought she'd dreamed had been real and were still echoing off the walls of her bedroom. It surprised her that no one in her apartment building called the police. Needless to say, afterwards she was unable to fall back to sleep. Dragging herself from the bed, she would sit in her darkened living room, nursing a cup of coffee in order to remain awake until it was time to start getting ready for work.

The other dream involved her night with Jaima, so different from the first. His hands gently roaming her body, his fingers caressing her every dip and curve with gentleness and reverence. How warm his mouth had been pressed against her lips, how he'd used those educated lips to explore her pussy, bringing her to orgasmic heights before thrusting into her with his powerful cock, tipping her into ecstasy as he kissed her cervix with the head of his cock. Those nights she would also awaken, shivering with want, flushed with heat, desire that could not be fulfilled with her hands or a battery-operated substitute. Nothing could take the place of the real thing.

Regrets were terrible burdens, and she was weighted down by the mother of all of them – not telling Jaima how she felt before he'd left. She'd sought him out that night for comfort and given over to the intense emotions he generated in her, the desire to share her body in a nonverbal expression of love, afraid that actually saying the words would have driven him away from the encumbrance such words men often associated with them. Might it have made a difference? Perhaps. Perhaps not. But if she had only said something, maybe he would have reciprocated, even in the smallest amount, giving her hope that they might have made a future together. On the other hand, had he at least admitted she was nothing more than a one night stand, she believed she could have accepted that and been able to move on with her life and the pleasant memories. And she would have loved him until the day she died.

She'd returned to work two days after the Taburons had left, taking one day to cry her fill, and another to allow the redness from her crying to fade so she wouldn't look so miserable in front of her coworkers and patients. She put on a happy face and went about her duties as usual, tending to her patients as best she could, ignoring the personal questions of her coworkers as much as possible, but daily her feet dragged towards the end of her shift and she was uncharacteristically the first nurse checked out to head home. Four weeks was beginning to feel like four months, today especially, as every minute took an hour and every patient seemed needier than normal. A few minutes was all she wanted, just a few minutes to rest her head, and she could go back to work with a smile on her face, no matter how forced.

She didn't hear the soft footsteps that had followed her into the room, but jumped when a hand gently landed on her shoulder, lifting her head to peer blearily over her shoulder at its owner. Dr. Tripp's smile turned into a frown as he saw her face.

"Jo? Are you all right?"

"I'm sorry, Dr. Tripp, I'm a little tired."

"You look exhausted and just short of falling over. What's up? Want to talk about it?"

She shook her head as she stood then thanked God he'd been near. For without his hand shooting out to catch her, she would have fallen over as a dizzy spell washed through her. "All right now?" he asked after a moment.

She nodded, her hands on the table top, leaning on it for support, taking deep breaths, fighting off the spinning in her head. She finally pushed off, straightening her back and smoothing her uniform with a deep breath. "Yeah. I'll just get back on the floor."

"No, you won't. Follow me," he ordered. Leading the way, he left the room, her on his heels, pausing long enough to tell the charge nurse that he was taking Jo for an hour. Down the hall he led, finally stopping by an open exam room, waiting for her to enter first, pulling the door closed behind him.

Searching through cabinets, Tripp found an exam gown and tossed it her way. "Three minutes," he warned her. "Change." He stepped out of the room to give her privacy, snagging a nurse as she passed to order several forms be brought to him for tests he would order for Jo, keeping an eye on his watch. He had the forms when he knocked on the door and opened it slightly to find she'd changed, standing by the exam table warily.

As he passed her to begin rooting through drawers he patted the padded table. "Up you go," he instructed. Resigned, Jo climbed onto the table, her legs hanging over the edge, her hands in her lap. Tripp placed an infusion set and several vacuum tubes on the table behind her, a long rubber tourniquet, several closed packages of alcohol wipes and sterile gloves.

Ripping open a wipe, he extended her arm, tucking it under his elbow and wiped a wide swath from her skin above her elbow to below it. Tripp repeated the process with a second wipe. "I've ordered standard blood tests, stat results, make sure you've not become anemic. I won't order an EKG or x-rays until I see the results of the blood work. You're not sleeping well, I take it?"

Several strands of hair slipped from her ponytail to drift around her face as she shook her head. "Not really."

"Just since those Taburons left, I take it?" He tied off her arm and drew on the sterile gloves. Ripping open the infusion set, he checked for a vein and pricked her. Attaching a vacuum tube, it began to fill. Tripp leaned down slightly to look directly into her eyes. "You fell for him, didn't you?" he guessed. "That injured Taburon. Jaima."

Jo's eyes watered slightly, but she nodded. "I broke the rules. I shouldn't have, but I did."

"Jo, if that was a rule, and unbreakable, then there'd be a lot of doctors and nurses kicked out of the profession. My wife was a patient when I met her." He switched out the tubes. "You're not the first and won't be the last." Tripp pulled an end of the tourniquet, removing it. "Did he love you?"

She shook her head. "I don't think so. He never said so, but I fell in love with him anyway."

"He seemed like an honest man. I'm sorry, Jo. You deserve better."

"I'm a fool, to believe in another man." Though she didn't talk about it much, Dr. Tripp, who'd been in residence since the day she'd started working, had been a good friend and gentle shoulder to lean on during those terrible days right after her marriage had gone to hell. A perfect listener, he given her a chance to vent her anger and frustration, not offering advice, just listening.

"Love isn't sane now, is it?" he asked keeping his voice light. No sense upsetting her more than she already was to his trained eye. "Isn't that why they say crazy in love?" He changed out another tube. "You went through a lot a few weeks ago."

"And I thought I had it handled. But between what happened at the house and Jaima, I'm not sleeping well. Hell, I'm barely sleeping at all."

Finished, Tripp pulled the infusion set and placed a cotton ball over the spot, bending her arm. Gathering the tubes, he set them aside, pushing a button on a nearby wall to call for a nurse to collect the tubes while taking his stethoscope from his pocket. "We'll see about taking care of that for you," he commented as he tucked her hair over her shoulder to the front. "Take a deep breath," he ordered. He listened to her lungs and heart, then felt the glands in her throat. A nurse grabbed the tubes and disappeared with them. While she still sat, he drummed along her back with his hands, then had her lay back in order to check her stomach. Supine, he felt her ankles to check for swelling, then offered her an arm to help her sit up. Passing her a sterile cup, he indicated for her to use the attached bathroom and fill it. Blushing, she scurried past him, holding the gown closed in the back. The door closed with a snick.

Straightening up, tossing used materials as he waited, the same nurse reappeared to hand him a paper. His eyebrows rose as he read the one test result, then thanked the nurse. Again he rummaged through the drawers, piling items on the table she'd laid on until he had everything he needed.

Jo returned, the closed cup in hand. Placing it on the counter, she glanced at the physician for what next. "Up again," he indicated, "lay back. Feet up." He pulled out the stirrups so many women dreaded, tapping them lightly. Obeying with trepidation, Jo settled down, her hands over her stomach as she took deep breaths to calm. "You've had OB exams in the past, relax," he told her, rolling a chair to the end of the table. He discarded the old gloves and pulled on fresh ones.

She sighed nervously, plucking at the edges of the gown. "The next time you have to open yourself up like this, then tell me to relax," she derided. He chuckled softly, spreading her knees apart. Warming the speculum in his hands before he inserted it, he then gently parted her feminine folds and put the end of the device inside, parting it to peer inside. With a long cotton swab, he took a sample, sealed it in a sterile package and set it aside. Tripp removed the speculum, coated his finger with lube and stood. "Take a deep breath," he told her, sliding his finger inside. His other hand he placed on her abdomen in order to check her internal organs, his eyes studying the wall behind her. Finished, he lowered her legs and snapped off the gloves. "You can sit up now."

"Was that really necessary?" she asked. "I know it's been a while since my last check-up, but I've not had any problems, except recently."

"What problems?"

"The tiredness, a general lethargy even though I have problems staying asleep and dream a lot more than before. I feel hungrier some days more than before. My breasts are tender, but that's happened on occasion."

"When was your last period?"

Jo's face screwed up as she thought. "It was due early last week. I guess the stress has thrown me off."

"How long has it been since your divorce?"

"We divorced three years ago."

"How long were you married?"

"A year and a half."

Tripp braced a hip against the edge of the counter, crossing his arms over his chest. "And you never got pregnant during that time?" She shook her head. "Let me ask you something. When you had intercourse with your husband, did he ejaculate inside you?" He touched her arm gently. "I'm not being nosy, but it's important."

Jo nodded. "Nearly always."

"And how did you feel afterwards? Think hard, Jo, be honest."

Jo thought, remembering. The times when they were first married, how gentle he'd been, caring and considerate, treating her like a queen. Then after four months, he'd decided that he wanted children, and his efforts became harsh, thrusting into her furiously after minimal foreplay, getting her just wet enough to penetrate. He'd fuck her, for it wasn't making love with the ferocity of the act, thrusting until he spewed into her, withdraw and fall to the side of the bed, going to sleep almost immediately while she lay, miserable and wanting, curled up on her side, her stomach turning, her body flushed and tingling. Once or twice, she fought to keep from vomiting as her abdomen cramped, deciding it was just a reaction to how poorly he'd used her.

"Any cramps, pain? Flushing, or other symptoms you wouldn't normally expect after having   intercourse?"

"Yes, maybe half the time."

"When did you last have sex?"

She flushed deep red. That was private, between her and Jaima. "Jo? I would really like to know."

"The night before the Taburons returned to their planet," she confessed, her voice nearly a whisper. "I spent the night with Jaima. I couldn't stop shaking because of what had happened."

Tripp nodded with understanding. He'd have been shaking like a leaf in a hurricane strength wind had he gone through what she had. "Well, I'm taking an educated guess here, but I think you couldn't get pregnant with your husband because you were allergic to his sperm. Your reactions to his ejaculate is typically a symptom. We could be sure if he would come in to take a few tests…" He dropped the idea at seeing her shake her head vigorously. "It's not common, but it does happen. He has children now, doesn't he?"

"Several, last I heard."

"Makes me even more certain then. As for you, you need to start taking better care. You're pregnant." Tripp waited as the news sank in, her eyes gradually widening in stunned surprise when she looked at him with disbelief. Tripp nodded, smiling. "You're six weeks, considering the last time you had sex and going by standard calculations. I assume your Taburon didn't use condoms?" She shook her head again, still in disbelief, her eyes rounded.

"You're sure?" she asked.

Tripp passed the test result paper to her. Being a nurse, she could read the results as easily as he. "First test on the list. Ordered it returned stat. Believe?"

"It's incredible. I never thought...I just...it's..."

"Wonderful, if you've wanted a baby. It is, isn't it?"

"Yes, it is. A baby, I'm going to have a baby." A smile split her face while tears filled her eyes as she gave over to the wonderful news. Her heart thumped in her chest as pictures of a child filled her head, her child, to hold and love. To love her back. To call her momma and bring her the latest crayon drawing that she would proudly display for all the world to see. A child who would fulfill her dream of family and continuance, to give her reason to go on and fight for everything she believed good and right. A child to enter the future, hoping the world would be a better place for her – or him – by the time he or she reached adulthood.

Then she sobered. She was going to have a baby, a Taburon baby, or half Taburon. With the atmosphere on Earth of general xenophobia, there was no way any child with Taburon blood would be safe from "them." How was she going to raise such a child and keep their ancestry a secret, especially if they had any of their father's traits, especially his eyes? They could get by with the hair, but the eyes would be a dead giveaway that her child was different and leave them vulnerable to attack.

"What?" Tripp asked as he watched the emotions flicker over her face.

"Everyone is going to know I'm pregnant. Everyone in the hospital will know."

"Look again. No name on the test requests, just initials, mine, and backwards."

She confirmed his statement with a glance, but there were still concerns. "He'll be Taburon, my baby."

Tripp nodded. "Half, yes."

"You saw what happened when one of them was here in the hospital. How can I protect my child if he looks like his father?"

"Maybe you should tell the father. Let him protect you, go to his world."

She shook her head. "No, I can't. He doesn't want me, not the way I need. We had sex. He never said he loved me or asked me to marry him."

"Maybe he'd change his mind if he knew."

"No, that's the worst reason to commit, because he feels obligated. I may not even carry to term."

"I don't think that'll be a problem. We managed to run some DNA tests on that man while he was here, and the physician, Sistan, volunteered blood as well. They're not totally human, about ninety-eight percent, but that's close enough. Besides, the queen had one child with a Taburon, and was expecting another. In my opinion there's no cause for concern there, at least not in that way." He placed a hand on her arm to give her a reassuring squeeze. "Let's worry about that in a few days. What I want you to do now, though, is go home, take a long bubble bath. I understand you gals like that kind of thing." He smiled to lighten the mood, the smile extending as far up as he eyes. She fell into his spell and returned the smile. Tripp was a good man, caring and compassionate. Rumor had it that he had enlisted and served one tour during the war in the Middle East and been so devastated by the severity of the injuries and the atrocities man could perpetuate another man that he'd not reenlisted and returned home more understanding and more charitable. There was also a rumor that his wife had not been nor was in the best of health, but he remained loyal to her though he could have exercised his right to divorce her and take another woman to his bed. He had no children that he ever spoke about nor any family that he mentioned other than his wife. "Have a healthy meal, lots of it. You're eating for two now. Sleep as long as you need. I'll take care of the shift nurse when she has her temper tantrum. Figure out what you're going to do over a few days. You might want to consider contacting someone connected with the Secret Service, maybe even the White House and let them know what's happened. They might be able to protect you." She nodded. "Can do?" he asked with genuine concern.

"I can. Thank you, Dr. Tripp. You've always been a good friend."

"Go on then. Get dressed and get out of here. Rest. I'd give you sleeping pills, but being pregnant kind of put the brakes on that."

"I understand. I'll try to rest, I promise."

Chapter Twenty-Three

"You're going to prune," McKenna declared as she entered the bath in their chambers. Radine, with a rare day off, and Rakenn were in the large tub, playing with toy boats, and had been for the last forty-five minutes. Rakenn kept sinking his father's ship, blasting the elder's corsair with bombing sounds of cannon fire. Of course, Radine let him, making sounds of sailors screaming as they fell overboard to drown in the deep waters of the 'king sea.' McKenna had burst into laughter the first time she'd caught them, her big Taburon husband and king, playing with the child on a two year-old's level. Rakenn, seeing his mother, had been frightened that they had been doing something wrong until his father had bent to whisper conspiratorially in his ear, shooting glances at the woman over his shoulder. The child had laughed, returning to his boat, shooting the father's toy and sinking it. Suggesting McKenna join them, his eyebrows bouncing suggestively, McKenna had laughingly declined. The games her husband had in mind for the two of them were not for little ears and eyes. And in the case of her husband, his 'ship' rarely sank.

Two year old Rakenn was already as tall as any human child of five. He followed his father everywhere, when permitted, and Radine had even taken him to the back of his *crufa*, one of the largest of the animals on the planet, much to McKenna's dismay. But the child had laughed with glee as they rode around the parade grounds, a fatherly hand holding on tightly. Her glare had had little effect on the two of them and she'd thrown her hands into the air, warning that they'd better not come running to her with cuts, scrapes and bruises, or Gods' forbid, broken bones. Inoa, when sought out for support, had waved her hand dismissively. Radine had been sitting on a crufa from the time he could sit up straight. She saw no reason for Rakenn to be treated any differently.

Radine righted the boats and gathered them together. "Time to quit, Admiral Rakenn. Mother has declared our war over." He stood, setting the toys on the edge of the tub and grabbing a towel. "Come here," he told his son. Lifting the boy out of the water, he put him on the floor and wrapped the towel around him, rubbing briskly until he'd stopped dripping. He draped a second towel over the boy's shoulders and with a fatherly swat to his ass, sent him running, squealing with laughter. Radine grabbed a towel for himself and started to dry, not missing the appreciative glance his wife gave him. Obviously he'd kept the bath water warm.

"You know he'll spend the next half hour mooning and terrorizing his nursemaid," she complained. The child had taken to running around without clothes, racing around their chambers and his nursery, his everything on display, an attendant hot on his heels. Unfortunately, he took after his father, since Radine could rarely spend more than a half hour in their bedroom without disrobing. Fine example the father was setting for the son. So far Rakenn had limited himself to their chambers or the nursery. McKenna dreaded the time when he escaped through the doors and headed for court. Crowned Prince or not, it would not go over well with many of the lords, ladies, and ministers who were constantly at court.

"He is a child who has discovered how much fun it is to go naked," Radine answered, pulling McKenna against his still dripping body, rubbing his cock, which always seemed to be engorged around her, into her belly. "Get naked with me and I will show you how much fun it is. I want to kiss you all over."

She swatted at his shoulder. "Behave yourself," she admonished. "I'm still nursing Avelda and not interested in getting pregnant again so soon."

"I will pull out before I come," he promised, bending her over his arm as he nibbled at her neck, a hand covering her breast to give it a gentle squeeze.

"As if that were reliable," she scoffed. Just to be perverted, she cupped her hand around his now fully engorged cock and squeezed. He groaned, bending to place his lips on hers, drinking in her taste in the kiss.

"Come to bed," he whispered.

"I have something you should see first," she diverted, slipping from his embrace. With a sigh he wrapped the towel around his hips and fastened it, ignoring the tent in the front of it, following determinedly as she led the way out of the bath. Her time would come, he promised himself, and he would delight in doling out a fitting punishment to their mutual pleasure. He hated the dress she wore, he couldn't watch her delightful arse wiggle as she walked in front of him. Though he could have sworn he saw an extra sway to her hips as she walked away. Vixen.

"What?" he finally asked, getting his mind back on business. "What has Jaima gotten himself into now?" he queried with a guess. He poured himself a glass of cool watered down wine.

Ever since their return to Taburon, Lord Jaima had been on a tear to see how quickly he could piss off everyone around him. He'd hit the training grounds like a dervish, the devil himself on his heels, looking for someone willing to hurt him 'accidentally,' something not one of his men was anxious to do. Even the king had not been spared his friend's desperation, Radine joining him once on the training field and ending up nearly actually fighting for his very life as Jaima lost his concentration, giving over to his emotional state. Only the intervention of other soldiers, stepping in to grab the man and physically pull him away had brought the lord out of the haze he fallen into and spared the king a serious injury. Jaima had instantly fallen to his knees to beg forgiveness, which Radine had readily granted, panting, out of breath, sweat running in rivulets down his face and back. He'd not realized how out of shape he'd been, especially when pitted against the zeal of a man in unrequited love.

The king stayed away from the mad man from that point on, instead receiving daily reports of his activities, each one making him grow more concerned about his friend. Finally, Rydul, Jaima's second in command, approached the king, begging for him to do something with the lord before the lord injured himself or forced someone to injure him in self-defense.

Realizing Jaima was hurting over Jo's rejection and not admitting to himself that he was in love with the Earth woman, and that he was looking for someone to punish him for the stupidity he'd displayed at not being truthful with Jo, as well as himself, Radine sent him on a campaign to tour all of the garrisons on the planet, evaluate their proficiency and bring them up to par if necessary. It would take him months to complete the task, especially since he denied him the use of an airship and made him go by crufa and sailing ship, giving the troops that bunked near the palace a much needed reprieve. Though the men who were to accompany him had been none too happy when told.

The hope was that by the time he'd finished, he'd have worked out his problem and return the Jaima they all loved. That he would have come to terms with what he had done and learned to live with the decisions he had made, no matter how much he hated them and himself. He had not been permitted to return even when McKenna had given birth to the royal princess six months later.

"You might be surprised," McKenna explained, reaching for a note on a nearby table to hand to her husband. He downed a long gulp of wine, setting the cup down as he took the note to peruse. She waited while he read.

"Gods' rods, this must be a joke!" the king exclaimed.

"Nope," she confirmed. "I spoke with Jo a week ago once I got that message."

The king started to laugh. "Oh, this is precious. And he doesn't know?"

"How could he? He's been gallivanting all over Taburon for the last eight months. We get reports weeks after he's left one place and is already on his way to somewhere else."

"We have to go to Earth, get this settled out."

"I know. How long will it take him to get back here?"

"About two months, if he's where I believe. Then he might need some time to get himself together. Such campaigns tend to allow a man to let himself go and get a little shaggy."

"Then we'll plan to leave a week or so after he's ready."

"He won't want to go," Radine warned.

"You are the king. Order him."

The look on his face when he turned to her let McKenna know that she was in deep trouble, and that he would soon be deep in her. He dropped the note on the table and tackled his wife, hauling her to the bed where he dropped her onto the mattress as he stepped between her opening thighs. "'Order him,' she says," mocking her, "'You are the king.' Why is it that never works with you?" he asked,

302

unhitching his towel. It fell to the floor, forgotten, his cock hard and pulsing. She giggled, spreading her legs further for him to settle between them as he leaned over her body, sliding her hands around his neck.

"Why do you always think with your cock?"

"Because he likes to kiss you too," he answered, tossing her gown out of the way and thrusting home.

Sky Clad Jaima

Chapter Twenty-Four

A throne room had been constructed in the largest area on the king's ship, the *Veleda*, two ornate chairs placed on a platform at one end. Behind the thrones, silky material hanged from the ceiling to grace the floor, wavering in an air controlled breeze. The banner of the royal house of Taburon rested upon the silk. Before the thrones was a crowd of people, Taburon and human, waiting for the beginning of the welcoming ceremonies for the start of new relations between the planets Taburon and Earth. This time though, Radine wasn't taking any chances. Only after careful scrutiny and with only specific people, he had convened this gathering on the *Veleda* where he could be more assured of keeping control of the situation. It was also the only way Jaima had agreed to be part of the group and attend. Stubborn to a fault, he'd absolutely refused to step foot on Earth ever again.

Off to the right, a door opened. King Radine and Queen McKenna entered, her hand set on his arm as he led her into the room. They were dressed in their rich clothes of state, his a uniform with medals on his breast, and she in a long dress of dark blue. Both wore crowns on their heads.

Behind them, garbed in a dress of dark green in Taburon style, Joanna Simon followed the royal couple. Her hair draped her shoulders in soft waves, longer than it had been the previous year when she'd tended to an injured Lord Jaima. Every Taburon in the room bowed to their king and queen, wondering who this human was and why she deserved a place of honor with the king and queen.

As for the lord in question, his back turned to the thrones, in quiet conversation with one of his officers, he stopped speaking when the officer's attention was caught by the entrance of the three, and he slowly turned. His knees nearly buckled at the sight of the young woman, his breath stopped, and his blood pulsed through his body as he automatically bowed with the rest of the group, his eyes never veering from the sight of the one person who'd allowed him to walk out of her life when he most wanted to stay. He had been a fool. He should have made her come with him, he should have told her how he felt, should have loved her for as long as it took for her to admit she needed him as much as he did her.

She was absolutely gorgeous, more so he believed, her face glowing, her eyes bright as she looked over the crowd, finally spotting him. He could see her chest rise as her breath caught, her skin flushing, and her head dipped to hide her reaction, but not before he saw that he was affecting her as much as she was him. He was so damned handsome and her heart sped up at seeing him again.

He'd had no idea that she would be here, that McKenna would remember the young woman who had spent days secreted in a house with them while he recovered from a gunshot wound and then bring her aboard the ship to have her stand next to her chair. The woman with whom he had shared an exquisite night of passion after they were nearly kidnapped by a mad man who had been McKenna's boss when she lived on Earth before becoming Queen. The woman who had refused to go with him to Taburon once the ship had returned to Earth to collect their wayward citizens. The woman who had haunted his dreams for the last year until he was sure he would go mad, taking his frustration out on his men until they had begged the king to do something with their seemingly possessed commander.

The woman he had fallen in love with, had been too stubborn to admit it to himself and had been too pigheaded to tell her before he returned to Taburon.

"For a Human, she's gorgeous," the officer commented softly, tilting in Jaima's direction. "Who is she?"

"Someone you need not be interested in," Jaima growled, facing forward fully. A surprised look crossed the officer's face as he also turned fully forward.

The king and queen took their seats, McKenna pointing to a spot next to her throne for Jo to stand. They waited for the general buzz of conversation to still and quiet to descend.

Radine stood. "The people of Taburon welcome the visitors from Earth and hope our future relationship will be fruitful. To this extent, I have appointed an ambassador, Janel, who will be our representative here on Earth." A general cheer and applause greeted his announcement as the man in question bowed to his king. Several of the Taburons surrounding him thumped him on the back in congratulations as the noise slowly abated and the audience waited for the rest of whatever King Radine was going to announce.

"Before we retire to a dinner meant to cement our peoples, there is one matter we must address. Lord Jaima," he called, his gaze zeroing in on his friend and 'brother.'

Puzzled, Jaima stepped forward, stopping at the bottom of the platform in front of his king. He had worn his best uniform, a white tunic over white trousers with polished black boots, his medals pinned on his chest, his sword's scabbard and hilt gleaming and hanging at his side. There were golden epaulets at his shoulders. His hair was tied back into a queue with a black ribbon. His eyes slid to Jo for a quick glance before he bowed his head and waited at attention.

Radine stepped down to stand in front of his friend, though he did not lower his voice. "Lord Jaima, did you or did you not once ask my queen permission to bring the woman, Joanna Simon, to Taburon?"

Jaima frowned, not knowing where this line of questioning was going to lead. "I did, Your Majesty."

"Why?"

Jaima hesitated, wondering why this was of any concern to any of the people here around them. He did not want to answer, but Radine was his king and friend and he believed there was no malice nor any intent to shame in his question. He searched for a heartbeat for the right words. "I wanted to pursue a relationship with Jo."

"You were unsure of your intentions?"

His eyes followed Radine as the king paced back and forth in front of him. "At the time, yes, Your Majesty."

"And now, My Lord? If you could ask again for permission to bring this woman to Taburon, why would you want her?"

Jaima looked at Jo. She was so easy to read, the hope on her face, fright in her expression, love shining from her eyes. She was so beautiful. He didn't know how he was going to be able to leave her again. If he had to remain on

Earth, he would, but his preference would be kidnapping her, hiding her away in his quarters and waiting until they left to return home before allowing her out. He slid his glance back to Radine, his king, his friend, his brother, his look one of absolute faith. And he knew that here and now, in front of all of these people, he needed to declare himself. "Because I was a fool, to know in my heart that she was the one to make me a whole man. But I listened instead to my head, where it spoke to me of duty and responsibility and not of love and compassion and companionship. I now know you cannot have one without the other and I am ready to finally and completely grow up to be a man, and need her as my wife and life companion."

"Indeed?" Radine asked, playing devil's advocate with relish. "Were you not the one who swore that he had no desire to be shackled by the chains of marriage, that he had no need for the pitfalls of love?"

Jaima shrugged. "Circumstances change, Your Majesty."

"So easily, My Lord?" Radine teased.

His head dipped slightly. "As you well know, my king, when the right woman comes along, it is as inevitable as it is unavoidable."

Radine smiled with memory before continuing. "When you came into your inheritance, you pledged your loyalty to me as your overlord and king. What will you pledge to this woman whom you say has captured your heart?"

Jaima drew his sword and held it point up in front of him for a second, then spun it around to point to the floor. Going down on one knee, he placed the point on the floor and held the sword by the pommel before him, facing Jo directly.

He swallowed deeply. "I pledge my life, my protection, my loyalty, and my love as long as I shall live. If she will accept me. These things, and all I have, are hers forever."

Radine spun to face Jo, his sword clattering, and with a wave, had her come down to stand beside him. "Well, My Lady, what say you?" he asked.

Her eyes had brightened more, though she frowned in what appeared to be consideration, also not above teasing this man who'd captured her heart and more. He'd put her through hell while she waited, alone and scared, in a strange place and without friends to lean on, and then gave birth to his son. "He is quite incorrigible, Your Majesty."

"Of that there is no doubt, My Lady."

"And he has a formidable weapon," she added meaningfully. Radine chuckled as McKenna suddenly hid behind a hand and snickered. Jaima growled softly, but only Radine and Jo heard it as he raised an eyebrow at the noise.

"That he does," Radine agreed, grinning. There were some things young men didn't avoid as part of their nature, and comparing 'weapons' had always been and would always be one of them, the king and his best friend in their younger years included.

Jo flushed deeply. "I meant his sword," she clarified before realizing the double entendre.

Radine's chuckle was louder, joined by several similar snickers from the onlookers. Glancing at his wife he saw she was having difficulty holding in her laughter. "As did I."

It took Joanna a moment to recover and the blush to fade. "I don't know, Your Majesty. A man who steps willingly into danger cannot promise his wife a long married life."

Radine faked a frown of concern. "You would have me release my best soldier, My Lady, the finest swordsman on Taburon?"

"No, Your Majesty, but I would ask that he always remember how we met and never repeat the circumstances."

Jaima growled again, louder, fed up with the teasing. "I will give up command if that is what you want, Jo. I will be a farmer or a weaver, a Gods' be damned poet, whatever you wish. But you have my promise I will remember." A poet? He had no idea where that had come from, but it had sounded good. Radine chuckled again and Jaima heard several sniggers from the watchers behind him. If he ever found out who, if they were any of his soldiers, they would be in for a well-deserved beating on the training field.

"Well, My Lady?" Radine repeated.

Sky Clad Jaima

Jo hesitated another second, dragging out the pain for this man she loved so much and who had treated her so callously a year ago. He'd only had to have admitted what he felt and she would have followed him to the edges of the universe. Instead, perversity had taken over and he'd allowed the best thing to happen in his life to drift out of reach. He deserved every second of their harassment, but she could see his patience was wearing very thin very fast. She smiled widely for him. "Yes, Your Majesty, I will take him."

Jaima's shoulders sagged with relief for a heartbeat before he rose, sliding his sword back into its sheath as he went to Jo. Standing before her, he stared down into her eyes, joy and happiness reflected back to him from the soft brown of her irises as he placed two fingers under her chin to tilt her head the slightest amount. "I love you, Jo," he murmured. "Marry me."

She laughed softly, tears gathering at the corners of her eyes as she nodded. "I love you too," she responded just as softly. "Yes."

Sweeping her into his arms, ignoring her squeal, her feet dangling off the floor, her body held tightly against his own, he kissed her, thoroughly and very publicly. The room

314

reverberated with applause and cheers as Radine, grinning from ear to ear, resumed his spot standing in front of his throne. Without looking he reached back for McKenna's hand, giving it a squeeze.

The king gave the couple a moment to indulge in their kiss before he cleared his throat, several times, in an attempt to catch their attention. Faces reddened at their open display of affection, Jaima lowered Jo back to the floor. "I will excuse you from dinner tonight," Radine informed them, his voice royal and commanding, "but you'd better be on the bridge in the morning…on time." Jaima grabbed Jo's hand and started to leave, stopping when the king spoke again with laughter in his tone. "Oh, and Jaima, sky clad is two days after we get home. I expect you to attend."

"We shall, Your Majesty," Jaima called over his shoulder, pulling Jo with him as they fled.

McKenna stood next to her husband, her eyes teary, watching the couple attempt to make their escape, hindered by friends who wanted to wish them congratulations. Radine lifted her hand to his mouth to place a kiss on the back of her fingers. He was pleased that his best friend and brother had finally realized the glory of love and found the right woman with whom to share it. He knew no other man who deserved it more than Jaima, who had earned it more than Jaima, who would make a better husband, and father, than Jaima. "Think he'll be surprised when they get to his quarters?"

"Floored, I expect. It would be interesting to be able to watch our Jaima finally brought to his knees."

Sky Clad Jaima

Chapter Twenty-Five

Impatient, having trotted at a fast clip the entire way through the corridors of the ship, dragging Jo breathlessly along behind and ignoring the questioning looks she shot at passing doors and corridors as well as crewmen, Jaima finally had her at his quarters and backed Joanna through the door to his rooms, his lips glued to hers as his hands worked to open the bodice of her dress. Had the doors not promptly closed behind him, she would have flashed her breasts at any passing crewmen.

His hands filled with her breasts, his mouth plundered hers ruthlessly. Panting, overwhelmed, she pushed at him. "Jaima," she breathed. He kissed along her jaw and down her throat.

"We'll be married within ten days," he said, nuzzling her neck, squeezing her plump flesh as he began another dive towards her lips, dying to show her how much he'd missed her and wanting to share nadryl to consummate his vows. His cock thickened and lengthened as her nipples tightened into hard buds. He walked her back towards the bedroom area of his quarters, one hand firmly planted at her back to keep her upright as he directed instinctively.

"Jaima, wait," she tried again, pushing at his chest, forcing him to step back.

He gave her a puzzled look as she replaced the bodice, refastening it. "I have to tell you

something," she explained.

"What could be more important than the fact that you've agreed to be my wife? I've missed you this last year. I swear I was losing my mind, not having you with me. I was a fool, Jo, to not tell you how I felt that day. But I'll never do that again. I'll tell you every day if you want. I love you, I want you for my wife." He pressed his lips to hers. "I have to admit, I lied to you." Her head cocked to the side in confusion, one eyebrow rising in expectation. "That morning, before Radine returned, you asked me what *olana* meant and I told you it was sweet. I lied. It really means dear one, for that was what you had become for me. I was afraid to admit it though, to you, even to myself. I've never been in love before and it frightened me more than any battle I've ever been in." He kissed her again. "I'm so sorry I never said it to you. I hope you can forgive me. I'm not a poet, Jo, no matter what I said about becoming one for you. I don't have fine words that rhyme. I'm just a soldier. Actions and deeds speak for me and right now I want to share nadryl with you. I have missed you terribly and I need to be inside you, to consummate our pledge with my body. I need to show you how much I love you by making love to you." The gold in his eyes sparkled with passion, seemingly shooting flashes of light uninhibited by his plea.

"And we have plenty of time for that, after I show you something," she insisted.

Gods' rods, she was going to make him suffer for being so thick-headed. Fine, he'd earned it. At least she didn't have any needles in her hands. He hung his head for a moment to regain control over his body, taking deep breaths. Finally he looked up. "All right. What?"

"Remember when I told you that I couldn't have children with my ex-husband?"

Jaima cupped her cheek. "I do not care anymore. You are more important. If we do not have children, I will live with it." He reached for her again. "As long as I have you, that's all that matters."

She batted his hand away. "I went to a doctor after you left and had him do some testing. After he asked me a ton of questions and took some samples, he determined I was probably allergic to my ex-husband's sperm, his seed, that every time we had sex, my body reacted negatively to it and I couldn't get pregnant." She shrugged. "Of course, perhaps I'm lucky because of it, otherwise I'd still be married to him and wouldn't have been available to fall in love with you. And without him to test, it was all supposition, but an educated one. So, in a way, it really was my fault."

"And it doesn't matter. We don't have to have children. I swear to you, Jo, I'm fine with it."

"But you don't understand. I can have children, just not with my ex, who I wouldn't go near now even if my life depended on it. No," she breathed softly, "I can have a child."

It took a moment for the words to penetrate his thick skull, but once it did, Jaima scooped her into his embrace, joy ringing in his soul. They could have children. No matter what he'd said before, a child would be the ultimate expression of their love, a promise of the future, a continuance of his line. Everything he could have wanted he'd now found – a wife and family – he was complete. And what better way to start than now, even before they were married, for children didn't appear as if by magic, but with sharing nadryl. Lots of it. All the time. If he got her pregnant tonight, things would be perfect.

Jo let him plunder her mouth for another moment before she pushed him away again, making him lower her to the floor. Was she going to make him wait until after the wedding? Hadn't she teased him enough already? They'd already shared nadryl a year ago. Maybe she wanted him to woo her. So not going to happen. He'd waited far too long, and was too determined to wait no further. He ached, his cock ached to feel the tightness of her sheath around him as he plundered her, bringing her to orgasm again and again. He remembered what it was like to hold her, to taste her, to have her wrapped around him and for him to feel as though he'd come home. Lying next to her, satiated, holding her, listening to her soft breaths as she slept, had been the most contented he'd been in a long time. No matter what he'd done in the last year, he'd never forgotten, and he'd never shared nadryl with another woman, not even his favorite *skala*, knowing it never could have been as glorious as it had been with his Joanna. "Jo?"

She took a deep breath to calm, her eyes bright with excitement, a smile gracing her lips. Instead of answering him, she went to the entrance to the quarters, waiting for the door to open. On the other side stood a Taburon woman with a baby in her hands, a baby she passed to Jo and withdrew, bowing. "Thank you, Seiga," Jo murmured to the woman before the door closed on her. Jo gave the baby a hug and kissed its forehead. The baby gurgled, reaching up to the woman with unsure hands.

Jaima was shocked, his knees turning to water and threatening to collapse. She'd had a baby? With who? When? Was he expected to raise another man's child as his own? To accept another man's child in his house and life simply because its mother was the woman he loved and planned to marry? Had she been so desperate for a child that she hadn't waited very long after he'd left to find someone with whom to share nadryl in order to get pregnant? How callous could she be to go from his bed to another man's before the sheets had even grown cold?

He'd been punched in the chest, hard, the pain worse than that he'd felt when the bullets had pierced him, yet she had him by his balls and he vowed he'd never recover from this betrayal.

But he had made a different vow before the king and queen and as an honorable man he would uphold it. He would marry Jo, and for all outward appearances, they would seem a happy couple. He would do what he'd thought about while recovering, establish her on one of his estates, keep her well and then for all intents and purposes, ignore her. She could raise her bastard child though it would never inherit a thing from Jaima. Whatever the child received, it would have to come through its mother.

Perhaps, if the mood hit, and he could get passed the thought that she'd given herself to another, he'd get beyond the revulsion of her having shared her body with another after him, he would visit her long enough and often enough to get her pregnant so he could have a legitimate heir, do his duty to his dead parents and his future. But he would never love her. Never tell her again that he loved her and share pleasantries as though they had a long and happy future together. Never open himself to letting her hurt him again.

She was still smiling as she walked up to him, cooing at the baby softly. "Did you have a good nap?" she asked the infant. "Ready to meet your father?"

She expected him to be this infant's father? 'How dare she!' he thought.

Jo ignored his thunderous gaze as she passed the baby into his reluctant arms. She knew he'd change his mind as soon as he looked at the infant she now gave over with trust. He had no choice but to take the child, or drop it. "I named him Jasim. He's beautiful, don't you think?"

After tolerating her touch in readjusting his arms so that he held the infant properly supporting its head, Jaima looked down into the child's face. The baby returned the gaze with bright eyes, curious eyes, eyes that were golden in color and Jaima frowned. The child was Taburon? But how?

With whom? There weren't any Taburons on Earth, yet this baby was one of his race. He slid his glance to Jo.

She sighed in exasperation. She resisted the urge to smack him upside the head. Honestly, men were so dense. She couldn't understand how they managed to survive sometimes, and he was the densest one of all. Couldn't he see the resemblance, that the baby he held was his own son? The boy was the spitting image of his father, right down to the golden color of his eyes. He'd been born that way and they had never changed, except to maybe deepen in color. The soft down on his head was the same honey gold as well. And if Jaima checked under the diaper, he would find that the baby sported his father's endowments there as well, though baby sized for now.

Knowledge finally dawned on the obtuse man. "Mine?" he asked.

She nodded. "Yes. He's three months old now, and growing fast."

"How?"

Now she really wanted to swat him, her arms lifting as though to follow through before dropping. Crossing her arms over her waist instead, she snorted indelicately. "As if you need instruction," she huffed. "One night, Jaima, one night and next thing I knew, I was pregnant with your son. That's why I went to the doctor. I was sick, I was scared, I found out I was pregnant, and stunned, and so very happy."

"Why did you not say anything?"

"Because I didn't know whether or not I would carry to term. I didn't want to take any chances that those people who hate Taburons and all outworlders would find out and try to hurt me or the baby. That they might try to take my baby and study him or experiment on him. That he'd be locked in a cage and I would never see him again. I insisted on protection when I found out and I'd gone into a witness protection program after you left and that didn't allow for much in the way of communicating with people I knew. After Jasim was born, I demanded that I be allowed to let McKenna know. That's why they decided to try again to reopen negotiations with Earth. That's why you're all here today. For my sake. For his sake. For *our* sake."

Taking the child, Jaima went to the couch to set him down, immediately stripping the boy of his clothes, touching the child along the way to assure of his existence. Once he was naked, Jaima held him up, examining him from head to foot. The baby gurgled the entire time. "He is well formed," he decided. The boy would grow into a fine warrior, a man with the strength to fight for what was right and good and protect the crown with his very life if it came to it. He would grow to be a friend to Rakenn, as he had become to Radine when they were children.

Jo giggled. "He's his father's son," she agreed moving close enough to palm her child's head softly.

Jaima's gaze landed on her chest. He'd thought her breasts had appeared different, fuller and more lush. "That is why your breasts are larger. You are nursing."

She settled herself next to him, standing before her lover and husband to be as he held their child like the most precious treasure in the galaxy. "And he has a hearty appetite."

"Was it difficult for you, alone and pregnant?"

"Sometimes. They set me up in a small house and gave me an income that paid the bills. As long as I kept a low profile, all I had to do was worry about staying healthy and pregnant. He wore me out while I carried, so I slept a lot, but it was all worth it when he was placed in my arms the first time."

Hugging the child to his chest, Jaima pulled her against him, burying his face into her side. She'd been right, sharing nadryl could wait a while as he soaked in the serenity that suffused him, cloaking him in its warmth. Jo's hands rested gently on his head, carding through his hair without looking for her eyes were filling with moisture. Now he understood the feelings the king had had when he feared McKenna lost to him and why the man, so proud and regal, had cried. Jaima felt tears fill his eyes and he would never again question or condemn the masculinity in crying.

Why he'd ever thought he could live without this escaped him now. There was nothing to compare it to that even came close to being better. This he would fight for for the rest of his life. This he would defend with his last breath. And he would take all of the ribbing Radine and McKenna slathered on him for his earlier misguided beliefs. It was worth it if he could come home to her and his child at the end of a trying training and know they would greet him with love. "Thank you, Joanna, for all you went through to have my son, and for giving me a family. I will love you, both of you, forever."

Sky Clad Jaima

Sky Clad Jaima

Chapter Twenty-Six

With his hand at her back, Jaima led Joanna up the path along the side of Lanzess Mountain. He had a small basket on one arm, she carried a blanket draped over one of hers. Sky clad was tonight, when, as tradition held, the Gods would give their approval for the couples on the mountain to mate, granting them a good future if the light was bright enough.

Of course, the couples had to present themselves to the moons of Taburon without covering, or 'sky clad,' nothing hidden from the Gods. And while the light shined on the mountain top, they had to indulge in at least one round of nadryl. It was tradition, a belief that the gods had once resided on the two moons, watching over the people below with benevolence, one that had been disproved many, many years ago, but the people enjoyed their traditions and this was one they kept religiously. Besides, it was just plain fun, with its suggestion of naughtiness at sharing nadryl outside in front of others.

The cloaks both people wore covered the essentials, since they wore next to nothing underneath. Jaima had donned a simple loincloth and Jo wore a similar covering, but had added a strip to cover her breasts, or at least hold them up, for they were heavy with the milk that she was feeding to the young Jasim. The child was waiting for them at a hostel at the bottom of the mountain with his nursemaid. While he was too young to be offended by what would happen, having a child on the mountain might have been off-putting for the other couples attending sky clad. So they would only be staying until the ceremonial light dimmed and they shared one round of nadryl, returning to the hostel before the night ended and sunrise.

Jo was aghast as they walked, averting her eyes from one side to another to avoid staring at couples already engaged in heavy petting, many of them naked and not waiting for the moons to rise. "You are a prude," Jaima whispered in her ear, a chuckle in his voice.

"No, I don't think so, but there are so many people."

"And they are so occupied with each other they will have no concern for us." Finding an open spot, Jaima dropped the basket and the blanket, spreading the latter on the ground for the two of them. He fell to his knees, pulling her close. When her cloak opened as she sat, she squeaked and overlapped the two sides to cover up. "You'll be naked soon enough," he commented.

"But not right now."

He chuckled. "You'll be naked and I will thrust my cock deep inside of you, sharing nadryl until you scream my name and come all over me. I will spill my seed inside you, so much that it will drip from your pussy as we walk back down the mountain, drops of both of us a trail anyone can follow." His head tilted in consideration. "Perhaps we shall make another baby tonight, as many result from nights such as this." His chuckle changed to a laugh at the flush that started at her forehead and crept down her throat until it disappeared under the collar of the cloak. Opening the basket, he took out a flask of wine and cups, then a dish of *entitans*, a sweet treat given to most couples for sky clad. Made from fruit and meat, they also contained herbs with aphrodisiacal properties to heighten and prolong the experience. As well as certain body parts, especially manly body parts.

Pouring a cup of wine, he passed it to her, filling his own cup. Unwrapping the dish, he broke off a large chunk of the treat, holding it out to her. She started to reach for it, but he pulled it back, his brow arching meaningfully. Getting the hint, she leaned towards him and bit off a bite, her cloak opening enough to reveal the cleavage of her bosom. He stared down the opening without reservation or shame, an eyebrow cocking up meaningfully. Turning the piece to where she'd bitten, he took a larger bite for himself, chewing with satisfaction.

Hearing a general cheer, they both turned. The sun was setting, its crest just over the top of the farthest ridge. As it began to finally disappear, a beam of light shot forth, rising into the sky to disappear into space. The cheers grew in volume, clapping added as the start of sky clad began.

Jaima finished his wine and sat forward, taking her cup from her to put to the side. Settling her in front of him, between his legs, they both watched as darkness fell, the sky turning bright red, then orange, then purple as night encroached. "Keep watching," he whispered in her ear, his hands delving under her loincloth to find her pussy unerringly, his lips teasing along the shell of her ear. On the trip back to Taburon, she'd had the hair of her pussy removed with a cream that not only took the hair, but killed the root. It was permanent and Jaima had enjoyed the smooth feeling of her numerous times since.

Now, as his knowing and expert fingers parted her folds, he found her already soaking wet. Stroking her lightly, he sought out her clit, covering it with her moisture, circling the little nub over and over until it swelled and poked out from under its hood. Jo grabbed his thighs and held on tightly, clutching at his skin until she'd left marks in his legs, her back arching, whimpers coming from her throat. One hand teased her clit remorselessly, the other plunged into her pussy, three fingers pumping her in time to her harsh breathing. Curling those fingers, he found her g-spot unerringly and rubbed it vigorously. "Come for me, *Onala*," he told her.

She tensed, her back arched as far out as she could get, and screamed. Her body spasmed, juices flowing from her to coat his fingers and hand profusely. Before she could scream again, his hands never stopping, he tilted her enough to cover her mouth with his, taking her cry into his mouth, forcing her lips to part so he could shove his tongue inside.

Once he wrung the last spasm he could from her, he kissed her gently, pulling his hands free. With his tongue, he licked the sweetness of her cream from them, slowly and tantalizingly from every, single one of them. "Delicious," he complimented, "sweet and precious. Better than even Bakkan wine." He nuzzled at her ear. "Thank you. You come so beautifully."

"So noisily," she corrected.

"I like noise. Lets me know I'm doing something right."

She leaned back and tilted her head to look up at him. "I don't know if you're being sexist or just obnoxious."

"I am pleased when I give you pleasure. If you will not tell me with words what I am doing is pleasant, then your cries of delight, especially when you come, are all I have."

"You want to talk during sex?"

"Why not? If I am doing something you do not like, do not want to do, or is hurting you, how will I know if you say nothing?" He clenched her chin. "I am not your former husband, Joanna. I will always treat you with respect and caring. I will give you what you want and need, or the opportunity to get it for yourself if that is what you wish. I cannot read your mind, though, you must tell me, sometimes outright. I am just a man, and at times I can be dense." She snorted. He wasn't telling her anything new there. Loosening his grip, he kissed her gently. "We will never bring him up again. He is dead and gone forever from your life, and your mind. Your life starts anew as of five days ago, when I asked to have you for my wife and promised to love you forever."

"I'm sorry, Jaima. I know he's out of my life, and I shouldn't let him have any control over me anymore. It's just sometimes it hurts, and words go very deep, and it's hard to get them out without some serious surgery."

"Nurse, heal yourself," he murmured. She chuckled, giving him a promising kiss. She would fight to forget all about her ex, he no longer existed, his words would no longer ring in her mind, and she had the most wonderful man to give her new memories and love incomparable to anything in the galaxy. Starting with the night he got her pregnant, the night she found love in his arms, despite him being thick-headed and stubborn, and yes, as dense as he said.

"Look," he indicated pointing out over the ridge. "Icide comes."

Along the top of the ridge, a crest was beginning to appear, the larger of the two moons of Taburon. It slowly rose, its light brighter than it had been in several years. "When Liva appears, we must disrobe and stand, waiting for the light to shine down on us. If the Gods will it, and the two join, and their light shines on us, we shall be blessed and have good fortune for the rest of our lives. It is then we should share nadryl before the light fades. Then we may go back to Jasim and home. A wedding awaits us there." His tone was acquiescent and stoic. "I am sure McKenna has gone overboard in preparing for it."

Joanna giggled. "I know she has, since she started planning it before you even proposed."

"Did she?" he asked, shaking his head. To assume he would have married Joanna as a forgone conclusion was taking their roles as royals just the slightest bit too far in his opinion. He would remember to return the favor to McKenna sometime in the future. With a sigh, he rested his chin on her shoulder while they sat together.

As they watched, Icide rose further until nearly half of the moon had crested the ridge. Liva started to rise as well then, her smaller size crossing over on front of Icide. In due time, when they had both risen, Liva would be totally encompassed by Icide, the smaller surrounded by her 'lover,' and the two would be in alignment. Only if conditions were right would the light from the sun hit the pair and reflect back to Taburon from the two moons, a shaft falling on the mountain. Lanzess was one of the few places where a single shaft of light would fall, and it only happened once a year at this particular spot. Couples waited all year for this night, though marriages were never postponed until after it any more.

Jaima rose to his feet, offering his hand to Jo to help her stand. "Strip," he told her, unfastening his cloak to let it fall to the ground.

"You're always telling me to take off my clothes," she grumbled, but stood as well.

Leaning close, he bussed her cheek. "I will never tire of you, *Onala*, and never tire of seeing you naked. I look forward to seeing you swell with our next child, but," he added, a hand over her abdomen as she started to talk, "I might be willing to wait a year, if you wish." His loincloth dropped and he stood, proud and fiercely erect, a warrior in his prime. She felt her heartbeat increase, pounding in her chest as the sight of the man she loved, tall and strong, and remembered him laid low, injured, hurting, fighting to push himself passed the injury. He was opinionated and staunch in his opinions, chauvinistic, but he put others before himself, ultimately thinking of their welfare before giving in to his own desires.

She thought of how he had struggled through the drugs and saved her and McKenna from a fate she couldn't even imagine. She loved this man more than life itself, and she was glad for how things had turned out in the long run. She had a husband who would cherish her, a child she'd always wanted, and someday there would be more children. A family she would love and protect, a man she would do anything for to protect and stand with. On Taburon, there were friends she could rely on, the king and queen, as well as so many of the soldiers under Jaima's command, for they trusted and respected their commander. She would never again be alone.

And she could still be a nurse. Pologa had offered to take her under his wing and show her how Taburons practiced medicine while learning from her the things she'd learned and practiced on Earth. Each had new ideas and old ones that worked well, enough that the experience would take a long time.

Jaima held his hand out to her as she shed the rest of her clothes and she placed hers within the firm grasp of his, facing towards the two moons, waiting with the many other couples as they also faced forward.

It seemed to take forever, but finally the moons were in complete alignment and not a single sound could be heard. The mountain itself seemed to have held its breath in anticipation. Suddenly, light poured forth from the moons, spreading in all directions, yet a single beam reached down to shine on the mountain, lighting it as if it were day. Loud were the cheers that rose, the applause drowned out by the voices of the couples as they turned to each other, embracing, kissing, falling to the ground to continue the intercourse they'd begun only minutes before while waiting.

Sky Clad Jaima

Jaima wrapped his arms around Jo, pulling her tight against his body, his body warm in the slight chill of the night. He attacked her mouth with his, a bruising kiss that he held as he lowered their bodies to the ground, stretching out over her, his legs between hers, separating them with his knees.

His cock lay on her thigh, heavy, pulsing, his hips twisting back and forth as he searched for the entrance to her pussy. With a small tilt, she offered herself to him, his cock now where it wanted to be most and he shoved forward, embedding himself completely with one thrust. She cried out as he thrust, but sighed as the head of his shaft kissed the entrance to her womb, buried so deeply she didn't know where he ended and she began. Bending her legs at the knees, he fell even deeper inside, groaning in ecstasy at being buried so far inside her he believed he would never find his way back out.

He started thrusting, gently at first, increasing the pace as she egged him on, locking her ankles over his arse, pulling him into her body with her locked feet. There was no foreplay now, just pure sex, hot, hard, fast and sure, one goal in mind – to reach orgasm while the light remained bright and full. His hips rose and fell as if he was trying to beat a record, each thrust forward a jolt to her, rocking her whole body, her breasts bouncing. As her blood boiled through her, as the emotions rose, as she felt electricity zing through her nerves, her breasts leaked, milk dripping from the nipples to dribble down the sides of her breasts and fall to the blanket.

Jaima lifted his torso and latched onto her right nipple, suckling, drinking the life giving fluid that she fed to their child, the taste sweet and warm. Giving over to her other breast, he drank from there. He'd been honest enough to admit to himself that he was jealous of their baby, the infant male who got a chance to nurse at her breast several times a day, the child for whom she bared herself to put him to her nipple at the slightest whimper. He hated the bras she wore to support her breasts, the padding catching the milk when she waited too long between feedings and began to leak, but he understood. He would have McKenna speak with her after the wedding about what Taburon women did to contain their breasts while nursing. In the meantime he'd offered to help, to relieve any pressure she might have felt by suckling her excess, but she laughingly fended him off. As long as Jasim was near, there was never any problem with an overabundance of milk.

Yet now he that had a chance to taste the essence of the woman he loved, the fluid she made from her own body to give to their son and he took it gratefully and found it delightful.

"Jaima," she panted, chanting his name over and over, "so close. Gods, I'm so close. Please, more. Harder," she pleaded.

He was happy to give in to her, slamming into her full force, not holding back. She would have slipped off of the blanket had he not held onto her, his hands at her shoulders. All around, the sounds of nadryl floated over the mountain top, broken occasionally by a cry of fulfillment, a hoarse groan from a man, or a scream of another's name as a woman orgasmed. For most of the people tonight, the night would be one of endless passion until the sun started to rise. Then they would drag themselves home, wherever that might be. Some would begin making plans to marry, others would find they were expecting as a result of this night. All of them would work towards fulfilling the prophecy of sky clad, perhaps the reason it was believed it brought good fortune, since many prophecies were self-fulfilling.

Sky Clad Jaima

But that was the last thing on Jaima's mind at the moment. He pounded into his woman, hard thrust after hard thrust, until she began a soft keening that grew into a wail. He felt her sheath spasm and tighten around his cock, traveling along his shaft in mind-blowing waves until he knew he was close to coming. His balls had tightened until they were hard nodes dangling between his legs, rocking, hitting her arse as he plunged into her body. Pulses of seed rushed through him from his balls to the tip of his cock and he tensed, holding still as he spilled himself deep within her, her sheath clenching on his cock as she joined him in the ultimate ecstasy, falling over the pinnacle together to stiffen, the clenching easing a little pulse at a time. When he emptied himself, he groaned, dropping his head into the space between her shoulder and neck. "I am sorry," he mumbled. "I did not take time to…"

She cupped his face. "It was wonderful, Jaima, I loved every moment." She kissed him before wrapping her arms around him, tightening her legs at the same time for a full body hug.

He lifted his head. "Joanna Simon, you have given me a son, you have given me your love and your body. Will you give me the honor of taking me for your husband,

344

becoming my wife and share whatever time the Gods give us with me?"

"I am the one honored, Lord Jaima, Commander of the King's Guard and the King's Army, and the commander of my heart. I have found the love of my life in you."

He sat back on his heels, gently withdrawing from her body, his cock glistening in the moonlight that still shone strongly. Holding out his hand, he asked her to take it. "Let's go home."

Sky Clad Jaima

Chapter Twenty-Seven

Jaima was dressed all in white, from head to ankle, highly polished black boots on his feet. Across his shoulders were gold epaulettes, a gold braid hung from his right shoulder to his right waist. Around his waist was a coal black belt and from the left side hung his sword, glittering in the light of the palace throne room. He was nervous, not because he was getting married, but because he was anxious to get it done and over with. He wanted to start his life with Jo and his son as soon as possible, taking them to one of his estates and showing her around.

There'd been little time for just being with Jo and Jasim. As soon as they'd arrived at Taburon, he and Jo had had to journey to Lanzess Mountain for sky clad. They had the nursemaid with them the entire time, except for when they'd actually participated in the ceremony. They had not been alone on the return trip to the palace, nor since, Jo being at the mercy of Queen McKenna and Queen Mother Inoa in preparation for their wedding. He'd spent time with Jasim, but not much with Jo and definitely not in her bed.

He was sure McKenna had arranged for the small interruptions that had plagued him when he'd found short periods of time to be alone with Jo upon their return from Lanzess Mountain. Some small wedding disaster after another kept them separated to the point of frustration and screaming on both their parts, for Jo needed him almost as much as he wanted her. Finally, after the fourth day of her machinations, Jaima made it a point to tarry around Radine as much as possible, grinning knowingly when McKenna tried to drag her husband off for a private moment but instead finding her husband deeply involved with the soldier and some matter having to do with the army or the guard. They reached a cordial peace on the fifth day, and both ceased the conspiracies, though Jo still hadn't given him any quality alone time the closer it came to the wedding. Finally, today they were being married and Jaima would gladly skewer the first person to interfere with his marital bed this night. For while his sword at his side was largely ceremonial, it was sharpened to a fine edge.

So now he waited at the foot of the thrones for her to appear, the general murmur of the watching attendees a soft noise in the background. King Radine and Queen McKenna sat on their thrones, also waiting. A priest stood near. In the front row of seats was Seiga, the nursemaid, holding a sleeping Jasim. With a moment yet to go, Jaima stood over his sleeping infant son and placed a light kiss on his head. He was so in love with this child, his heart swelled every time he saw the boy and held him in his arms. The child was the greatest gift any person could have given him, short of the mother herself, whom he was about to marry.

A soft herald of trumpets announced her arrival and the general buzz silenced as everyone turned to watch the bride walk up the aisle to meet with her groom. Jo was in a dress of off-white, the bodice tight around her breasts, gathered under her bosom and flowing freely to grace the floor in a full skirt that drifted around her feet. Her hair had been rolled on top of her head and set with jeweled pins. Around her neck and from her ears hung *vireck* jewels, the gems the dissipated stones that provided the source of energy on Taburon and highly valued as both a source of energy and beautiful jewels in their second life. Jaima had sent them to her in the morning to wear with her dress, sure that the color would complement her eyes. He'd been right, he decided, as he watched her walk up towards him, her eyes bright and alluring, full of hope for the future.

She carried no flowers. Instead, her arm was draped over that of Sistan, the Chief physician on King Radine's personal ship, the *Veleda*. They had spent nearly a week on Earth when Jaima had been shot, Jo his nurse during his recovery. She had fallen in love with him during that time, against her better instincts and professional code of ethics. He'd found her beautiful and wanted to share nadryl with her, but had not admitted to himself that he actually loved her until it was too late and he was on his way back to Taburon. Since Sistan had been the person she knew best other than the queen, and her own father was deceased, she'd chosen the physician to walk her to her groom.

Sky Clad Jaima

Jaima smiled as Jo approached. She was beautiful and he loved her beyond any thought of love he'd ever considered. This was a love that encompassed his heart as well as his head and body, and now that he had it, he would never give it up in any way, shape or form. He would die before he would allow her to leave him or anyone to take her from him.

As she neared, he took a few steps closer to take her from the physician, bowing his thanks to the man for bringing her this far. Sparing the baby a quick glance to make sure he was still quietly sleeping, Joanna placed her hand over his arm. Together, they turned to face the king and queen, the priest moving forward to perform the ceremony.

The actual marriage was short and sweet, a reminder of what it meant on Taburon to be wed, an exchange of vows to love, honor and respect each other, a pledge to do whatever they had to do to stay together, create harmony, and work to a better future for everyone. Sealing their vows with a kiss, they started to turn to face their well-wishers. The king clearing his throat stayed them.

Radine stood, pulling a piece of paper from a pocket inside his coat. He smiled at his friend and brother, happy for the man that he'd found the same kind of love that he shared with his McKenna, that Jaima would never be alone or feel left out, especially since Radine had taken a wife and started a family. The king was not a stupid man, he knew that Jaima often felt out of place when he shared dinner with the couple, watching them in their happiness and family life. He was a beloved uncle to the two royal offspring, but not a father, and Radine had seen the longing in the other's eyes, driving him from the palace and away from his family for months on end before the news had arrived and they'd returned to Earth.

Now they had things in common again, if Jaima ever left the poor woman alone and out of their bed. Except for the short time he'd spent on the bridge the day they left Earth orbit that last time, the couple had not been seen once the entire trip back to Taburon. Though the food left outside their quarters had disappeared on a regular basis.

Radine unfolded the paper. "Before the actual celebrating begins, I would like to read this letter written by King Tylene, my father, prior to his death. It was written for Lord Jaima to be read at his marriage. My father had hoped to read it himself, never expecting it would take so long for either of us to marry. Instead it was passed down to me for that day to read." Queen Inoa smiled and wiped a tear from her eye at the mention of her husband. He would have been so proud of both Radine and Jaima, the children of his body and his heart.

"'My Dear Anason, You came into our lives under the worst possible circumstances, the loss of your parents, but we took you in with the greatest amount of joy and love in our hearts. You became a part of our family, growing up with Radine, getting into all of the trouble only two young, ambitious, intelligent men can get into. We have been so proud of you, watching you grow into the fine man, fine soldier and great swordsman that you have become, as well as the best friend of our beloved Radine. You embody all of the things that make Taburon what it is today - you are its strength, its beauty, its compassion and its loyalty.

'Today you take a bride for wife. I hope she is everything that you wish for in a woman, and that she understands the great gift she is about to be given. I want her to realize that she holds your heart in her hands as you do hers, and that they both need tendering every minute of every single day. Be happy with each other, care for each other and never forget that love will conquer all adversity if you truly love.

'You are a lord within your own right, but today I grant you this one thing as my gift to you and your bride. Today I make you as equal to your brother, Radine, and crown you Prince of Taburon and your bride Princess of Taburon, no longer anason, but son and new daughter. I wish you both the greatest of joys and a long happy life together. With all of our love and hopes, Tylene, King of Taburon and Inoa, Queen of Taburon.'"

Radine looked up from the letter. "And Radine, King of Taburon, with McKenna, Queen of Taburon." The shock that was on Jaima's face was palpable, his chest rising in pants of disbelief, and he sank to his knees as Radine stepped down from the throne to stand before him. From the side, a young guard from his own regiment came forward with a pillow on which sat two crowns. Radine picked up the larger one.

"Your Majesty?" Jaima questioned, his voice breaking, tears welling.

"I agree with my father, brother, and I am so very happy for you." He set the crown on top of Jaima's head, adjusting it so it sat straight, then took the second crown. Indicating for Jo to kneel, she did, shaking as the crown was placed among her curls and settled. With a flick of his wrist, both people rose. "We can have the loyalty oaths taken when you return," he said softly. "Then you can sit on the throne in my absence on occasion," Radine added, reminding the other that he had always said he'd never wanted to experience that particular 'pleasure.' Jaima allowed a momentary look of distress to cross his face before he swiveled.

Jaima glanced at Jo. Her eyes were also wet, but for the man she loved instead of for herself. Of course, she was stunned. A lowly nurse who happened to fall in love with a warrior who was also a lord, the best swordsman on an alien world and held in high regard on his planet. Now she was a princess. A girl could never have dreamed things would turn out this way. But she'd learned that Jaima and Radine considered themselves brothers before today and acted together as brothers whenever they could.

Now they truly were, and while Jaima would never inherit the throne, unless every one of Radine's children died - and he would never wish that on his brother - to be formerly raised to the level of actual brothers made this day all the better for the warrior who had nearly given his life to protect his king.

As Radine returned to his throne, the attendees rushed to congratulate the couple on their great fortune, sweeping them along on the tide of their happiness to the reception that followed. Jaima would have been hard put to remember any of the actual words, though he responded appropriately. Still in a state of shock at the honor, he had to keep reminding himself, when he heard the title 'your highness' used, that the speaker was talking to him. He was a prince. His son was now a prince, and all of his children would carry the title down through the generations until the day came that no one would consider them less than royal, that how it came about no longer remembered. He started with surprise when he considered that someday, one of his descendants could become king or queen.

But that was in the distant future, and today he was the happiest man on the planet.

EPILOGUE

Radine strode through the corridors of the palace, his attention buried in a tablet of writing as he walked, automatically stepping around people in the halls without looking up, yet never taking his eyes from his reading. Turning right around a corner, he glanced up for a heartbeat, checking his whereabouts, never slowing in his stride, then glancing back to his papers.

Jaima had taken to his new position like a fish to water. Of course, having spent the majority of his life in the palace trotting along with Radine as the other learned statesmanship for his future gave the new prince a distinct advantage in absorbing his new responsibilities. And he handled them with great aplomb and diplomacy, as well liked as a prince as he had been a non-royal lord.

He still trained with the men, and still commanded the Guard and Army, but found new respect from them – as well as a distinct feeling of being allowed to win at their mock sword fights. Jaima, once he realized what was going on, roundly berated each man, put him on extended duty, and jumped back into the fray hell-bent on proving that even though he was now a prince, he was still expecting the best from his men all of the time no matter who the opponent.

Joanna had joined McKenna in her efforts to form a solid clearing house to gather information about other planets and peoples to pass onto Earth, to report on the conditions of women who had migrated and the advantages for the future for women who wanted to see if there were better chances for them somewhere other than Earth. She was happy on Taburon, working with McKenna and Pologa, lending a hand when needed, especially in the nearby town if a family found themselves in need of nursing assistance.

Sky Clad Jaima

Jasim was growing like the proverbial weed, already walking well and talking, his best friends Rakenn and Alveda with whom he spent a number of hours under the watchful eyes of the royal nursemaids. But every night, when his papa came to fetch him, he gleefully raced to the sweating man to jump into his arms and join him in a bath for an hour or so of water games while they cleaned.

Joanna had been aghast when she discovered that Jaima had started riding with his son, sitting the child in front of him on the impossibly high crufa, frightened that the boy would fall to his death if Jaima ever lost his hold. The child, on the other hand, was giggling with delight, egging the animal on with his little body the way he'd seen his father do.

After suffering her berating, he instead put a wooden sword in the child's hands and was teaching him to sword fight, deciding that twenty-one months wasn't too young to start training the son of the greatest swordsman on the planet. In fact, he taken some ribbing from his men, wondering when he was going to start training the boy. Joanna nearly fainted, but finally simply tossed her hands into the air and went in search of some sanity from McKenna. Unfortunately, the queen couldn't offer any reassurance, having gone through the same thing with her own husband and son not that long ago. The two women commiserated together, plotting how they were going to teach their husbands a lesson.

With his abilities as a royal well established, Radine had been concerned that the prince had not signed off on the manifest for the ship that was heading to Earth well before sunset, taking supplies and relief personnel to the embassy in the Capitol. Keeping track of the supplies and personnel had been one of Jaima's new duties, since many of the personnel were chosen from the Guard because of their skills at command and security. Having had no success in getting the prince to respond to requests for his attention, the captain had turned to Radine to get his intervention in the matter. Thus the king's journey through the halls of family wings of the palace to the quarters of the prince in the middle of the day, tablet in hand.

Reaching his destination, he passed through the sitting area to stop in front of the entrance to the bedrooms. He lifted one hand and rapped on the door. Hearing a muffled voice he believed responding, he pushed the doors open, entering without looking up. "Jaima," he started to say.

Sky Clad Jaima

A muffled squeal brought his head up sharply in time to see sheets and blankets float up across the bed and settle upon a figure, hiding it from view, blonde hair flying. His intended target, whose buttocks had been prominently raised over his bedded companion, swung around so quickly he nearly fell from the bed, grabbing a pillow as he twisted, plopping it over the exposed male genitals, now covered, an extremely reddened and very peevish look on the owner's face.

Radine spun on his heel to face the door. They were close, and since they'd grown up together from the time they were six and five, respectively, had seen each other naked numerous times, but this went beyond the pale. He hadn't wanted to see Jaima's naked backside any more than he'd wanted to find his mother in bed with the palace physician in the middle of sharing nadryl– both of whom he saw nearly every day and fought hard to keep the memory at bay. He hoped he wasn't scarred for life. "Gods' rods, Jaima," he exclaimed, "it's the middle of the day!"

"Gods' rods, Radine," the other replied with disgust. "If you remember, it's supposed to be my day off," he added. "Jasim will never get a brother or sister at this rate," he mumbled.

Sky Clad Jaima

Glancing hesitantly over his shoulder, Radine saw the couple was as decent as they could get, considering the circumstances. He cleared his throat loudly, inclining his head. "Yes, well, I am sorry, Jo. I guess I forgot. If you could but give me a moment, I'll get out of here."

Jaima slid his glance to the side to check with his wife. Radine saw the blankets shift as she nodded. Lifting a finger, the naked man made a spinning motion for the king to turn his back again, adding an accompanying scowl. Suppressing a chuckle, the king spun around.

Rustling bedclothes told him that Jaima had slid from the bed, his feet thumping to the floor confirming it. He made a disgusted sound. Several curse words followed.

"Jaima!" Jo hissed, "language."

"Where are my pants?" he asked of her, his voice lowered so he thought only she would hear. Radine choked back a laugh.

A feminine giggle was followed by a sigh of defeat that sounded more like another curse and then the sound of heavy footsteps as Jaima walked across the room. The wardrobe opened, a drawer was pulled, then slammed closed. Hushed curses came on the heels of Jaima dressing in a pair of training togs. "All right," he indicated, going closer to the king, stepping within his peripheral vision. The sooner he got this done with, the sooner he could get back to sharing nadryl with Jo, trying for their second child. Jasim was nearly two years old now, and it was time for a sibling. They were giving it their best effort. They were trying to give it their best effort.

At least it was fun trying.

If the king would leave them be for the afternoon.

"I wanted your approval for this schedule," Radine began, showing Jaima the papers he had been holding. He ignored the half-dressed state of his friend and brother, his bare feet stark against the dark tile flooring.

Jaima felt like busting his king in the jaw for this simple matter. "You came here for this?" he asked, his voice rising with surprise. He promised himself that he'd get even – someday - in a big way.

He gotten his revenge on the Queen for her interference in his attempts at finding time alone with Jo between sky clad and their wedding by making sure Prince

Rakenn and Princess Avelda received treats and toys every day for a consecutive two weeks, disguising them as gifts from an anonymous loyal subject that she could not refuse, presenting them to the children not only in front of the queen but the court. The children had been delighted with their presents making it difficult for McKenna to scurry them – the toys - away so her children were not spoiled shamelessly. When she'd found out the truth, he'd bowed and grinned with unabashed delight while Radine laughed helplessly and Jo smirked behind her hand.

"The ship is leaving before the sunset, the stores are being packed even as we speak. The captain asked for the final approval several hours ago, but you weren't responding to his requests."

Jaima took the sheaf and studied it closely. "It seems fine to me. Rydul is going?" he questioned with surprise.

Radine nodded. "He asked for the assignment."

"He's my best man. I don't know that I want to let him go for six months."

"I think he's chomping at the bit to test himself outside of your direct influence. He'll be in charge of the security at the embassy. And he wants the chance to explore another world that he didn't get when you were injured. You know he was excited about going to Earth."

"Yes, there was that," Jaima agreed, remembering with little fondness of the days he'd spent, first unconscious in a hospital bed and then confined to a house as they hid out while he recovered and waited for the return of the ship to take them home. He'd been shot by a man dead set against the arrival of the aliens and that one of them had dared to marry an Earth woman. The fanatic's response to rectifying the 'problem,' as he saw it, was to kill the king on his first official visit to Earth. His bullets had been taken, in defense of his king, by Jaima.

Of course, the time spent on Earth had given him his wife and son, for he'd fallen head over heels for the pretty nurse who'd volunteered to care for him in and out of the hospital despite the danger to herself. She'd felt the same. Neither wanted to admit to their true feelings, blaming what they were experiencing on lust and a healthy dose of curiosity. They'd beat around the bush for several days, coming together then pulling apart. Neither had counted on the hatred of one man, his lust for revenge for a slight he'd never been given, who'd invaded the house with ill intent where they'd been staying. Jaima had saved the inhabitants from the evil man, killing him though he'd himself had been drugged and near collapse. It wasn't until after the danger had passed that circumstances brought them into the same room, the same bed, and the same thoughts, falling into each other's arms passionately and completely, spending the night together but getting very little sleep. Jasim had been the result, though Jaima hadn't known about it until the child had been three months old and still on Earth. He hadn't offered any commitment before he'd returned to Taburon, and she, not wanting to force the issue, not wanting a commitment for the wrong reason, hadn't asked for one.

Rydul was a loyal subject, second in charge of the King's Guards and a commander in the Royal Army. A few years younger than the present king, he'd come up through the ranks as many a man did, proving himself over and over instrumental in helping Radine keep his crown when he first came into it and was challenged for the right to rule. The loss of Radine's father had hit the young soldier as hard as it had the king, the elder adored by the young officer and taken under the old king's wing several times during his growing years. He'd been given an estate for his dedicated service though not a title. So he was just a soldier, a high ranking one, yes, but simply a soldier.

He loved his work, he loved his king, and he loved to expand his knowledge as much as possible, taking on challenges that other men found daunting and throwing himself wholeheartedly into the task. During that fateful voyage to Earth, he'd been in charge of the guards so the king and Jamia could concentrate on the meetings that would occur between the royals and the humans. He'd had command for a full half hour before word had come that Jaima had been shot and all soldiers were to return to the ship and remain on board. Then his only job had been to keep peace among the men who'd thought they were going to have some leave on a new world and were now unhappily confined to their ship.

In the year and six months since their return with Jaima and his new-found family, few words had been exchanged between the Taburons and humans while a very small, very well-guarded contingent established an embassy on Earth to improve relations. A location had been searched for, a building secured with defenses the Taburons could control and coordinate with the humans, and furniture had been made special for the large warriors since human furniture was a foot or so too short. They had hired a human as a driver and obtained a vehicle outfitted for their size and protection. It had all taken time, the search, the coordination, and the approvals from all parties. The embassy had been set up now for three months and the guards there were ready to return home as new soldiers were sent out to relieve them. Only the ambassador and his secretary would remain on a permanent basis, guarded by both Taburons and human soldiers provided directly by the President of the United States. Every six months they would rotate personnel until the Taburons could be assured that their people were safe from fanatics and xenophobes bent on chasing them off the planet. And while the personnel weren't officially confined to the embassy, excursions out into the city were not readily encouraged. The Taburons had learned that familiar faces made for more easily remembered targets and thus, the rotation policy.

"Well, I guess I can't deprive him of the chance to explore a little. He knows the dangers and how to conduct himself. He's a good man, intelligent."

"Then sign off on it, and I'll make sure the captain gets it in time." Jaima scrawled his signature across the bottom of the page and gave the papers back to Radine.

367

"Now, if you don't mind," Jaima hinted.

"I guess you won't be joining McKenna and me for dinner?" Jaimas response was to scowl at his king. "Guess not. Well, then, carry on. Enjoy your evening." He started to leave the room when an unusual dark shape above his head caught his eye, halting him in his tracks, and he glanced up. Jaima's pants hung from the chandelier overhead, swaying gently from a soft breeze coming in through the opened windows.

Radine snickered loudly, his shoulders shaking in repressed laughter, a masculine groan on his heels as his friend realized what had caught the king's attention. Figuring discretion was the better part of valor, and knowing he would certainly be using the discovery as ammunition in the future, Radine left the rooms, pulling the door closed quietly. Through the door he heard pounding footsteps and the lock on the doorknob turned with a resounding click. He grinned at the masculine growl that issued through the wood of the door, followed immediately by feminine giggling and a definite squeal. Muffled laughter echoed through the room and Radine pushed away from the door, suddenly uncomfortable in his trousers. He needed to visit with his own wife. And very soon.

Sky Clad Jaima

Turning a corner onto the corridor that led back to the main part of the palace, Radine, looking for a private spot, went several feet before ducking through a narrow archway, pulling up short. He'd come face to face with a portrait of a woman that startled him at first until he remembered the name of the person in the portrait. She had been the first queen of his line, Kadric, his grandmother ten times removed. He had had his family history drilled into him from the day he could understand words and it all came flooding back as he stared at her picture. Helping her husband, his grandfather Madine, secure his throne with a firm, decisive hand had earned her the nickname The Tigra Queen, comparing her to one of the planet's most ferocious predators. Time had softened her reputation to match the sweet features painted on the canvas, though there was still a hint of hardness in her eyes.

Radine grimaced faintly, shifting his hips, then shrugged. Kadric had also been something of a lusty woman, giving her husband nearly ten children, of whom three survived to adulthood. So he was certain she would understand as his hand slipped under the waistband of his trousers to adjust himself more comfortably. His people knew he loved his wife, and loved sharing nadryl with her, but it wouldn't do for him to encounter any of his lords or ladies in a pronounced engorged state, not at this time of day. Taking several deep breaths, he brought his rampant thoughts under control, as well as his swollen cock and nodded once with reverence to the portrait before turning to leave the niche.

"Rydul," he called, catching sight of the young officer in question as he continued back to the halls of the main palace. The officer was heading in the direction of the throne room, six or seven steps ahead of his king. He stopped immediately and turned, bowing as Radine approached.

"Your Majesty," he greeted.

Radine held out the tablet. "Jaima signed off on your assignment to Earth and the manifest for the supplies. Would you be so kind as to make sure the captain gets this as soon as possible?"

The other took the papers. "Of course, Your Majesty."

"Looking forward to going?"

"Yes, Sire, I am. I didn't get much chance to see it the last time."

"Well, let's hope you do this time, and without the same results." He clapped a hand on the soldier's shoulder. "We will miss you here, especially the ladies. McKenna tells me that since I and Jaima have married, there have been quite a few of them to sets their sights on you."

Rydul had the grace to lower his head slightly to hide the blush that started to creep up his throat. "I could never compare with you or the prince, Sire," he admitted with embarrassment.

Radine grinned unabashedly. Jaima may have been the best swordsman on the planet, but there wasn't anything shoddy about Rydul's skill with a blade or laser weapon. Whenever he contested with the prince, he always gave the man, only a few years older, a decent run for his money. Radine himself often sweated whether or not he would best the officer, not having as much time to practice as he always wanted.

And the ladies, watching from the sidelines and balconies overlooking the practice yard, twittered and giggled and flirted as much with the younger warriors as they had with the two older men. With the king and prince spoken for, it was only natural that they turn their attention to the next in line who had the ear and favor of the king, even if he wasn't a lord. After all, he was still young enough to earn a title if he wanted one. Or had a wife to egg him on.

"Never doubt your own abilities, Rydul, nor your appeal. You wouldn't have gotten as far as you have without it." He thumped the other's shoulder several times. "Take care, Commander, and enjoy your time on Earth, but don't have too good of a time. I'll expect you to keep me up to date with full reports. This embassy is very important to the queen. I'd hate to disappoint her."

"You have my word, Sire. All will be well and I shall keep you informed." His head bowed as the king turned to leave. Holding the tablet close, he went in the other direction to deliver the manifest before finishing his own preparations for his journey, a new confidence in his step.

Sky Clad Jaima

Book One of the Sky Clad Series

Sky Clad Radine by Karen L. Milstein

King Radine of Taburon has delayed finding a wife and queen for ten years, content with ruling his planet by himself and enjoying the charms of women. But his mother's constant nagging and parade of eligible women sends him to Earth in a pique, determined to find someone to satisfy both the needs of his planet and his own.

McKenna Primm has just quit her job after being sexually harassed by her boss one too many times. When her car dies on the road, she is rescued by a tall alien who is perhaps the most handsome man she has ever seen.

Determined to find a woman who wants him for himself and not his crown, keeping his true identity a secret, and believing he has found the perfect mate, Radine asks her to come back to Taburon with him as his bride. Little does she know how much her life will change if she accepts his offer.

ISBN 13: 978-0-9863295-1-7

Published by Geminorum Publishing

Available from Amazon.com, Barnes and Noble.com, or on Amazon Kindle

Sky Clad Rydul

by Karen L. Milstein

Book Three in the Sky Clad Series

Coming January, 2016

Captain Rydul had been looking forward to his tour of duty on Earth as head of security for the Taburon Embassy. But six months is a long time to be away from home and as his tour is drawing to a close, he finds himself anxious to get home.

That is until a fight between the humans who want the Taburons gone and those who support them breaks out in front of the Embassy, injuring the one person who has held his attention for months. Beautiful, red headed Kathryn Tehyr found the huge warriors fascinating from the day they'd first arrived. From across the street she spent her lunch hour surreptitiously watching the tall, handsome aliens, hoping for a glimpse of one of them. She is saved by Rydul when a rock thrown in her direction knocks her unconscious.

Little can happen between them in the short time he has left on Earth, and he returns home, regretting that he hadn't had a chance to get to know Kathryn better. So he is surprised when she is among the first of invited colonists to arrive on Taburon six months later and he decides to start a relationship to see where they might go together.

But other danger has arrived with the colonists, danger that might threaten not only Rydul and Kathryn, but all Taburons, forcing them to sever all but a few ties with humans forever.

Biography

Karen L. Milstein is a writer and nature photographer who prefers the out of doors to cities and large crowds. She is a huge fan of sword and sorcery and enjoys reading all types of books in her spare time, especially science fiction, fantasy, romance and romantica. She lives in Palm Beach County, Florida, with her husband, son, and a small pride of rescue cats. She is also an enthusiastic player of Dungeons and Dragons. Fergus, the dragon in her first book, *Fergus and the Princess,* is real and sits above her computer to give her inspiration.

Sky Clad Jaima

Other Books by Karen L. Milstein:

Fergus and the Princess, A Lasker the Storyteller Tale

Young Adult Fantasy

There are several truths about dragons that everyone knows: they are excellent poets, they can't resist a riddle, and they love things that sparkle. When 16 year old Princess Ciara is discovered sitting in her garden dressed for her upcoming birthday party with jewels in her hair, she is plucked up by a passing dragon.

Everything she knows about dragons she learned at her father's knee – and HE HATED THEM! But when she is kidnapped and forced to spend time with Fergus, a very purple dragon, she doesn't know what to believe.

As she deals with magical creatures, impossible riddles, and daring escapes, Ciara finds she must decide for herself just how evil – or good – dragons really are.

Lasker is a wandering storyteller who travels from place to place to tell his tales for the price of a tankard of ale, a warm hearth, and a crust of bread. With him as his companion is a young widow who writes down the stories for posterity.

ISBN: 978-0-9863295-0-0

Geminorum Publishing

Available at Amazon.com, Barnes and Noble.com, or Amazon Kindle

Sky Clad Jaima

www.ingramcontent.com/pod-product-compliance
Lightning Source LLC
Chambersburg PA
CBHW072112250626
47159CB00007B/2417